VEGAS DAZZLE SERIES

Book One

Vegas Dazzle

Diane
Live each and every day
to the fullest.

Love Pam Jackson xoxo
God Bless

VEGAS DAZZLE SERIES

Book One

Vegas Dazzle

Pam Langsam

PMB PUBLISHING

PMB Publishing, LLC
Denver, CO

To book this author for your live event please contact
PMB Publishing at pmbpublishing@vegasdazzle.com.

Visit us on the Web: www.VegasDazzleSeries.com
Like us on Facebook: Vegas Dazzle Book Series
Follow us on Twitter: @VegasDazzle, @PamLangsam

Cover design by Amy de Leon Petzel: www.deleonpetzel.com

First paperback edition April 2011
10 9 8 7 6 5 4 3 2 1

ISBN-13: 97809832871-0-0 (pbk)
LCCN: 2011906259

To the memory of my dearest friend Michelle Appleby who unfortunately left this world behind way too soon, I miss her each and everyday. And to my twenty-three year old cat Goober, who will always hold my deepest–darkest secrets ... ;-)

Acknowledgements

Writing a book is a journey of learning about one's self. I couldn't have done this without the support of my family and all of my great friends! Especially my husband Michael, who is my true soul mate, I love you dearly; My son Bryce, who is the best part of me, hugs and kisses; My mother and father, who gave me a childhood full of travel and adventure, and to my sister Kaylee who is dear to my heart. To my wonderful friends Amy de Leon Petzel and Kris Davis for being so creative, talented and absolutely awesome! Katherine Carol for being a true spiritual friend and Isabella Cass for just being herself; My dear friend Patrick Griffith, who does a Mobster's voice like no other and held my hand through the finish; Holly Samler for being so supportive and a great cheerleader. Finally, a special thanks to my editors for all your hard work and much appreciated red marks. To everyone else, thank you for your support and love. I love you all! You rock! ;-)

Love is patient, Love is kind, it does not envy, it does not boast, it is not proud, it is not rude, it is not self-seeking, it is not easily angered, it keeps no records of wrongs. Love does not delight in evil but rejoices with truth, it always preserves and never gives up. And now these three remain faith, hope, and love. But the greatest of these is love.

1 Corinthians 13

in·tris·ity

[in-tris-uh-ti]

–adjective

1. a supernatural level of excitment; a
    powerful transformation of energy.

Origin:

2010- Pam Langsam

Famous Quotations

"Together you are whisped away on an adventure of immaculate love, danger and intrisity
that alters your world forever."

    -- Vegas Dazzle Summary

1

Prince of the Mob

My chest is bursting. It's on fire. Running frantically, I search inside the dim, unlit building, looking to the back for a fast way out. I race for the emergency exit. I kick hard on the metal bar, and the door flies open. Adrenaline pumping, I make it halfway down the alley, where I check over my shoulder to see if anyone is chasing me.

The fresh, yet hot night air relieves the pressure from

my erratically beating heart. Taking a short breath, I realize the insane, uncontrollable situation I'm in. Placing both my hands over my face, I take in another breath, this time deeper, and wipe the dripping sweat from my brow. Checking out my location, I notice that I'm in a dark, paved alley surrounded by shadows cast from the walls of the old buildings on either side. The black, starless sky hovering above me glows with the neon lights of Fremont Street one block over.

I hate this place.

Taking another breath, I feel a sensation flowing through my body that I just might survive another night of my god-forsaken life ...

As the door comes crashing open, terror once again fills my bones. Sweat is streaming out of every pore of my body. To my relief, it's only Mateo and Tony falling on each other at my feet on the disgusting smelling ground, groaning through their heavy breathing about their pain and agony.

"What happened to you Dario? Where the hell did you go? How could you leave us in the midst of the battle?" hissed Mateo.

"Battle? ... You two always have to take everything to a level that is so completely out of control! You aren't satisfied unless you see not only fear in someone's eyes but also blood gushing from some part of their bodies! You're both clueless ... and in case you haven't noticed, we aren't in a war zone here—this is Las Vegas.

Mateo, Tony and I have been friends ever since I can remember—my two best friends, partners in crime. Now, when I say crime, I don't mean running amok like a bunch of low-life, trouble-making teenagers. Stealing a few candy bars here or there or bustin' a few heads once in awhile, this is *not* what I'm talking about. Crime means life or death, crime means our lives, crime means family ... the kind of crime that goes back for generations. Organized crime that has been running this town way before I was born and way before my father was born ... The kind of crime described by most people as the Mob. Crime is what makes Vegas ... Vegas. And unfortunately, the Mob is my family.

"Hey! What the hell is going on with you lately? You haven't been yourself, and you're going to get us killed if you keep this shit up! Dario, hello, are you even listening to me?"

Tony's yelling at me as he picks himself up off the foul street, but all I can think about is how I don't want to do this anymore. I don't want to be here anymore, and I can't tell anyone or they will have me knocked off, which in Mob terms means killed!

"I hear you. I know. I just have a lot on my mind lately." I say with a hesitant voice. How do you explain to your two best friends that you wish things could be different; that you wish sometimes you didn't know them; that you wish you didn't know the *"Family"*—including your own father. A day doesn't go by that I'm not riddled with fear. I wish my dad were just a dad. Instead, he's the boss of all these powerful—crazy people!

Quickly pulling myself together, I realize that there are two bodies still inside the building I've just escaped from.

I'm not even sure what the final outcome was for either of them. I'm just praying neither of them is dead!

"So how did the two of you leave it inside? What's with the Larson brothers?" I ask.

"They're alive, just knocked out cold," Tony says. "Mateo wanted to finish them off—he's so sick of their bullshit excuses all the time—but I yanked him off when he started to bang their heads on the pavement. I told him they got the message. None of us can get money out of dead guys."

"Then let's get the hell out of here before anyone sees us!" I holler over my shoulder. I begin racing down the alley with Tony and Mateo close behind.

Reaching the end of the alley, we stop abruptly to check things out. That's when we notice the Larson brothers' posse hanging out around their car, waiting for their idiot bosses to come out. There's no other way out, seeing as how the other end of the alley is a dead end. Lucky for us, they're a bunch of moron idiots who like to stand around acting like they're tough guys while chain-smoking cigarettes and drinking beer.

I'm beat. Adding more violence to my evening—or should I say morning, seeing that the sun is starting to make an appearance on the horizon—is not what I want? Not now.

But my cohorts have other ideas.

"Let's go get them!" Mateo says, nodding his head in the direction of the Larsons' posse.

"Yeah boss, let's nail them," Tony adds.

"Not tonight guys," I state, leading them up the

rundown street away from the Larsons' misfits. I know I'm going to get a load of slack from Mateo. But I really don't give a shit anymore—I'm the one that calls the shots around here anyway. I just want to get the hell out of here, and the sooner, the better. Knowing we can cross back over to Fremont Street from the next block over and get back to the Horseshoe where we parked the car is all that matters to me. Maybe then I can get some badly needed shut-eye.

As we walk briskly down the street toward our car at the Horseshoe Casino, Mateo is grumbling and complaining behind me about how I'm getting weak. He hasn't wanted to mention it lately, he says, but now things are really getting out of hand. I've heard his ramblings before and ignore him as I take in the scenery around me.

Vegas is different these days. All the lights are still here, brightening up the night, but there's a different energy in the city. The city's trying to replace or renovate all the old buildings. I actually appreciate how they are trying to clean up downtown and make it a better place, a place without all the crime and poverty. What the hell is going on, I can't believe the thoughts that are bouncing around in my head. Crime is part of my family. Appreciating "nice things" or "pleasant surroundings" isn't usually in my vocabulary.

Then I overhear Mateo say to Tony that if I don't pull it together, he's going to have to let my dad know about my situation. Normally, I would ignore him, letting his opinions go in one ear and out the other. But when I hear his comment about my father, something inside me snaps! I spin around with anger in my eyes, grab his shirt and throw him up against a nearby wall.

Placing my face right into his, I demand, "Just *who the hell* do you think you are talking to? You work for me, not my dad—and not only that, you're supposed to be my friend—someone who covers my ass when I need help! What do you think; you can run off like a little kid and tell on me? Don't ever threaten me again! Do you hear me?"

Still holding him up against the wall staring into his frightened eyes, as he slowly nods his head yes. At the same time, Tony is trying to pull me off of Mateo, telling me to ease up ... "We are all on the same team Dario ..."

• • • • • • • • • • • • •

The car ride home is silent, just the way I want it. I'm tired of the same old conversations about the Vegas scene and our lowlife job of making it ours, controlling every-one and everything around us. I make Tony drive so I can be dropped off first. I just don't want to deal with them anymore tonight.

As we pull up to the gate of my family's compound, Tony lowers the window of the driver's side door to put the code that opens the gate into the box. I'm still steamed.

"Don't bother. I'll walk from here."

I know they are both confused, seeing that they always drive me in and almost always come into the house for breakfast or some kind of eating frenzy after one of our "encounters." But not tonight—I've had enough of them and this entire evening.

I open the car door. Just before getting out, I turn to

the two of them. "You've got the Larson brothers' blood all over your clothes and faces, and you stink. Clean up. Do you understand me?"

Mateo looks hard and long at me before nodding, his face reflecting a deep aggravated scowl as he sighs disgustedly.

Surprisingly, Tony is more civil. "No problem boss, we'll catch up with you in a little while after we have all gotten some ZZZ's. I think we all need a little extra today."

"Don't call me boss, Tony. Dario will be just fine."

"No problem boss ... I mean Dario. See you later."

I get out of the car knowing Mateo will get out of the back seat and move to the front. He always does. I leave the front door open for him as I step away. With major attitude, he opens the back door, jumps out of the car, slams the door shut and gets into the front, slamming that door, too. He motions to Tony to drive.

I stand and watch the car back down the long drive and head north, until I can no longer see it. Deeply inhaling the crisp morning air, I finally feel like I can breathe. I take in another deep breath as I soak up the awesome bright orange and yellow sunrise expanding around me throughout the whole Las Vegas valley.

I take my time walking up to the gate. Then I enter the code, push the gate open and secure it behind me. I walk onto the grounds of the main house. As I try to figure out if I'm hungry or too tired to be hungry, I run into one of my dad's bodyguards on watch.

"Had a falling out with the boys?" Frankie asks.

"No, why would you think that?"

"Not like them to drive away, the way you guys like to eat and all after a long night ..."

"I just wanted some time away from them. I get tired of these all-nighters. I mean, you are here every morning. Don't you ever just want things quiet once in a while? Sometimes, I just want to stop ... and breathe ... and look around. Like, I just noticed this beautiful, awesome sunrise we're having," gesturing with my arm toward the valley.

"Awesome sunrise we are having? Are you nuts? Are you okay, Dario? Since when do Tony and Mateo drop you off at the front gate so you can enjoy sunrises by yourself? Awesome sunrises? Should I be worried?" Frankie squints and takes a close look at me.

"Really, it's not a big deal," I say, trying to sound light-hearted. "A little bit of change never hurt anyone. We had a crazy night, and I just want to get some sleep and wasn't in the mood to entertain. That's all. Like I said, no big deal... Have a good one ..." I push pass him and continue up the path to the house.

We live on this huge compound that my parents built when they got married 17 years ago. It used to be so far south of the Las Vegas Strip that we didn't have neighbors for miles and my parents would joke about how we almost lived in California.

But things have changed over the years. People now live a little closer to us in this development called Seven Hills. My dad bought enough of the land around us so that no one could ever be our next-door neighbor, but if I drive down the hill a bit, they are close enough. One of the cool things about Seven Hills is that it has an incredible country club called Bonita Palms that my parents actually joined. It keeps me sane, for the mere fact that I get to hang out with normal people and escape the madness of my family—and my secret life after it gets dark.

Walking up to the house, I notice the landscaping and how everything is manicured to perfection as always. I marvel at the wonders of the desert and all the magnificent flowers, plants and trees. It's as if all the gardeners who work for my father have studied the landscape paintings that hang in museums. As I turn to see if I'm being followed by Frankie, I glimpse at the valley behind me, noticing for the first time ever the lights of all the Las Vegas Strip casinos and hotels turning off right before my very eyes. What an unbelievable sight! It really is stunning. Stunning ... did I just think that word ... stunning?

If anyone saw me standing here enjoying such a little thing or knew what I was thinking, they would check me into the nearest crazy house. Mateo's right, something isn't right with me. I don't even understand it myself. I wonder why I am in this life—Vegas Mob prince—and whether or not I can turn my back on it. Up to just a couple of weeks ago, I didn't care about anyone or anything except the family and getting a job done. Whatever my father wanted me to do, I did. I lived for people being afraid of me. I lived for running this town.

Something is happening to me. I don't get it. It all seems to go back to that one night, the night the dreams started, the dreams that are changing everything ... the dreams that are not only changing my life ... but the dreams that are changing me.

2

Innocents of a Secret

Nothing will ever be the same. My life, as I've known it, has changed forever. As the private jet accelerates down the runway, gliding upward into the dark gray-clouded sky, I peer out from my window seat, taking a last glimpse of the picturesque English countryside of Cambridge. All I can think about is how angry I am at my parents for making me move to Las Vegas. Tears fill my eyes as I think of losing my friends ... my best friends ... gone forever.

"Taylor, aren't you excited? Isn't this the most amazing adventure?" my mom asks.

She doesn't get it. I know she means well, but nothing is exciting about leaving behind the first place I've considered home. All I can do is stare at her. Overwhelmed with sorrow, I have an achy feeling in my heart, as if part of it is being ripped out of my chest. I close my eyes tightly, remembering how wonderful my life has been the last six years in England. I hurt, my whole body feels weakened by my sadness.

We moved to England from the United States, California to be exact, just after I turned 10. We lived in the cutest, quaintest village named Fenstanton, nestled just outside of Cambridge in a home next to St. Ives on the Great Ouse River. Like most kids, I never really knew many details about what my dad did for a living, except that he was a corporate pilot for some company in Cambridge, and that's why we moved to England in the first place. That is, until he accepted his new job with some fancy hotel and casino in *fabulous* Las Vegas called the Beauvallon Resort and Casino.

My mom always says *fabulous* when she talks about Las Vegas, but what could be fabulous about a place that has already made me feel so awful? I don't want to move there.

Exhausted from this crazy day and surrendering to the soothing hum from the jet's engines, I lean my head against the headrest. I feel tears seep out of my eyes again as I shut them. But soon, I begin to drift off into a deep, calming sleep.

Suddenly, I find myself falling into one of the bizarre, realistic dreams I've been having a lot lately.

I'm wandering through a deep canyon or valley—a place I have never seen before. It's dark and eerie, and the moon is full and intense, its bright light beaming down, allowing me to see the path in front of me. I notice the most beautiful, passionate, yellow-orange and red flowering plants around me. Lining the canyon walls, they are surprisingly comforting, as if they are guiding me like arrows pointing the way.

Glancing up into the dark-blue, starry sky, I realize that the walls of stone surrounding me extend up so high I can barely see the tops of them. I feel my heart drop as my body fills with fear.

The swaying of my gown surprises me, and I suddenly realize I'm wearing the beautiful white nightgown that my mom had given me for my birthday last year. I've never worn it before—I always felt it was too elegant to wear to bed.

The air around me is warm and soothing. It wraps itself around me as if gliding me along. I'm not really sure where I'm going, but my feet seem to be leading the way on their own as they feel the deep sand below them. I can see in the near distance that the rocks fade away, leading to an opening. It's so peaceful here under the dark starlit sky, yet I have an unsettling feeling in my stomach that the peace is just a mask, disguising what's really going on.

As I approach the clearing beyond the canyon walls, I see miles of sand and desert surrounded by more mountains and valleys in the distance. Suddenly, my eyes focus on something not far off, a car, a black SUV to be exact. I hear men's voices—voices that are not familiar to me and that rapidly send a deep, chilling sensation throughout my spine. The feeling almost takes my breath away.

Reminding myself that this is only a dream, and urged on by my curiosity, I move closer. From the tone and loudness, I can tell that the men are arguing intensely about something. I can't hear clearly enough to know what's being said, so I move even closer, slowly sliding myself along the canyon walls until I come to a large boulder that I am able to hide behind.

Terrified to the core of my soul about what I might see, but again spurred on by my own inquisitiveness, I peer around the boulder. I now can tell that it's three young men. Not really men, yet, more like teens just a year or two older than I am. Two of them are digging a hole in the sand, a very large hole. Uncertain why anyone would be digging a hole in the middle of the night in what seems to be the middle of the desert, I continue to watch in fascination.

The third teen is farther away and seems to be retrieving a very large black duffel bag out of the back of the SUV. When he turns around and heads toward the other two, dragging the bag behind him, I realize that I recognize his face. It's the face I have been seeing quite often in my dreams, a face I do not know, a beautiful face I can't stop thinking about, even during my waking hours.

All of a sudden I can't breathe. My heart seems to stop beating, and my feet feel as if they are encased in concrete! Frightened, I want to run, I have to run! I have to get out of here before anyone sees me. Before "he" sees me! What is he doing here? What are they doing here? Why am I here? It takes everything I have to force my dreaming body to turn and run!

I run until I'm tripping over my nightgown, my beautiful, elegant nightgown. It's ripping at the *hem as I fall down a steep embankment. With furious speed, I tumble down through all the beautiful flowering plants I had seen before—plants that are now poking me, scratching my skin and pulling at my hair. Scared, I'm falling ...*

Waking up abruptly, wide eyed, I find myself on the airplane with my mom standing over me, touching my shoulder.

"Taylor, wake up honey. Are you all right?"

With a deep breath and a quick couple of nods, I assure her I'm okay. Fear still in my bones and still short of breath, I let out a sigh of relief that the dream is over. Yet, I'm still yearning for the gorgeous and intriguing young man from the dream, the boy that dwells within me ... Who is he? Why is he there, every time I have one of these strange dreams?

3

Strange Endeavors

As my mom returns to her seat, I shake off the intense dream. Why do I keep having these dreams? And with the same guy in them all the time?

Okay, earth to Taylor. I bring myself back to some sort of reality. It hits me that the United States has to be just a few hours away. I haven't stepped foot on American soil since my family moved to England—it feels like such a long time ago. I know the country has changed, most likely as much as I have. I'm not really sure what to expect. Of course, I've seen America on the telly and in movies, but who knows what I'm really in for? The adrenaline runs through my veins as my anticipation builds.

Glancing around, I start to realize how unbelievable this jet is. My mom was right—this is an awesome plane. I especially love the soft, creamy leather seats that have allowed me to sink into such a deep slumber and let me feel comfortable through this agonizing and depressing day.

Dad has let me fly with him a few times, but I have never been on a plane like this before. They haven't missed a thing. The plane even has the largest flat screen telly I've ever seen hanging from the front bulkhead—where, of course, I see my sister Mckylee has made herself quite comfortable wearing headphones and enjoying a movie. Thankfully, she's not bothering the rest of us like she usually does. For once, she's not nagging me to entertain her.

Mckylee isn't really that bad, but we've never been very close. She just turned 15 last month, which makes us about one and a half years apart. The problem is, we have absolutely nothing in common, which is why she seriously gets on my nerves sometimes.

"Can I get you something to drink or a snack?" The flight attendant practically scares me to death as she taps me on my shoulder. I had forgotten we even had a flight attendant.

"No! No, I'm fine, thanks," I answer as I drift back into thought.

Still extremely tired, I don't want to deal with anything right now, especially my family. Not interested in my sister's movie, or in her either for that matter, I decided to hang out in the back of the plane. My eyes drift to my mom, who is sitting kitty-corner to me in the middle of the plane and seems deeply absorbed in some book. My dad is nowhere in sight. I can only assume he must be in the cockpit, hanging out with the other two pilots.

Resting my head on the seatback again, I can't help but glare at my mom. How could she do this to me? How could she take me away from all my friends and a place that I love? I'm still so angry with her! Staring at her I find myself backing off. Sophia, my mom, is really okay. My friends all thought she was cool for a parent. That is, when she isn't trying to ruin my life. Seeing her now, looking at her face that doesn't look like it's stern, I remember all the awesome afternoons we had back in England.

My mom was the head chef at a restaurant back in St. Ives. I would visit her often after school, enjoying one of her magnificent creations, which varied from exquisite entrée dishes to unbelievable deserts like her mouth-watering cheesecake. Sometimes she would surprise me and my friends with an incredible English Tea spread out and loaded with an array of "sweeties" that makes my mouth salivate just thinking of them.

Chef Sophia was known to be one of the best chefs around. She did all her training at a premier cooking school in France, called Le Cordon Bleu, and she has the most amazing liking for all types of gourmet foods. All I know is that I'm really going to miss my afternoon visits with her at the restaurant. When we were packing, she told us she has been thinking about opening her own cooking school in Las Vegas, which I think she would be really incredible at. I guess we will just have to see. But right now, I could care less. Las Vegas can never be as great as what I had in Cambridge.

It always surprises me how different Mom looks when she isn't wearing her chef's coat and her hair isn't pulled back. She has the perfect figure and the most eye-catching, curly, strawberry blonde hair that falls just past her shoulders. She loves clothes and is always styled in the latest designer outfits, and she has the cutest shoes. She's very *trés chic*, as they say.

Trés chic is definitely not my style. Mom is always trying to get me to dress up in cute, girly clothes, but that's not me. I love my jeans, sweatshirts and tennis shoes. *Trés* Taylor I call it. Needless to say, I guess I am a bit of a tomboy, and fancy clothes like my mom wears really aren't my cup of tea.

She turns around abruptly and catches my stare. I try to play down my intense glare by pretending to be fooling with my hair, but don't quite pull it off.

"What's up with you Taylor? Why are you staring at me so strangely?" she asks.

Knowing I need to back off my bitchy attitude, I answer sweetly, allowing her to think I'm getting over it. "Nothing. I was just thinking about how pretty you are when you're not working in the kitchen and how I'm going to miss visiting you at the restaurant back in St. Ives, that's all," I quickly turn away to avoid any further unnecessary conversation.

I really wish she would just leave me alone right now. I

know my mom worries about me, but I'll be fine. I never stay mad very long, but right now I need to be alone. The plane jolts, and I know we're descending. But something must be wrong. There is no way we are in Las Vegas already.

"Where are we? Why are we landing so soon?" I shout out to anyone who may be listening.

Just then my dad, Robert, emerges from the cockpit. "Hey, Sophie can I have a word with you?" He waves at Mom to join him up by the cockpit door. My dad is the only one who calls my mom Sophie; everyone else calls her Sophia. I think it's kind of cute that he does that. I watch with anticipation while my dad has a quick word with her. As I study them, I'm reminded that they are quite the couple. I admire how handsome he is—six feet tall, with wavy brown hair and blue eyes. I can see why my mom was attracted to him from the first time they met. He promptly finishes by giving her a quick peck on the lips, and then re-enters the cockpit.

Slowly turning around, Mom informs us that we're stopping for a brief layover in New York to refuel and pick up something for my dad's new boss. I can't believe it—just like that, England is in the past. New York is suddenly here. I have such an empty feeling inside my belly. I feel like none of this is actually happing. It's like I'm dreaming, I am just so out of it.

But nothing seems to faze Mckylee. She says she's starving and needs something to eat. I overhear Mom say that lunch is being delivered to the plane from one of Dad's favorite Italian restaurants (well, it's really more like dinner to me since it's around 5:30 in the afternoon in Fenstanton, but I guess it is lunch time here).

Mckylee perks up. "New York? I never thought I would ever get to see New York. It's so exciting." Well, neither have I. And I guess it's kind of exciting. Sort of. I'm not sure how much excitement we're going to have, since it's not like we're going to spend any real time here.

From the plane's window, the city looks massive. I can't believe all the tall buildings and bridges that seem to connect the city to all its neighbors. It's like a giant spider web reaching out in every direction. I can almost feel the pulsating energy coming from this huge city as we come in for our landing. I look down at all the cars and see what looks like people hustling everywhere in masses. Before I can blink, the plane is on the ground.

After taxiing, the plane comes to a stop at a small terminal. Dad emerges from the cockpit, telling us lunch will be here in a few minutes. He says he's ordered for all of us, from one of the finest Italian restaurants in Manhattan. He looks at Mom and winks, adding that he personally guarantees it will be the best Italian we've ever eaten. I'm famished, and Italian does sounds really yummy right now. It's been a long time since I've had some good, much less great Italian food. I can hardly wait for it to be delivered.

After Dad promises us our forthcoming feast, the two other pilots emerge from the cockpit. Moving out of their way, Dad sits next to Mckylee. One of the pilots heads toward the exterior door and opens it. The other tells my dad he will be back shortly. Through my window, I watch them walk across the tarmac and disappear inside the terminal.

I stand up, stretch my legs and then say to my mom, "Hey, if it's okay, I'm going to get off the plane for a minute to get some fresh air and check out the terminal while we wait for lunch. Then I can tell my friends that I was in New York."

Whatever I said, it was the wrong thing. Catching my mom's glare, I notice she's shaking her head no with a beady look in her eyes. It's a little odd that she doesn't speak a single word, but I know that beady look. She doesn't think it's a good idea for me to leave the plane. I get the message. It's completely clear not to ask again or to question her.

Still not quite sure what that was all about, I sit back down in my seat. Why is she acting so weird? I'm left with a bizarre feeling that something isn't quite right. As my dad makes himself comfortable, he turns the telly to the local news. I'm beyond glad he turned it on, for the mere fact that it breaks the awkwardness that, all of a sudden, surrounds us in this small space. It's still a little weird, Dad and the news—he never cared about news on the telly when we lived in England.

Planted in my seat with the clear understanding not to get out, I notice out my window a nice-looking black car approaching the plane. It parks a few yards away. Good, I think, lunch must finally be here. But wait, no one is getting out.

For some reason, I can't stop watching the car. Now I'm thinking to myself that a car parked right next to the jet seems a little weird—a car that just sits there with no doors opening ... it's almost like it drove itself there. It feels even odder that no one gets out. The windows are so dark I can't see inside the car. I look around the plane to see if anyone else has noticed the car, but the only thing the others seem to be noticing is the news on the telly or their book.

A slight chill runs through the center of my body as everyone is acting as if the car isn't even there. Is it really possible for no one else to notice?

Slumping into my seat, I maintain my silence after my mom's look. I'm not going to mention the black car to anyone. Things already seem a little weird around here ... okay, a lot weird, but it's not my problem. Especially with no one talking to each other. I try to avert my eyes and not look at the car, but I'm finding it impossible not to glance over once in awhile to see if it is still there. Has someone opened the door yet? It's like a magnet. I don't know what it is about the car ... something ... something tells me that it's trouble.

I physically shake as a chill runs through my body. All I can think about is how strange all of this is and how I feel that everyone is pretending like nothing is going on or has happened. Hello ... doesn't anyone see that there is a big, black car right by this jet besides me? I'm not even sure what the heck is really going on. All I know is that I'm feeling really freaked out!

The black car is still just sitting there. I can now barely make out that there is a driver inside it. All of a sudden I catch sight of our two pilots emerging from the terminal, slowly walking toward the rear of the car—the trunk, to be exact. As they approach it, the trunk suddenly opens like magic. Someone who is inside the car must have done it, as no one has gotten out. This is getting weirder. Now, they each grab the opposite end of a large black duffel bag that looks quite heavy by the way they are lifting it. One of the pilots accidently drops his side of the bag on the ground as he slams the trunk closed. The car then quickly drives away. Nope, it's definitely not food from the Italian restaurant!

I find myself holding my breath as I try to figure out what is going on and what will happen next. Together, the pilots walk with the oversized bag towards the plane. I assume they're placing it where the luggage is kept. I hear a loud thump below.

A mad rush of fear comes over my body. I know that bag! I remember seeing it before. It's like the bag I saw the guy, that beautiful, intriguing guy, dragging across the sand in my dream just a few hours earlier! I can't even tell anyone because they would think I've gone completely mad. Am I mad? I'm beginning to think I must be with these crazy dreams I keep having.

As I sit here trying to figure it all out and wondering why I'm the only one who seems to think none of this is normal, another car approaches. This time, it's not black. My dad hurriedly gets up and leaves the plane, joining the other pilots on the tarmac. After what looks like a quick conversation, Dad has his wallet out and is handing cash to the driver. This must be our food. All three of them, bags in hand, climb the steps to our plane. They rejoin us as if the black bag exchange had never occurred. They take the bags of food to the galley, where the flight attendant tells them she will serve it up promptly.

They act as if everything is normal. And what's with Mom? I can't help wondering how she can engross herself in a book. It's like she is oblivious to everything. She hasn't looked up for a single second to at least pretend she's aware of her surroundings. Meanwhile, my sister is watching the news as if she is enjoying it—when she hates the news. I mean, we could have all been murdered and no one would have even noticed it coming.

What is happening to me? To my family? I've never been afraid in my life, and now all I feel is fear in every pore of my body. I wish we could just turn around and go back to England and pretend that we never got on this plane this morning, like none of this ever happened ...

Solar Phenomenon

Before I know it, we are once again airborne. There is none of that "fasten your seat belts," spiel from the flight attendant over an announcement system like there is on a commercial plane. The door just closes, and we take off. Each of us is in our own space, our own section of the plane. It's raining hard, with huge gray clouds making it difficult to see the city below. As I look out, I can see hints of lightning flashing.

We are in the air, yet my mind is still obsessing on the strange bag pickup in New York and how weird the pilots, including my dad, acted back at the airport. Even stranger was my dream and the boy—that gorgeous boy. Thankfully, the flight attendant distracts me from my thoughts.

"Are you ready to eat? I have a plate prepared for you, if you want to pull the tray out from the side of your seat." She smiles at me while holding a plate of scrumptious looking food.

"Most definitely. Thanks." I reply as I release the tray and pull it out. She places the plate in front of me and hands me a linen napkin with silverware rolled up inside.

"What can I bring you to drink?"

"A coke would be great. By the way, do you have any garlic bread?" I ask.

"Sure. I'll be right back with your coke and some bread for you."

Not wasting a single minute, I unroll the silverware from my napkin and dive in. Everything looks and smells so good. My stomach is doing a happy dance. For the first time ever, I feel no need to pick through my food. I don't even care what's on my plate—I'm starving. There is some sort of pasta with a marinara sauce and melted cheese, which I decide to try first. That is definitely yum. The beef is so tender I can cut it with my fork, and the salad is just right. The flight attendant returns promptly with my bread and soda.

Incredible, delicious smells surround me. With everyone eating, there is a comforting silence in the cabin. My mom and dad are eating together, and Mckylee is back in front of the telly, watching another movie and enjoying her lunch. For a brief moment, I feel … well, I feel content.

But only for a moment. Then, I remember overhearing the flight attendant inform my mom before we landed in New York that the flight from New York to Vegas is about six hours. I swear this has already been like the longest day ever in my life! It's bizarre to think that I woke up in England and I'll be going to sleep in Las Vegas almost 24 hours later. Crazy, really … I feel like it's been days since I was last in England hanging with my best friends. All of this is just a little over-stimulating to my already over-working brain.

This lunch is so good, I hate to finish it. Dad was right; it is the best Italian food I've ever eaten. Handing my tray back, I decide to watch a movie to get through the next six hours, and I join my sister in front of the telly. As I take the seat next to Mckylee, she smiles at me and hands me a set of headphones. That's the first time I have smiled back at my sister and felt really glad to be hanging out with her. Boy, is that a change of events. Things really are changing in the weirdest ways. But it's all good, I suppose. And I could get used to this huge screen.

After two movies, a few sodas, popcorn, and small snacks that the flight attendant keeps bringing us, we finally feel the plane's decent into Las Vegas. We're really here! I can't believe it. Looking out the window, I see nothing but brown, lifeless mountains and dirt … or is that sand? When Mom and Dad told us we were moving, I had read that Las

Vegas is smack in the middle of a desert. Now I can see this is true. Not one blade of grass or a single tree to be found for all the miles I can see out my window. With the sun beginning to set off in the horizon, I am thankful there is still enough light for me to see the ground below.

As the jet continues its descent, I search for some sort of life, looking for the city that I will soon be calling home. Finally, I notice something that could sustain some sort of life—a large body of water. I can actually see boats cruising across the water's surface. Wanting to share the sight, I tap my sister on the shoulder while pointing frantically out my window.

"What?" she yells a little too loudly because she still has her headphones on. Slowly, she removes them so that she can hear me.

"Mckylee, look out the window! ... There's a lake in the middle of the desert ... It is huge! You have to see it," I insist.

She quickly leans over me to look out my window.

"Wow! You're right, that's huge. The boats look so little from up here."

"I know, but how awesome is it that there's a lake? I didn't know there was anything here like the river back in St. Ives. This is so cool," I say.

Before we know it, we are seeing more and more signs of life. Out of nowhere, it seems, houses become visible. Lots of them.

Suddenly, the cockpit door flies open, and my Dad joins us in the cabin, a sort of fun energy bursting from him.

"I'm so excited we're landing just as the sun is setting! Now we can see all the bright lights of the city. We couldn't have timed our arrival into Vegas any better," he says.

I can honestly say my dad never gets excited about anything, so being the good daughter that I am, I play along with his enthusiasm. Besides, his excitement is definitely making all of this way more fun.

I have seen Las Vegas before on the telly and in movies, but I've never seen it firsthand, so I'm a little intrigued—although I can't show much enthusiasm and allow my parents to think, even for a minute, that I'm okay with their decision to move us here, at least, not yet.

As we approach Las Vegas for our landing, I can't believe my eyes! The view takes my breath away. The sun is going down over the mountains, and the skyline is full of pinks, yellows, oranges, reds and blues—as if a painter had squirted various tubes of paint randomly across the sky. I don't ever recall seeing such an awesome sunset in my life! It's unbelievably picturesque.

Wow! As tired as my body is, I'm now full of anticipation and excitement! Dad's mood must be rubbing off on me. The plane seems to effortlessly glide into a turn, leading to its final approach, and then an even more unbelievable sight takes my breath away! The Las Vegas Strip! All lit up in its full glory. OMG! I have never seen so many lights in my life. I hear everyone's ooohs and aaahs in the cabin, and suddenly feel as if I can't breathe from all the excitement. I can't believe I am going to live here!

The sight is almost surreal. There is an Eiffel tower just

as in Paris, France; a beautiful pyramid, as if we're in Egypt; and a purple guitar coming out of the roof of a building saying, "Hard Rock Hotel" on it. Then in the blink of an eye, the plane touches down.

We're here; were finally here. Las Vegas, our new home. I'm surprised at how close the airport is to the Las Vegas Strip—it's cool to be able to see all the hotels right outside the airplane's window. As we taxi to the executive terminal, I'm having mixed feelings. On one hand, I am excited to be here; on the other hand, I'm feeling very sad. Somehow, I know that I won't ever be going back to Fenstanton. I just know once I step off this plane, things will never be the same.

I'm amazed at my family's anticipation and excited energy. Everyone seems to be caught up in the moment. I can't wait to get off of this jet and experience for myself what Las Vegas is really all about.

With the plane finally stopped, the pilots kill the engines. Dad quickly opens the airplane door to our new lives, just as if he were a butler at a fancy house welcoming us inside. Mckylee and I jump out of our seats, rushing toward the opened doorway. The hot, intense air hits me like a bolt of lightning, filling my lungs as I breathe it in.

As my eyes drift off into the horizon, I watch the sun's final descent behind the mountain peaks. Mckylee and I can't believe how incredibly hot it still is without the sun even shining. It's beyond bizarre. It's as if someone has sucked the regular air out of us, replacing our lungs with a heater that has been turned on full blast.

Glancing over at Dad, I ask, "Why is it still so hot out here?"

Mom breaks in. "That's what happens in the desert; it stays warm all the time, day and night."

"It has to be at least 100 degrees still!" I complain.

"This is nothing," says Dad. "Wait till the daytime when the sun is shining. That's when you'll experience the full intensity of the hot desert sun! One hundred degrees is nothing in Las Vegas."

• • • • • • • • • • • • •

As I catch my mom's eyes narrowing, I quickly turn to gather my things via an order from my dad. A car is already waiting for us just outside where our plane has stopped—a limousine to be exact. A long, beautiful, black limousine, I can't believe it. I've never been in a limousine before. The only time I've even seen a limousine is in London when an ambassador drove by—or someone of importance anyway. This is insane.

"Is that limousine really for us?" I ask, watching the driver load our luggage into the trunk.

"Yes, the limousine is for you and your family. In Las Vegas, limos—that's what most people call them—are a dime a dozen," one of the pilots who has overheard my question responds.

"Thanks," I reply with some hesitation, a little put-out that he answered and not my dad or mom.

I quickly make my way to the limo and get in. Just as I

situate myself in one of the black leather seats, I notice out of one of the dark, tinted windows another car pulling up to the jet—a car I have seen before, but I'm not sure where. A black SUV, I can't take my eyes off of it for some odd reason. I swear I've seen the car before, but where?

My mind racing and my heart beat increasing, it hits me! This is déjà vu! It's the car from my dream!

Just as quickly as the SUV arrives, the two front doors fly open and two men jump out.

My heart drops!

The sight of them takes my breath away ...

I recognize them immediately. How could I forget those faces? Oh ... my ... gosh ... those are the two guys that were digging a hole in the desert in that wild dream I just had hours ago.

Is this even possible?

I feel as if I'm losing my mind!

I'm trying my hardest to maintain complete calm on the outside, so that no one thinks I'm crazy. But I'm starting to wonder if I could be losing it.

I don't dare take my eyes off of them.

I know they are here to pick up that duffle bag off of the jet. Then just like that, they walk over to the plane; each one grabs a handle on either side of the bag and lifts it out of the baggage compartment, and they walk back to the SUV. Magically, the back hatch opens; then lifting the bag, they place it inside the car. The back of the SUV automatically closes, just as it had opened. They walk to the front of the car, jump in, slam their doors and drive away quickly.

Most definitely, déjà vu! This is without a doubt related somehow to my dream!

Unable to comprehend what has just happened, I am once again left with the strangest feeling. I don't even notice that our limo has started to drive away until I see other cars pass us by on the road, as I am still staring, shocked and confused, out the window.

5

City of Lights

Staring out of the limo's window trying to remember what they call someone who sees things that haven't really happened yet, clairvoyant maybe? Out of the corner of my eye I see an incredible sight. A huge building with the name "Mandalay Bay" displayed across the top of it in massive letters. It shimmers of gold with the last rays of the sun hitting it as it descends behind the mountains. This seems to be the first hotel on this end of the Las Vegas Strip! It's absolutely amazing!

Mckylee finds the button to open the sunroof and stands up as if she's in some crazy movie while tugging at me to join her. A little hesitant but curious, I make my way up through the sunroof and stand by her side. My eyes are dazzled by the implausible sight before me, the whole Las Vegas Strip in its full brilliance!

"Is this amazing or what?" Mckylee shouts at me as the limo enters the gateway to this fabulous city of lights! And it's our new home!

"Unbelievable! Absolutely unbelievable!" I shout back while mesmerized by the huge hotels and glowing lights that line the road before us. It does feel like I'm in a movie.

As a warm breeze hits my face and whips through my long, brown hair, something is released inside of me. I feel free! Free to live and enjoy my life, free to be a little wild, free to be crazy, free to be myself! My heart assures me that I belong here, that I am finally home. I reach my arms to the sky, close my eyes tight and yell at the top of my lungs, "I'm free!" Opening my eyes and gazing down the fabulous Las Vegas strip, I shout, "This place rocks!"

To my surprise, Mckylee joins me in my yelling spree, raising her arms to the sky, too. "Woo Hoo!" she shouts. "How awesome is this?"

The people crammed on the sidewalks hear us as we pass and wave, adding their cheers to our giddy enthusiasm.

This is one of the most exhilarating moments of my life! This is a part of me I didn't even know existed. Who am I? And where have I been my whole life?

We pass the famous hotels, one after another. The New

York, New York, with its enormous rollercoaster and the MGM with its huge lion and its glowing eyes welcoming all the guests. People are everywhere—walking, hanging out, dancing on patios, cruising by in their cars. The crowds! It seems like thousands of people are everywhere, up and down the sidewalks, intoxicated by the intrisity of the Strip. Live bands are playing music. This place is insane!

The City Center is so huge it's unthinkable, and the Planet Hollywood hotel looks like a place I want to be, with its huge mall right on the Strip.

In my excitement, I haven't realized that my dad has been trying to pull us back down into the limo until he pulls us so hard, we practically fall on top of each other inside the car.

"That's enough ladies! What has gotten into the two of you? I have never seen such behavior out of either one of you before," he says, seeming half amused, though speaking in that knock-it-off voice only parents use.

"Sorry. We were just having fun," I say.

"That's fine," our mother chimes in, with a serious look on her face. "I understand this is all a little overwhelming. It's just that we are almost to the hotel, and you two need to act like civilized young ladies. This is where your dad works, and he expects you to respect that."

Mckylee and I both nod, implying that we understand her when, really, all I can think about is how amazing it was to feel the air on my face and how alive I felt for the first time ever.

I had almost forgotten that we're staying at the hotel

where my dad is working until our house is ready. Mom is having our new house painted and all the floors redone—not to mention the minor detail that we also need furniture, seeing as we don't have any because she got rid of it all back in England.

I'm not complaining by any means. If this hotel is anything like the ones we've just driven by, I can hardly wait. I'm not sure what a five-star hotel looks like, but I bet it's unbelievably awesome. It's beginning to feel like we are on a long vacation.

The driver informs us that we are pulling up to The Beauvallon Hotel. This is it; this is where we will be staying for the next few weeks. This is where my new life begins. I put down my window so I can get a better look as we pull up the drive. It's enormous! I've never seen anything quite like it before! It looks like it should be on the French Rivera. The driver pulls up into the front entryway, and I feel nervous butterflies swarming around in my stomach. The car comes to a stop, and this really cute guy in a very nice suit opens the limo door for us. As we each step out, he introduces himself as Mr. Kyle Thomas but insists we just call him Kyle. He informs us that he is our personal host and is here to help us get acquainted with our new home here in Las Vegas.

Turning to my dad I ask, "What is a personal host?" Grinning, he replies, "I'm not really sure but I'm thinking he is kind of like a butler?"

"A butler? We have our own butler? Really?"

Kyle informs us that he has arranged to have a bellman

take our things to our room and then invites us to follow him, leading us through the hotel doors. My eyes take in the endless action going on around me. Everything seems flawless. I've never seen so many beautiful people in one place. Everyone is tan, healthy looking and dressed impeccably, with perfect hairstyles. Which makes me realize, I must look like a complete mess. I am definitely in trouble. My butterflies have now turned into knots, and I'm feeling overwhelmed!

The annoying noise from the slot machines is ringing in my head. It's enough to drive anyone crazy. They are everywhere, hundreds of them across the massive casino floor. The people sitting at them feed them coins as if the machines were wild, starving animals at a zoo! I have never seen anything like this before!

"Can we put some money in one?" I ask.

"No, and don't even try," Kyle responds quickly. "The gambling age in Las Vegas is 21, and there is no tolerance for anyone under 21 gambling, ever. Security is everywhere, even in the sky." He points to the cameras in the ceiling above us, which seem to be covering almost every inch of the casino floor. That's a lot of cameras, I think to myself.

I share my concerns about the intense noise surrounding us. "You'll get used to the noise," my mom says. "That's one of the things that make Las Vegas, *Vegas!*"

As we continue across the casino floor, my body is beginning to revolt. All I really want is a bed, a comfortable bed that I can sink my aching body into. I am so tired and over stimulated. I am ready for everything to just stop!

After walking for what seems like forever, we exit out of what I'm presuming is the back of the hotel. The landscaping is amazing. It's tropical with a variety of trees and plants that I've never seen before. Everything is lush and green and there are even cages with these huge beautiful—colored parrots that greet us. It's amazing. It's awesome.

Just off in the distance I can see what I assume is the pool, all lit up and glowing a shimmering blue. We walk a few more minutes, and then we finally come to our room ... if that's what they call it. It is really a house, or villa as Kyle explains as he opens the door. It has four bedrooms and even its very own pool. That's great, I think—but really I just want a bed. I'm so exhausted!

Kyle holds the door open, and we all enter. He directs my parents to the master bedroom down the hall and then points out the three remaining bedrooms to Mckylee and me. They are all the same, he says, but I don't even care which room is mine. I walk into the closest one and yell goodnight to everyone. Closing the door behind me, I collapse on top of the bed. I just want to sleep; I want to sleep for an eternity! Sweet dreams I tell myself as my head hits the pillow and I pass out ...

6

New Beginnings

*L*ying here half asleep utterly sucks. Not to mention I'm absolutely freezing to death! Forcing my eyes open, I realize I'm lying on top of some bed that is completely made, with all of my clothes still on—except for my shoes.

I'm completely disoriented. The room is pitch black, so I'm not even sure if it's day or night—although there's a slight sliver of light creeping through the drawn curtains, hinting that it's daytime. There's a steady flow of cold air coming in from somewhere. How long have I been sleeping?

Rolling over, I try to find a light of some sort and catch sight of a digital clock that reads 6:42 A.M. It's way too early to be getting up! Then I realize that this is Las Vegas, not England, time. No wonder I'm disoriented. My body clock is off, way off. Bits and pieces of the last 24 hours begin to fill my head. I don't know if I lost part of a day with all the travel, or gained part of one.

Fumbling with the light on the nightstand, I finally manage to turn it on. I sit up and quickly survey my surroundings. *Awesome* is the first word that pops into my head. Is that a bathroom? Yes, I have my own bathroom! This is great because I seriously need to brush my teeth. They feel extremely gross and nasty, the result of our traveling for what seemed forever and me finally collapsing on this bed. I do have one slight problem though. I don't even know where any of my things are, including my toothbrush.

Still confused, I make my way to the bathroom and splash water on my face. Then I cup my hands, sipping the water that collects in them and rinsing my mouth. The water tastes so good, almost delicious. Glancing into the mirror, a sudden sadness fills me as I remember that I am no longer in England. Will I ever see my friends again? My ragged looks don't help the way I feel. I decide I still need a little more sleep—after I find my toothbrush, that is.

Walking back into the room, I notice my suitcase sitting by the door, almost as if it's saying, "Hey there, you aren't alone ... I came with you. I'm here too."

"Thank you to whoever put this in here for me. I so love you," I say aloud. I'm sure Dad must have set it here for me last night after I collapsed with total exhaustion.

Remembering that I am still wearing rumpled clothes from yesterday, I open the suitcase and begin to dig. I guess I was thinking ahead when I packed, because right on top are some comfortable clothes to change into. I pull on sweatpants and a long sleeve shirt because I'm still absolutely freezing. We didn't have air conditioning in England; no one I knew had it. It was so hot outside when we landed and drove from the airport; I can see why people have to have it here. But, this doesn't feel like air conditioning, it feels like air freezing!

With a little more digging, I finally find my toiletries bag and then my toothbrush. Mission accomplished.

I finish up in the bathroom and, still freezing to death, make my way back to bed. This time, I lift the beautiful cream duvet and climb in, pulling the covers over me nice and tight. With my head lying on one of the softest pillows I think I have ever felt, I start to feel the warmth spread through my body once again.

Staring at the ceiling, I contemplate my life. I can't believe how awesome this place makes me feel, how it seems like I belong here, even though I was so devastated leaving England just yesterday. It *was* yesterday, wasn't it? It's as if England doesn't even matter anymore. How is this possible? What is happening to me?

I try to clear my mind and get a little more sleep. But I can't let go. All of a sudden, I'm drifting back to yesterday at the airport, remembering those two guys picking up that huge, black, duffle bag. What was in that bag anyway? Why did my dad seem to pretend that nothing was going on outside the plane in New York?

And what was with the loud thump it made below me in the luggage area on the jet? The bag seemed to be really heavy, judging from the way everyone was hauling it.

The even bigger question is: was the dream I had on the plane a *"this already happened"* or a *"future of what is going to be"*? Then it hits me. Either way, if those two guys were here in Las Vegas, physically here, so is my mystery guy.

Oh my gosh! He's here, I just know it! The beautiful guy from my dreams really exists!

How can this be?

All of a sudden, I can feel his energy inside of me, inside my heart. It's as if my heart is aching for him, yearning for him. As weird as this sounds, I know he is very near.

Completely freaked out and unable to make sense of what is happening to me, I decide that sleep is not what I need. What I need is to get out of this room. I need to clear my head of all these crazy thoughts. I need distractions.Now!

Leaving my room, I make my way down the white marble-lined hallways toward the main part of the villa. This place gets more and more outrageous with every step. The main living area is elegant, with carved moldings and huge chandeliers. The furniture is made out of woods that I've never seen before with cloth and leather upholstery. The room is laid out like those magazines my mom would look at as she slowly turns each page.

The villa has every amenity any human could possibly ever need and then some. It even has a flat screen TV. I can see that there are small circles of mesh-like material on the ceilings and around the rooms, similar to the speakers in the old boom box I had at home. But these are framed, almost as if they are part of the villa. I wonder if it's some kind of a sound system? This place is nicer than any house I have ever lived in or even the mansions and chateaus we visited in England and Europe.

As I enter what seems to be the kitchen area, a sweet woman with an unfamiliar accent greets me.

"How are you? You must be Taylor. I'm Malia."

I nod "yes" as she continues, "I am the housekeeper. If you need anything, just let me know. Your parents are out on the patio if you are looking for them."

Processing everything—we have a housekeeper? My mom must be loving this! I manage to reply, "It's nice to meet you Malia ... yes ... I am looking for them. Thanks."

"Can I get you something to eat? Maybe something to drink?" she offers.

"Yeah, that would be great. Can I get some coffee by any chance?"

"You will find coffee and juices outside on the patio where your parents are. But if you want something to eat, I will prepare you something."

"Food would be great. I'm starving. I'll take anything that looks like breakfast! And thanks."

I head outside to join my parents, completely amazed at what I've just heard.

The patio is as wonderful as everything else in the house. It's lovely with a huge area rimmed with an 8-foot wall lined with palm trees and flowers. Did I say it was huge? And did I mention the pool nearby, with water that glistens like the most perfect blue sea? Protecting this idyllic spot from the blazing sun is an awning with two large palm fans pushing the air to create some sort of breeze.

The weather is just right and the hot air instantly soothes my skin. It feels lovely, as I'm still freezing from the cool air inside.

I greet my parents with a huge grin.

"Good morning," I say, announcing my presence.

"Well, aren't you in a good mood this morning," my mom says, returning my smile.

"Can you believe it? We have our very own housekeeper. How crazy is that? She even cooks!"

Dad chuckles as I reach for the cool–looking pitcher, I'm hoping it's full of my new favorite beverage, coffee. Not disappointed, I pour myself a cup and sit down.

Half listening to my parents discuss everything they have to do over the next few weeks, I find myself drifting off–to my mystery guy. I try to remember every little detail about him, but don't come up with much. How much can you remember from a dream? All I'm really sure of, at this point, is that I know him. I don't know how I know him, but I do. I also don't know how I know that he's looking for me, just as I am now looking for him. But I know this, too.

Malia arrives with the yummiest looking breakfast I think I have ever seen. She hasn't missed a thing. There is scrambled eggs with cheese melted on top, French toast, bacon, potatoes and fresh fruit, all arranged on a plate like a piece of art—art I'm going to eat and enjoy every bite of.

"A little hungry there?" my father says.

Ignoring him, I take my first bite. This has to be one of the best breakfasts I've ever had—or maybe I'm just so hungry, it only seems that way. Mckylee finally joins us, announcing her hunger as she begins to pick at my plate. Thankfully, Malia appears.

"Good morning. You must be Mckylee? I am Malia. Can I offer you some breakfast?"

When Malia leaves with Mckylee's breakfast order, she turns to me, eyes wide. She starts grilling me on what she has missed so far.

"So what's going on? Who's Malia? What are Mom and Dad talking about? What's happening?"

"I don't know," I say, not in the mood for talking.

"They seem so serious," she continues.

"I really don't know. I haven't been paying much attention. Something about the house I think. Why don't you just ask them yourself?" I had forgotten what a pain in the neck my sister can be with all her questions.

• • • • • • • • • • • •

It's wild how hot it's getting out here and so fast! I'm starting to burn up with all these clothes on. I quickly finish eating so that I can get inside to the cool air. Talk about confused—one minute I'm freezing and the next I'm on fire.

"I'm going to go inside and take a shower," I announce as I push my chair back and stand up.

"Sounds good. We just need you to be ready to take off in about an hour," Dad tells me.

"Why?" Mckylee chimes in between bites of French toast.

"Yeah, why? What are we doing?"

"You'll see. It's a surprise. Don't ask any more questions please, just be ready," he says.

I excuse myself, grab my plate and head inside. Malia once again appears out of nowhere and takes it from me.

"How was everything?"

"It was wonderful. Thank you so much." I tell her as I head back to my room.

I have no desire to go anywhere. After the last two days, my body is telling me it needs a day off, a day to do nothing. But complaining about it won't get me out of going, so why bother.

I head straight for the shower. I instantly feel the warm steam fill the room. The water runs over my skin and feels amazing as it washes away all my thoughts and clears my head. I feel my shoulders relax. My mind and body are telling me to stand here forever and let all my confusions wash down the drain.

Then out of nowhere, a mad rush of energy fills my body. Now what?! He's back! Once again I can see his face ... and I swear, I can hear him, too. He is talking to someone about ... no ... I'm just imagining things. How can I hear someone else's thoughts? ... This isn't even possible

... what's happening to me? ... I don't understand any of this!

"Someone, anyone ... please explain to me what the heck is going on!" I shout aloud, over the rushing water of the shower.

How the hell can I hear what someone else is thinking? And how can I hear someone I don't even know?

I grab a towel from the rack and wrap it around me as I step out of the shower and onto the cold tile floor. I take a seat on a chair that I didn't notice before.

Focusing, I imagine his face. I try with all my heart to hear him again, to listen in on his thoughts. I can't. There's nothing. He's gone ... Who is he? What does he want? And what does all of this mean?

Innovations

I've driven up to my dad's hotel a million times, but this time it's different. I feel this unbelievable sensation running through my body—like a higher energy, almost a vibration. I feel powerful. I feel free, I feel ... I feel *her* ... This is completely different than in my recent dreams. I feel as if she's closer to me, closer to my heart. All these feelings, these vivid dreams suddenly seem to be vibrating through me ... *I have to find her.*

I pull into my spot next to the valet stand and park the car. All of sudden, out of nowhere, I swear I hear water running, as if I'm in the shower or something. "Do, umm, by any chance, you hear water running?" I turn and ask Tony, who is in the passenger seat.

Looking at me a little strangely, he shakes his head. "No. Why would I be hearing water running right now, Dario?"

Maybe he's right ... maybe I'm hearing things ... but somehow, I just want to confirm my own craziness. Still, I think I can hear her voice in my head, wondering if she can hear me, the way I can hear her. Then all of a sudden she's gone ... poof! Just like that. Crazy.

"Is everything okay, dude?" Tony asks.

"Yeah ... it's all good. Let's roll." I get out of the car, trying to shake off the strange thoughts running through my head.

"Hey, do you know what your dad wants to see us about?" Tony says as we approach the hotel's front door.

"No. Do I ever know what he wants to see us about?" A uniformed bellman holds the door open for us. "How's it going today?" I say, giving a nod.

The Beauvallon is my Dad's baby. His pride and joy. He runs this place day and night, living and breathing it. He believes everyone is an idiot, and no one can run a casino the way he can. His bottom line is: trust no one! Sometimes I wonder if he even trusts his own flesh and blood. He loves to brag that he does all this for me and that someday all this will be mine. There is one major problem with that: I don't want it. I don't want any of it. Of course, I haven't told him this little bit of information, but trust me, he doesn't care what I want. It's really all about what he wants.

We walk across the casino floor toward the elevator, and there she is again. In my head. Why now? Why all of a sudden can I hear her as if she's standing next to me? What's going on? Who is she anyway? And *why can't I stop thinking about her?*

As we approach the elevators, one of my dad's security guards greets us. Dad always has some big thug standing guard.

"How's it going Dario ... Tony?" he says.

"Great. We're here to see my father." I push the button to the private express elevator that goes directly to his penthouse office.

"He's expecting you," says the guard. The elevator arrives, and we step inside.

Gross, I hate how this elevator always stinks like cigarettes. I can't believe that some of Dad's idiots actually smoke in elevators or just smoke so much that the stench of them lingers everywhere. I stick my hand in the biometric reader for clearance. Can we say my dad is a little paranoid? The door closes and we are on our way up to the 63rd floor. My dad has completely convinced himself that no one can get to the 63rd floor without him seeing them first, but I say if someone wants you badly enough, they'll find a way to get to you no matter where you are.

The elevator doors open, and there he stands. Mr. Mancini, as everyone else calls him, greeting us as if he is actually happy to see us. I know better. He's just pleased that we're here to fulfill one of his little tasks.

"Hello boys. How are you? Staying under the radar, I hope. Can't have my best boys drawing any attention to themselves now, can I?"

"Everything's good," I answer short and direct. "So what's up Dad?"

"We had another incident in New York two days ago, and I need you boys to go with Mateo tonight to take care of the package that arrived yesterday from the city. It's critical that it is done tonight. You need to meet Mateo out at the warehouse. And Dario, take the Suburban instead of the Escalade this time ... I don't want any shit in my Cadillac. Understand?"

"Sure thing Mr. Mancini," Tony says, kissing my dad's ass as usual. It makes me sick. "We'll take care of it. You don't have to worry about a thing."

It's crazy to me how afraid everyone is of my dad. He doesn't frighten me. He's just a man in an expensive suit with a lot of money that tells everyone what to do, and they do it. I'm just another puppet in his little army—one who is getting tired of this game.

"Sure Dad, we'll get it done. Anything else?"

"Nope, that will do it. You boys are free to go now." He walks off toward one of his video viewing rooms. The only reason I know this guy is my father because Mom keeps telling me so. I'm not really sure if he's capable of being a real father. To be a real father, he would have to stop acting as if I were one of his employees and, instead, treat me like a son.

• • • • • • • • • • • •

"Let's get going Taylor," my dad says, knocking on my door.

"Just a minute," I yell back in a complete panic.

Checking the clock, I realize my hour is up, and I'm not ready. I will have to address my mind-reading problems later. Knowing I have to get ready fast is enough to think about right now, considering I don't know what to put on. What does "ready" mean here? I guess that would be "Vegas ready"—looking fabulous, like all those people outside our villa.

I've never thought much about my appearance before. No one seemed to care about how anyone looked back in England. Now, I'm struck by how inadequate I feel. I don't have any shorts to wear; my suitcase is stuffed with England clothes—sweats, jeans, sweatshirts and sweaters for that damp corner of the world. I have no choice but to put on a pair of jeans and a T-shirt, even though I know I will look foolish and be blazing hot. Mom and Dad promised us a shopping spree as soon as we got here. I hope it's in their plans for the day. I realize that my normal frumpy hairdo—hair pulled back in a ponytail—will also have to do. And so will zero makeup, since I don't own any.

"Let's get going," my dad yells, knocking on my door again.

"I'm coming!" I grab my purse and leave the room.

It's really glaring out here. I need sunglasses big time. I never needed them in England for the mere fact that most of the time it was gloomy—overcast or rainy. Our villa is set near the main hotel's pool area, which is packed. Around the pool, tons of people soak in the hot sun rays, perfecting their tans, something that doesn't happen very often in England.

"We need to check that out soon," I tell Mckylee as we walk by.

"I know. Look at all the people out here!" she says, scanning the area.

We make our way into the hotel, which is unbelievably elaborate. All the hallways are lined in white marble etched in gold and black designs. The halls lead to the main casino floor, where the marble gives way to carpet in a funky design that looks somewhat retro yet feels inviting. Trying to keep up with my dad and still see everything around me is virtually impossible. I can't wait to see more of it when we're not in such a hurry.

We walk to the hotel lobby, out the front doors and over to the valet drop-off and pick-up. I can't imagine why we're at the valet, seeing as we don't even have a car yet, but Dad approaches one of the attendants and talks to him for a few minutes. Then the guy leaves. When he returns, he hands Dad a key and points to this beautiful, metallic silver Mercedes sedan parked in front of the hotel.

Dad walks toward the car, while Mckylee and I, in complete awe, stand there like a couple of idiots.

"Are you ladies coming?" Dad waves at us to join him, and we make our way over. I'm not paying much attention to anyone around me when I run right into ...

My body is on fire from his touch! Instantly our eyes lock, as if we are in a place where the two of us stand alone. I've never seen eyes like these before: green, blue and brown, all mixed to create their own unique color. He is the most beautiful guy I have ever seen. My eyes drift up to his wavy brown hair and brilliantly bronzed-skinned face. Did I say that my body was on fire? I feel as if I can't breathe.

"Excuse me. I'm so sorry. I didn't mean to almost knock you over," he says as he gazes into my eyes.

"Dario, are you coming or what?" his friend shouts at him from the parked cars near where my dad is standing.

I catch a glimpse of my dad looking at me strangely. I know he is wondering what I'm doing. I am even wondering what I'm doing, and I'm also wondering what just happened. But at least I know one thing for sure as I watch my mystery man walk away. I now know the name of the guy I've seen in my dreams over and over.

Dario.

Perceptions

I can't take my eyes off of him. He walks over to this incredible black Corvette and gets in. His words surround me—it seems I hear them everywhere, interrupting my own thoughts at times. I can hear him more clearly than ever. I'm beginning to assume that he must be able to hear me, too. What is this connection ... him and me?

"I can't believe I just bumped into her, she's nothing like any girl I've ever met in my life. She's incredible. She's so sweet and

innocent and her touch ..." I hear racing though his mind as he starts his car. He looks into the rearview mirror to get a final glimpse of me. I walk to our new car and open the back door. Before I get in, I watch him as he drives away. Concentrating, I try to extract the words that he is saying, but with no success.

"Taylor, get in," Mckylee insists.

"What are you doing?" my mother says. "Let's get going."

As I lower my bum onto the softest black leather seat I have ever sat in, I'm still a little dazed by my unusual encounter with Dario. What an intriguing name, Dario... I can't believe the way his touch made me feel. Not like sparks, but there's definitely an energy running through us. And his smell ... well, he smelled absolutely ... delicious. I still can feel him as if he were part of me, as if he swooshed right through me.

"Oh my gosh ... that guy that practically knocked you over was so hot! And his car ..." Mckylee whispers under her breath so our parents can't hear.

"I know. He was pretty unreal." This time, I am telling her the complete truth ... this Dario *is* totally unreal.

As I sit here in silence, looking out the window, Dario is the only thing on my mind. Mckylee starts asking Dad a million questions about the car and seems to cover all the questions I might have asked. I am thankful for this, seeing as I'm not in the mood to talk to anyone right now.

I can't believe this is Dad's new company car, part of the benefits he's getting for being a pilot for the Beauvallon resort. I can't believe this is our life now—we went from boring Americans living in a small village in England to living like the rich and famous in Las Vegas.

I decide I have to be prepared for just about anything from this point forward. Las Vegas is so different from Fenstanton. First, we didn't have a lot of big highways there, and here they seem to be everywhere. Within just a few minutes of leaving the hotel, we have already been on two different highways—huge ones: Interstate 15 and now 215. We don't call them interstates in England, they are called motorways. Also, we didn't have any mountains back home, and they are all around us here. And where is all the grass and trees? Fenstanton was surrounded by the most luscious countryside. Here, there is dirt everywhere. They want to call it a desert, but the bottom line is it's just dirt. I mean, I thought the desert was supposed to be sandy ... no, this definitely looks like dirt.

The car ride is silent, as everyone is preoccupied studying our new surroundings. We pull off the highway at an exit named "Eastern" and make a right turn at the end of the ramp. The first thing I notice is an In-N-Out Burger on the left side of the road. I can't believe it! I thought In-N-Out Burger was only in California. They were one of the things I missed the most when we moved to England. And here they are, in Las Vegas!

"There's an In-N-Out!" I excitedly point out to everyone.

"Can we eat there later?" Mckylee asks.

"We'll see," Dad says as I try to take it all in.

"Where are we going?" asks Mckylee.

I don't need to hear the answer. For some odd reason,

I'm pretty sure we're going to check out our new house. I don't know why, but I am sure of it.

. . . .

"Dario, what's up? Why are you being so quiet? Can you believe that chick almost knocked you over?" Tony says.

"She didn't almost knock me over, I ran into her. Why don't you text Mateo and tell him to meet us at Capriotti's on Eastern. I'm starving."

I am trying to change the subject. Tony will never understand what's happening to me and what the girl means to me. *The girl.* Hell, I don't completely understand it myself. But her touch! It was like she was filling every part of me, making me feel completely whole. It was like she could move in and out of me, the way a ghost moves through walls. And her smell! She smelled so incredibly sweet and delicious, not like anything I have ever smelled before in all of my 16 years of life! What is with me? I can't believe I just thought a girl was "sweet" and "delicious."

The way she makes me feel, I know it's meant to be ... whatever "to be" means. I know it sounds dumb, but I have to be with her. I don't care what anyone thinks or says.

Pulling into the parking lot, we can't miss Mateo. His car is parked sideways, taking up two spots, and his music is blaring, as if he were some idiot who thinks he is the only one that matters. He is so embarrassing to be with; it's like it gets worse every time we go out—especially now that my dad has us doing more and more of his dirty work. Mateo is starting to think he is invincible, untouchable. I think he's totally out of control.

"Why does he always have to attract so much attention to himself?" I say to Tony as I park the car as far away from Mateo as I can without making it too obvious that I wished I didn't know him anymore. Why do I so want to get away from these guys? I've been around them all my life, and suddenly everything they do and say is bugging me to no end.

"I don't know why you let him get to you. Just ignore him. That's what I do." Tony and I get out of the car and walk toward the sandwich shop, gesturing to Mateo to join us. I am so over all of this shit, I really am.

Capriotti's makes the best sandwiches around. The "Bobbie" is like eating a homemade Thanksgiving dinner any day of the week. The best thing about coming here is they know us and take care of us without saying a word. The second our cars pull into the lot, they start making our sandwiches. By the time we get to the counter, lunch is ready—to perfection.

"Hey Dario. How's life treating you today?" Mikey greets us from behind the counter.

"No complaints. Life is good," I reply as he hands me a bag with our sandwiches and some chips.

"Any drinks today boys?"

"Sure. We'll take a few sodas. Thanks." I hand him a twenty-dollar bill, even though I know damn well he won't take it, because our food is always on the house. I like to offer it anyway, so I can at least leave it as a tip.

"No, we're all good here Dario." he states, just as predicted. I throw the twenty into the tip jar.

"Thanks guys. We'll see ya next time," I nod as we walk toward the door.

Then Mateo throws his two cents in. "Yeah, we'll see you next time boys, and these sandwiches better be right."

"Why do you always have to be such an ass Mateo?" I sneer at him once we're outside.

Without giving him a second to answer, I head to my car. As I get in, I shout to Mateo to meet us at my house. Tony barely jumps in before I speed out of the parking lot.

Feeling frustrated with Mateo and extremely tired of all his shit allows me to deepen and confirm my thoughts about how sick and tired I am of all the bullshit I have to put up with on a daily basis.

"Dude, you've really got to chill and back off of Mateo before this gets out of hand," says Tony. I hear him, but I pretend not to listen or even care.

Driving up to Seven Hills, I remain silent and allow myself to cool down and get a hold of things. Obviously, nothing is going to change any time soon, so I might as well just deal with it all.

I allow myself to drift off, visualizing my mystery girl's face. Instantly, I feel a sense of calm. *Who is she?* All I know is that I need to know her ... I must know her. And I need to find her again as soon as possible. Something inside of me knows I need to be with her.

Approaching the gate to my house, we find two guards standing watch. We never have guards standing watch.

Something isn't right ...

• • • • • • • • • • • •

Turning the corner and up some sort of driveway, I hit Mckylee in the arm and point up the drive at a set of luxury gates with the name **"Bonita Palms"** on them in beautiful, black scripted letters. "I knew it! I knew we were coming to see the new house," I say excitedly to everyone in the car.

"Wow, Taylor! How incredible are all these homes? How awesome is this place?" Mckylee says.

Bonita Palms sits up on a hillside overlooking the entire Las Vegas valley. Coming in, we passed a big boulder with the words *"Seven Hills"* engraved in it as the car headed up the hill. Is this the township we are in?

The main entrance to the subdivision is lined with huge palm trees. It's so picturesque it's as if we are entering the grounds of a castle. Dad pulls up to the gate and stops at a small building that sits in the middle of the two driveways. He lowers his window.

A man in a uniform greets him. "How may I help you sir?" I can't believe we have a guarded gate!

"I am Robert Dove, the new owner of the house on Ridgeway Drive," Dad informs the guard.

"It is nice to meet you, sir. I have a set of keys here the Realtor left for you." He reaches for an envelope, and then passes it through the window. "Do you need directions to the house?"

"No, we're good, thanks. Have a nice day," my dad says as the gate opens as if we were royalty, and we drive through.

The first thing I notice about all the houses is that they

are very different from the ones back in England. Most of the houses in England are much smaller and quite quaint, each one unique. These houses are huge, and all are pretty close to the same color: varying shades of tan. They all look alike.

"Why are all the houses so similar?" I ask.

"They all have stucco on the outside painted in shades of the sand to protect them from the heat," my mother tells me. "The color helps them stay cool inside."

It's so exciting to finally see the neighborhood and house in real life. Before now, we have only seen a few pictures that the Realtor sent by email just before we got on the plane a few days ago. Mckylee and I also looked at it online through Google Earth, but the real thing is way better.

We turn a corner and pull into a driveway. "So, what do you think so far?" Dad asks.

My sister and I are speechless, too amazed to reply. "It's massive!"

"Vegas, we're home!"

Our house is two stories with a front yard landscaped with grass and lots of palm trees, unlike other houses on the block, which have desert plants. I definitely prefer the grass look. We did just move from England, after all. A beautiful set of Spanish tiled stairs lead up to the house and seem to invite us into our new home. The big front doors are made of wood with intricate carvings of flowers and vines on them.

I just know the house is going to be amazing. Dad opens

the door, and, once again, I feel like I am dreaming and this isn't really my life. How could so much change so quickly—and in such an unpredictable way?

9

Revenge

"What's going on Frankie?" Tony asks as he rolls down his window.

"The shit has hit the fan! That's what is going on! The Larson brothers think they can mess with Dario's dad. And as we all know, no one messes with Mr. Mancini."

"What are you talking about?" I ask. "What could the Larson brothers possibly do to require us to plant two guards at the front gate?"

"And all around the entire house," says Frankie. "Those jerks tried to kidnap your sister at the mall about an hour ago! Thank the Lord Dito had driven her to meet her friends. He just happened to be sitting outside waiting in the car when the stupid idiots walked out with her and ran smack into him."

"What? Are you kidding me? Where is Arianna now? I'm going to kill Jake and Zack!" I shout at Frankie, rage building in my voice.

"She's fine. She's in the house with her friends."

"Can you believe this shit, Tony?" I say. "Who do those guys think they are?"

I quickly drive through the gate and park at the side of the house. Mateo rushes up to the car, just as I'm getting out. I had forgotten that he had been driving right behind us.

"What's going on Dario? What was Frankie telling you? Something about Arianna and the Larson brothers? I'm going to destroy those guys ... I told you to let me finish them off the other night!"

"Let's get inside so I can talk to my sister. And I need to see how my dad wants to handle all of this."

I'm doing all I can to seem cool on the outside, even though I'm raging on the inside. I can't believe how stupid some people can be ... trying to kidnap my kid sister! Entering the side door of the house, I find my mom in the kitchen with our cook. They are baking something. Mom only bakes when she is completely stressed out!

"Where is Arianna? I need to talk to her. And where's Dad?"

"I think she's out by the pool with her friends ... but Dario, please don't upset her. She is trying not to be too upset about what happened today. And your father is in his office with some of the guys."

"Why don't you two go find my Dad in his office? I'll meet you there after I talk to my sister," I direct to Tony and Mateo as I head out to the pool.

No matter what goes down now, it isn't going to be pretty. No one is going to take this one lying down, and that means the Larson brothers most likely won't live to see another day—which won't be good for any of us.

Seeing my sister and her friends sunbathing and swimming around like nothing happened puts a smile on my face. She is pretty tough for a 14-year-old. I open the door and step out onto the slate stone surrounding the pool.

"Dario, you're home!" Air calls out at me. "Air" is what I call her when just the two of us are together, a little nickname I use. She runs over and gives me a big hug, getting me all wet.

"How are you? How are you really?" I dig deep with my question as we have a pact to be there for each other, no matter what, and to never lie to one another.

"I'm okay. Really! I knew nothing was going to happen to me when they walked me out the door where Dito was sitting. It's all good. Really."

"Are you sure?"

"Yeah, I was a little scared when they grabbed me. But I knew I was safe when I saw Dito."

"I'm glad you're okay. I don't know what they were

thinking—and who knows what Dad has in store for them. If you need to talk later, let me know, and no going anywhere without taking someone with you, do you understand?"

"Yeah, Yeah. I've already gotten the lowdown from Daddy," she tells me as she heads back to her friends.

I go to my dad's office to see what the buzz is. I am so mad, I want to kick the shit out of those two idiots, but I know they most likely have a death sentence on their heads at this point, so there's nothing more I can do it about it. My dad says it's all business when you involve his family, so you don't involve his family unless you want to die ... at least you don't involve his family the way the Larson's just did.

• • • • • • • • • • • •

"Taylor, you're not going to believe your eyes when you walk into this house." Mckylee says. She has entered the house a few steps before me and now has a look of complete awe on her face. I soon understand why. The entry opens to the most elegant living room I've ever seen. It's paved with beautiful marble floors and has high ceilings. There is a breathtaking fireplace, and just beyond, at the room's edge, there's the most amazing spiral staircase that winds up to a veranda above. The room is unfurnished, but "wow" is the word that keeps running through my mind.

Looking at Dad, I ask, "Did you win the lottery or something?" He laughs and explains that he is making a lot more money with his new job, and it's important to him and Mom that we live in a nice neighborhood with the best schools.

No wonder Mom sold all of our furniture and stuff in England. She wants a fresh start, and we are getting it! Dad has made all this happen.

"Come on ladies, I want to show you the bedrooms I have picked out for you."

Mom and Dad climb the spiral stairway, leading us on a grand tour of our new home. Mckylee and I stay close on their heels, not wanting to miss anything. The first stop is my room. I can't believe I have my very own room with an adjoining bathroom that connects to what my parents call "The Hangout Room." Mckylee's bedroom is across the hall. I am so happy I don't have to share a bathroom with anyone ever again! In England, Mckylee was always using my stuff and taking things that didn't belong to her.

Mom and Dad's room is at the other end of the house. I thought my bedroom was huge, but theirs is gigantic! It has a sitting area with a fireplace in the wall that can be seen from both the sitting room and the bedroom. Their closet is called a "walk-in"—and "walk-in" is right. It's the size of two of our rooms in England. If it wasn't upstairs, my Dad could park his new car in the closet and still have plenty of room to hang all their clothes.

Off of the sitting room is a set of French doors that open to a deck overlooking the whole Las Vegas valley and strip. As I open the doors and walk outside, Mckylee comes in from the hall and joins me. Neither one of us can believe any of this!

Checking out the view and our amazing backyard, we are thrilled to see the beautiful aqua blue shimmering pool below. I've died and gone to heaven? Standing on the deck, I realize I can also see into many of the other backyards. I almost can't believe what my eyes are seeing—every house as far as I can see has its own pool! It's absurdly crazy.

I hear the doorbell ring and walk inside to see who could possibly be here, since we don't even know anyone yet. From the veranda, I watch my dad head toward the door.

"That must be the interior designer I hired," my mom says to us as she enters the hallway. "I felt that it would be much easier to have a designer come in and help me since I don't know the city yet and I need to have things done quickly. Like the floors, painting, and new furniture. Not only that, but your dad's boss offered the designer and I wasn't about to say no."

Mckylee and I decide to hang out and listen in on what our parents had planned for the house. The designer lady hands us catalogs to look at for new bedroom furniture. After we come to an agreement with our mom on our furniture, the two of us decide to head out to the pool while they finish up. A little while later, Dad comes out to the pool.

"Are you ladies ready to get out of here? We're done for the day and we're ready to leave."

"We're starving! Can we go and get some lunch at In-N-Out Burger?" I ask.

"Well, today is your lucky day because that is exactly what I was thinking."

• • • • • • • • • • • •

"Dario, I'm glad you're here. I need you," my dad says as I enter his office at the back of the house, my body still pumped up from the adrenaline rush I felt when I heard that the Larson brothers had tried to grab Air.

"Yeah, sorry. I stopped by to check on—."

"I am so sick of the Larson brothers and the shit they think they can get away with," he says, cutting me off and slamming his fist down on his desk. "The only reason I have allowed any leniency toward those boys and their so-called posse is because their father has done some work for me in the past and always has been a straight-up guy. But enough is enough. Mateo just informed me you stopped him from killing them the other day. Is this true?" He is speaking with the demeaning tone I have come to hate.

"Yes, that's true. It wasn't the time or place for things to go that far. I stand by my decision for the time and situation." As I say this, I'm thinking that maybe it is my fault they attacked my sister. If I had let Mateo take them out, it never would have occurred. I just don't believe that death is always the answer. But maybe my dad's way is the right way to handle those thugs.

Dad is silent for a moment. I don't know what he's thinking, but I can't miss the fact that he's glaring at me. "Well, everything tonight goes as planned for the three of you. I need that situation taken care of ASAP, and I will have Anthony and the guys take care of the Larson boys," he says.

"I want to go with Anthony," says Mateo. "Dario and Tony can take care of the other shit without me."

"Mateo, I know you want to be with the big guys, and I commend you for it. But not yet, your time will come, trust me."

The way my dad praises Mateo for wanting to be a killer makes me sick! I've had about all I can take for now ...

"I'm out of here—unless you need me for anything else," I tell my dad. "And tonight is taken care of." I exit the room exhaling a deep breath of relief that the meeting is over.

10

New and Improved

I just love it when my family and I are all on the same page—life is so much easier that way. We all love In-N-Out Burger, which was just as I remembered it—absolutely delicious! Now once again we're back in the car, destination unknown.

"So where are we off to now Dad?" I ask, hoping we are going back to the hotel. Dad doesn't disappoint me.

"Your mom and I thought we would head back to the

Beauvallon and get a little shopping in. How does that sound to the two of you?"

Mckylee and I just look at each other, grinning. I am so thankful I didn't have to beg not to go anywhere else, and on top of it all, we are going shopping! I'm so ecstatic! It will be great to get some hot weather outfits, as it's clear our England clothes won't work here. When we lived in England, clothes were no big deal. But here, everyone looks so amazing. It's time for me to embrace all this shopping ... I mean, look at all these awesome stores. What girl wouldn't love it?

As we drive up to the valet, I find myself looking for Dario's car. Unfortunately, there isn't a car parked in the spot where his awesome black Corvette was before. I know he'll eventually be back, and I don't want to miss him. Exiting the car and heading up toward the main entrance we are once again greeted by a doorman, this time by name.

"Hello Mr. Dove and family. How has your day been so far?"

"It has been quite successful to say the least," my dad answers as he walks through the open door.

"That's good to hear, enjoy the rest of your day," the doorman replies.

"We will ... thank you, and you do the same."

Standing in the front lobby as my parents debate which way to go to find the shops, I am mesmerized by all the slot machines. I don't understand how people can sit for all those hours and give their money away! It just blows me away!

"Hello Dove's. How are you all today? And what can I help you with?" Kyle, our host at the hotel, asks as he approaches us in the lobby.

"I'm so glad you're here Kyle. We are trying to find our way to the shops. The girls need to pick up a few things," Mom explains.

Waving his arm for us to follow, he leads us down one of the many large hallways off of the lobby entrance.

It seems so unusual to have a mall in a hotel. I guess maybe if you win a lot of money, you need somewhere to spend it all, right?

"Hey Kyle, we need a store where we can buy swimsuits and really cute summer clothes. Do you have any ideas?" I ask while trying to keep up with his fast pace.

"I would suggest the Quiksilver store. You were given a gift certificate to that store and many others in your room. Did you get them in the welcoming basket on the coffee table in the family room?"

"I saw the basket but didn't look in it yet." Mom says.

"I'll run back to your villa and grab the gift cards and meet you all at the Quiksilver store," Kyle offers. "How does that sound?"

"Wow," Mckylee and I both say at once.

Feeling downright great, I lead the way to the store, praying it's going to be a good—no, a great—shopping day, one where I find a lot of cute clothes that fit me perfectly. Arriving at the Quiksilver store, I know in an instant I'm in the right place. The bathing suits hanging on the walls are endless and racks of cute summer clothes surround me.

I've hit the jackpot—and without all those crazy bells going off in the casino!

My praying seems to be paying off. Mckylee and I find tons of outfits and have a blast trying them all on. The sales-girl helping us is really interested in us because she thinks our English accents are way cool, which is kind of strange to me. We don't think we have an accent—she does! We tell her about moving from England to Las Vegas and how we need to add some American flair to our wardrobes. She is having as much fun helping us as we're having shopping.

After trying on every bathing suit I think is remotely cute, I decide on three of them. I also grab a couple of pairs of fun flip-flops, some really adorable shorts and quite of few T-shirts to match. I even find some adorable (did I just use that word again?) sundresses, skirts and blousy tops—amazing for a girl that hates dresses and anything girly-girl. The salesgirl even suggests we get a few zip-up sweatshirts that she calls "hoodies." I guess they're in style, as she insists they're a must. We both pick three, in different colors.

Kyle must have stopped by while we were trying things on, because my dad now has a hand full of gift cards. After finding dozens of amazing things to buy, I'm completely in shock when my parents tell me to get all of it. We have never had a shopping spree like this before ... ever. Even my dad, who is usually not so cool, gets some stylish swim shorts and clothes. He's strictly a white-shirt, dark-tie and dark-slacks guy, so seeing him with these almost-frivolous items makes us both laugh out loud.

Reaching for our many bags, our salesgirl tells us that

she will have them delivered to our villa and then points us in the direction of more stores. We head into the mall, following our mother, who seems to know exactly where she's going. She walks right into a store called Louis Vuitton. I have never heard of Louis Vuitton before, but I'm assuming it's a handbag store, seeing as there are handbags on all the shelves and in the cases.

Mckylee, Dad and I take a seat on a bench off to the side. Before we know it, a saleslady is asking us if we would like a beverage—she suggests a soda for Mckylee and me and a cappuccino for Dad. We nod our heads and, at the same time, watch my mom walk around the store checking out all the bags. She's like a kid in a candy shop! She finally sees one she is interested in—not too big, not too small, and I love the way it hangs on her arm perfectly. Is that me thinking this? Who would have thought I would be thinking about purses, much less a purse that hangs perfectly?

"So what do you all think?" she asks us.

"I like it," I say, getting up to join her at the counter.

"What about that one, though?" I suggest, pointing to a chocolate brown one with this intricate design that I instantly love. The handles are actually beautiful ... I can see my mom carrying that purse—it's amazing.

"It's cute and looks like something you would carry."

She nods approvingly. "Can I see that one too, please?" she asks the saleslady.

Mom models the bag for us and decides she likes the one I picked out the best.

"Who would have known you had such great handbag

taste? There is hope for you yet, Ms. Taylor," she says, then turns to the saleslady. "How much is this one?"

I wasn't quite prepared for the answer, which is still registering in my brain. Did she just say $1,200 dollars for a handbag? A purse to put stuff in and carry around in the car with you? What!

"I'll take this one, and I would also like my daughters to each pick out a bag for themselves."

"What! Did you just say Mckylee and I can also have one of these handbags as well? Or am I hearing things?"

"Yes, I said you could both have a bag of your own. So pick one out before I change my mind," she says.

I look over at my dad, who just smiles and shrugs his shoulders. You don't have to tell me twice to pick out some fancy handbag. I'm all over it! I think she has lost her mind, but who am I to say no to a free, no-questions-asked Louis Vuitton, whatever his name is. Mckylee and I try a few different bags. I decide on a cherry black, patent leather one, which is absolutely stunning, and Mckylee picks a silver, patent leather bag, completely different from mine. The sales lady tells me that my color is an Amarante—who would have known!—and Mckylee's is Gris Art Deco, which means silver. We both giggle when we hear this, never would we have thought up such names for cherry and silver.

"You know what I'm thinking Mckylee? Seeing as how we both got totally different bags, we could share them, and it would be like having two bags each."

"I'm in!" she agrees. "I love the bag you got!" We've never really been the sharing types, but I have a feeling things are starting to change. I take everything out of the ugly handbag I have been carrying for at least a year and move it into my new handbag, so I can exit the store in style. I have never had any style before, so this is a good start. I ask the saleslady to just throw away the old one, because I don't think I'm going to need it anymore.

After the Louis Vuitton store, we make many more stops and end up buying a lot of new things—including plenty of shoes to match all of our new outfits. I have never had a real passion for shopping, but I have to admit I'm having lots of fun. I've never been shopping where I can have practically any and everything I want! And Mckylee and I are basically the same size, so we really get twice as many new clothes. We both realize this sharing thing has lots of benefits.

With so many bags and not enough hands to carry them, we all decide it's time to quit and head back. This whole shopping stuff has made me hungry.

"What are we doing for dinner? I'm starving!" I announce as we head through the hallways toward our villa.

"I arranged with Kyle to have dinner in tonight. Malia is preparing us something special. How does that sound?" Dad asks.

"Like what?" Mckylee chimes in, shouting from behind because she is walking so slowly.

"You'll just have to wait. I want it to be a surprise!" he jokes, holding the door to the pool area open for us.

I'm hit with a blast of hot air as I walk through the door, but this time it feels good on my over-air-conditioned skin. I take a deep breath, releasing it nice and slow as I look at the lavish pool area. Reaching the villa, I've never been happier to be home. I can finally stop moving.

Dad opens the front door, and we all get a whiff of something incredible. I know this smell: Mexican food! I haven't had any good Mexican food forever! This place totally rocks!

11

Secret Lair

Completely aggravated, I head down the hall **to gather the guys.** With every step, I get more and more pissed off. I can't believe I have to dedicate another night of my life to covering my dad and the family's asses. Not to mention having to deal with Mateo and all his riotous bullshit for the next two or three hours. This night is going to be agonizing!

"How can the two of you sit there and play that dumb

Xbox hour after hour? We have more important things to do?" I direct my growing irritation toward Mateo and Tony, who are sitting in my family's theater room, hashing out a game of Halo online with a bunch of other Xbox junkies. "Hello ... is anyone even listening to me? It's getting late and we need to get out of here before this escapade takes all night! I don't want to be with you fools longer than I have to! I'll be in the car—don't make me wait!" I bark at them as I head out of the room and down the hall toward the family room to say goodnight to my mom and sister.

I always say goodnight and give them each a kiss on the cheek, wishing them sweet dreams before I head out or go to bed. I'm superstitious, I've never missed a night, and I know if I did, that would be the night something bad happens to me. I guess they are like my good-luck charms, or something like that ...

"Hey Mom, the guys and I are taking off and I'll be back late, so don't wait up, you too Arianna. You need to get some sleep, okay?" I give each of them a kiss on their left cheeks; it's always on the left side—another superstitious thing I guess. Then I give Arianna an extra-long hug.

"Dario, please be careful and be safe," Air whispers to me as I let her go and leave the room, Mom's "I love you" following me.

"Love you too, Mom!" I holler back from down the hall.

Exiting the side door of the house, Mateo and Tony behind me, I appreciate, as always, the one thing I like about my dad—his compulsiveness about cars: black cars to be exact. He loves black cars—and lots of them!—and I get to drive whichever one I want as long as it's available. Except, that is, when we have a job to do. That's when I drive one of the many Cadillac Escalades, all of them in his favorite color—black. They are all equipped with souped-up engines and are bullet proof bumper-to-bumper. That's his insurance against any crazy fool that tries to take one of us out.

Mateo slams the house door behind him, and we jump into the closest SUV, me at the wheel, since I really don't trust Mateo's newfound *"I think I'm invincible"* act when he drives these days. He has always been a bad driver, and now he thinks he owns the road. It's become downright scary.

We sit in silence as I drive down Eastern toward the Blue Diamond highway. My father has a secret hideout ... he calls it his "lair" in Blue Diamond, a small town about 30 minutes west of Vegas. He was explicit when he told us, in his office earlier, about our mission tonight. "Pick up the package and dispose of it in the desert." Which means six-feet under.

"I hate doing these dumb, useless jobs. I want to be where the real action is," Mateo says, breaking the silence that was lingering heavy in the car.

"Oh yeah," I say, "I'm so sorry for wasting your valuable time. Picking up a dead body from a meat locker out in the middle of nowhere and driving out into the desert to dispose of it isn't exciting or dangerous enough for you?" My voice is sarcastic and undercutting.

"You're just jealous because I have what it takes to take care of a situation and you don't," he snarls back at me.

That statement is so stupid I don't feel the need to

comment. I have no desire to have someone else's blood on my hands, and if that's what Mateo thinks makes him a man, he can have it.

"You two are like a bunch of old women," Tony says with a grin, at least I think it's a grin, trying to break the tension. "You both sit around and argue about the dumbest things, and I have to listen to the two of you constantly bicker with each other. Get over yourselves. Doesn't it count for anything that we have all been like brothers since we can remember? That has to count for something, doesn't it?"

Tony's right. Our friendship should come before all the rest of this crap we are constantly dealing with. It's been getting harder and harder for me to see through the pressure my dad puts on me daily. I so want the stress out of my life. I know that I'm taking it out on Mateo. He's just so damn dedicated to the Mob and the family and all the things I don't believe in anymore. He wants in; I want out.

Every time we pull into Blue Diamond, I get an eerie feeling deep in the pit of my stomach. I hate it here. If this town only knew the deep, dark secrets hidden in the house on the hill at the end of the dirt road, no one would ever want to live here.

My grandfather built this house on his secret piece of land about a quarter-mile out of town toward the Red Rock canyons. It was far away from his crazy Vegas life—kind of like a personal retreat. It was a place where he could pretend for a minute that he was a normal person who liked a quiet evening by the fire reading a book. That was, until my dad took over running Vegas and the family. When he found out about his father's secret house and his land out in the middle of the desert, he had a different type of retreat in mind. My dad decided it was the perfect place to create his own little undisclosed lair, a hideaway built underneath an oversized, three-car garage at the back of the property.

Driving up to the garage, you could never tell that there were more levels to it, added many feet below the ground's surface. Actually, there are two levels, which contain lots of rooms: rooms for storing arms, drugs, money and even people—dead people that is, in a very large freezer, where the bodies remain until someone can dispose of them.

When I say money, I mean money that the government doesn't even know exists. It's called the "skim"—the money that comes off the casino floor and into bags that are brought here before anyone has noticed it was there to begin with, money that is never reported as income to the IRS. All that cash is trucked away daily from the casino and stored in this huge vault with a combination that only my dad and the guy that delivers the cash to the house know. That way, if anything goes missing, Dad knows who to knock off first—which is where the Larson brothers messed up big time. They thought they could skim a little off the skim and no one would notice? Well someone noticed, all right! They used to be in charge of driving the packages to the first drop—that is, until my Dad put an order out for them to be "dropped," or, in other words, exterminated!

I pull onto the dirt road and drive through rugged territory. Soon, the garage appears. As usual, one of the guards on the inside garage is opening the door. I quickly pull in.

Before I even turn off the SUV, the guard immediately closes the door behind us. Let the fun begin!

"Hey boys. How's it going tonight?" one of my dad's idiots asks.

"Life is good," I lie as I glance over at Vincent's car parked down a few spots.

"What is Vincent doing here?" Mateo chimes in.

"He and a few of the guys brought one of the Larson gang's guys in to ask him a few questions," the guard says. "I guess he wasn't cooperating out on the streets, if you know what I mean." He acts like he knows what he's saying, but he's probably never been down in the lair. He probably doesn't have one idea about what really goes on down there.

An elevator sits behind a fake wall, built to look like metal shelves full of auto parts and tools. The wall moves when you open one of the toolboxes (the red one, to be exact) on the third shelf and press a roll of black electrical tape inside it. The tape is really the button that allows access behind the wall—very James Bond like.

Tony does us the honor of opening the wall, and we all walk into the next room. I push another button to quickly close the wall, then the button to the elevator, and we all stand in silence waiting for it to arrive. I'm mentally preparing myself for the unthinkable; I don't know what's going on in Tony and Mateo's heads. I just hope I'm not too late to save someone's existence, there's no telling how far Vincent will push something.

The elevator arrives, and I take a deep breath as the doors open, hoping no one is inside. Empty just what I was praying for. I can tell by Mateo and Tony's faces they are glad it is empty as well. Vincent can be a little hard core, and you never know what he is dealing up. We all get in, and I push the button to level 2.

"How bad do you think my dad is torturing him?" Tony breaks the dead silence of our ride down.

"I'm sure pretty bad. Your dad is crazy and doesn't know when to stop," I reply. I so don't want to be here, knowing I'm not going to be happy to see whatever is going on.

Vincent, Tony's dad, is known as the "enforcer," and no one messes with him. He is the craziest and cruelest man alive and isn't afraid of anyone. He will kill someone for just looking at him. He doesn't give a shit! Vincent and my dad have been together since they can remember—kind of like Mateo, Tony and I. He is my dad's right-hand man, his "enforcer," always looking out for him and taking care of his dirty work.

If you ask me, I think my dad just uses him because he's another idiot who specializes in the art of brutality and will do what he is told and beyond. But I know one thing for sure: Vincent is the most crooked person around, and I wouldn't trust him for anything.

The second the elevator doors open, I can hear it. The loud pitch of whatever moron they have down the hall in the so-called "tool room" wrenches through my entire body.

"Let's go check out which one of those dumb idiots they have decided to torture and what the hell is going on," Mateo suggest as he heads briskly down the hall toward the loud screams of an agonized human, male by the sounds of things.

Mateo barges into the large room as if he's going to get in on the action. There's only one problem with that: no one gets in on Vincent's action.

"What do you think your doing, Mateo? Get the hell out of here right now!" Vincent yells out at the top of his lungs as Tony and I come rushing through the open door.

"Great! Let's just have a f–ing party now that everyone's here!" he shouts. In front of him we see the Larson's younger brother tied to a chair with blood dripping from every part of his face ... Vincent's hand is gripping a baseball bat.

"Have you lost your mind? What are you doing Vincent? You've got the wrong guy! He has nothing to do with the two brothers we have our beef with!" I shout at him as I walk toward the boy to untie him.

This guy has to be about the same age as I am and has never been involved in his two older brothers' shit. He's pretty strait–laced, with a clear head on his shoulders. I've seen him around at a few school parties here and there and he minds his own business. He's even on the honor roll at school. Vincent has definitely screwed up here.

"I suggest you take your hands off of him if you know what's good for you, Dario!" Vincent demands as I continue to untie the guy.

"I guess you'll have to beat me too, then, because you have the wrong guy!" I persist. Seeing that his feet are like Jell-O, I help the boy stand, throwing his arm around my shoulder and propping him up against me. I don't think he knows where he is now or even who is rescuing him—he's completely incoherent.

"I'm warning you Dario!" Vincent yells, his face turning beet red and the veins popping out along his neck. When I turn my back, ignoring him, he grabs my shoulder from behind. Spinning around, I tell him through clenched teeth that he is done for tonight. With the look he gives back, I know he wants to club me with the bat, but I move his victim out the door and down the hall toward the elevator anyway. Tony and Mateo are right behind me.

I'm surprised to see them both with me, especially Mateo. "I figured you'd stay with Vincent, Mateo."

"You did the right thing here, Dario. This kid wouldn't hurt a fly for one thing, and for another, I know for a fact he has nothing to do with his older brothers. Hell, his mother left the other brothers and their dad to try and give this kid a different life," Mateo says. Then he grabs the other side of the guy and helps me carry him onto the elevator.

12

The Beauvallon

*T*he next morning, I notice through a small break in my curtains that the sun is just beginning to rise. I never wake up this early! The time change has everything to do with this—it's already afternoon in England. My body doesn't know if it's coming or going!

Lying in bed, I can't stop thinking about the strange encounter yesterday with Dario. I feel so drawn to him. Bumping into him is the most mysterious thing that has ever happened to me! Knowing that the gorgeous guy from my dreams really exists has taken everything to a whole new level.

"Knock, Knock, hello … are you awake?" Mckylee asks, entering the room.

"Not really … kind of, I guess."

"I just wanted to tell you that Mom and Dad are up and out by the pool. If you want to join us, that's where we'll be."

"Thanks, but I'm going to stay in bed a little bit longer. I'm still a little tired, but I'll be out eventually." I snuggle deep into my covers. I just want a few more minutes to daydream about my beautiful mystery guy.

I wish my friends from back home were here. How great would it be to share all this with them: this fabulous hotel, my incredible new house and, especially, my hot mystery guy. Thinking about my old friends makes me feel lonely and homesick. But lying here in my own self-pity isn't the answer. Not only is it making me miserable, but hungry, too. In fact, I'm starving! It dawns on me that if I get out of bed, I can eat another one of Malia's great breakfasts.

If I called my friends back home and told them that we are staying in a villa with a butler and a wonderful house-keeper who is an unbelievable cook, they would say I was lying. I would think I was lying, too—if I weren't living it myself.

• • • • • • • • • • • •

The door flies open, sending my body into defense mode. I must have been in the deepest sleep, because even though the disturbance has caused me to jump out of bed, I'm still completely disoriented.

"What!" I yell at the shadow in my doorway, unable to make out who is standing there.

"Sorry to scare you Dario, but your dad wants to see you in his office right away." I recognize the voice ... as the door closes again.

I grab my phone off the nightstand to see the time. It feels like the crack of dawn. I can't believe my dad is getting me up ... it's only 8 a.m. What could he possibly want now? I was up practically all night taking care of his shit.

I throw on a pair of jeans and a T-shirt and start walking down the hall, desperately trying to get last night's story clear in my head for the boss's inquiry.

"Hey Dad, what's up?" I ask, entering his large office. I see all of his men sitting around him, as usual.

"Have a seat, Dario." He points to one of the chairs in front of his desk. My heart is racing. I hate it when he treats me like I'm one of his peons who is about to get a scolding. I'm his only son. Why can't he talk to me in private? I feel like he uses me to prove to the guys that no one messes with him—not even his flesh and blood. Noticing Vincent sitting off in the corner, I sit down and prepare myself for the worst.

"So, you want to explain to me what went on last night? I'm a little confused and I need to hear your story," my dad says.

"There is no story. I went out to the house in the desert to get rid of the trash that you wanted us to take care of, and Vincent over there was beating on the wrong guy. A kid. About to kill him, I might add. A guy that's my age and has never had anything to do with the Larson brothers you're looking for, except for having the same blood running through his veins. I took it into my own hands to get him out of there and dropped him off in a wheelchair outside Sunrise Hospital and left. By the way no one saw us. Then I made my way back to the house in the desert with Mateo and Tony, went to the meat locker, grabbed the trash from New York we were supposed to dispose of and took care of it. Which, I might add, took a few hours."

My Dad looks over at Vincent. I sense that he's not too pleased with what he has just heard. "Is this true? You had the young Larson, the one whose mother left her old man to squirrel him away from his brothers and him? You seemed to have left that part out of your story."

My father is glaring at Vincent. I know that look. You could drop a pin on the floor, and the sound would echo throughout the house.

"Yeah boss, but I know he knows something. I know he knows where his brothers are ... I'm sure of it!"

The tension in the room is like a time-bomb ready to explode. Dad looks at me and says, "Dario, I'm sorry I woke you up. You did the right thing. Can you do me a favor and make sure the boy is okay and that his hospital bills are anonymously taken care of?"

"Yeah. Sure, Dad. I'll take care of it," I nod my head, in

shock that he actually stood by my decision.

"Okay then, you can go back to bed now. I'm sure you need some sleep." I stand up to walk out of the room when he readdresses me. "Hey Dario, thanks for taking care of the New York situation for me."

"Yeah, no problem. Anytime."

I am amazed that he just thanked me, that he just supported my decision. Is my Dad feeling all right? He actually made me feel like I'm his son for the first time in a long while.

Entering my room, I fall face down into my pillow. Then I remember that I have to get up in a few hours because the guys and I are having a pool party at the hotel in one of the cabañas. I'm so tired I wish I could blow the whole thing off. But I can't. I won't. Because I need to find her—the girl I can't stop thinking about, the girl who I know is staying at my dad's hotel. Too tired to think even about that, I drift off to sleep.

• • • • • • • • • • • •

"Good morning Ms. Taylor. How are you this morning?" Malia greets me as I walk out to the patio.

"I'm doing pretty good, considering how early it is. How are you today?"

As I approach the table by the pool where my family sits, I notice Mckylee is already in her swimsuit, ready for a day of sunning and swimming. I am so looking forward to lying by the pool all day, doing nothing and hopefully getting some sort of tan. I am glad we have our own private pool, because I'm so pale I can't bear for anyone to see how white my skin is.

I'm still feeling a little delirious from the time change. Thank goodness there is coffee on the table. I really love coffee with cream and lots of sugar. I've only been drinking coffee for a few months. Before that, my parents always insisted it would stunt my growth. But one day I had a sip of coffee at the market in St. Ives, and I've been hooked ever since.

I'm finally starting to feel more alive as Malia brings me another breakfast like yesterdays. While eating, I listen to my parents ramble on about all the things they have to do today. I'm glad that they have agreed to let Mckylee and me stay at the hotel to get in a little pool action.

Finished with my breakfast, I excuse myself to change into my swimsuit. I have never really been into swimsuits, but I've never needed them in England. Now I have a feeling they will be a big part of my wardrobe.

Back in my room, I choose the black and pink bikini, throw my hair into a ponytail and return to the pool. Mckylee has already set up the lounge chairs for us. They have big, comfortable green and brown striped cushions that Mckylee has covered with soft pool towels. I plop down on one and instantly feel the warmth of the sun on my body. I can't believe that it's only 10 a.m. and the sun is already so hot. But it feels yummy on my desperately pale skin!

Lying with my eyes closed, I hear our parents say

goodbye as they take off on their mad adventures to tackle Mom's never-ending list. Hopefully they will be gone all day, because that leaves me in charge. And when I'm in charge, we don't have to do anything but be lazy.

Soon, the sun's rays are blistering. The only way to cool off is by jumping in the pool. Thankfully, there's this shelf in the pool just big enough that we can lie in the water and tan at the same time And Malia has other wonderful ways of cooling down.

"How would you ladies like one of my strawberry pina coladas?" she asks. "Virgin, of course."

"Yes please, that sounds incredible," I respond.

In a few minutes, Malia comes back outside holding two glasses filled with a yummy red frozen drink.

"Here you are, ladies," she says, handing each of us a frosted glass.

"Thank you so much!" Mckylee and I exclaim in unison.

We each take a sip, and I look down at my body, feeling lucky that I tan quickly, without burning. By the end of the day, I will be well on my way to looking somewhat normal for around here.

Feeling refreshed, I get out of the water and lie in my chair. Soon, I sense myself drifting off from the warmth of the sun.

"Okay, I know you're here. Where are you?" A now-familiar voice is speaking in my head. Not completely asleep but drowsy, I wonder if I'm really hearing his voice or just dreaming.

"You're not dreaming. I need to see you again and I know

you're here at the hotel. The Beauvallon. So am I," the voice persists.

"I don't even know you, and I don't understand why I am able to hear you as if you are talking to me."

"I am talking to you through my thoughts, through our thoughts. I didn't think it was possible myself, well for sure anyway, until just a minute ago, when I decided to test it out. It works!" the voice continues.

"To be honest, this whole thing is starting to freak me out, I don't get how you can keep jumping into my thoughts ... who are you? Why are you in my head? ..." I respond.

"Then don't you think that we need to meet to figure out what's going on between us?" the voice continues. *"I'll be at a cabana by the main pool at noon. Meet me there."*

"I don't know."

"Why not? You're already lying out at a pool now, aren't you? Just come to the other pool and be with me."

"How do you know I'm at the pool? Can you read all of my thoughts?" I ask, feeling a little pissy and a little intrigued both at the same time ...

"The more I talk to you, the better I'm getting at it. I'm not trying to scare you. That's the last thing I want. All I want to know is why we can read each other's minds and why I keep seeing you in my dreams." The voice is now soft, almost caring.

"I'll think about it. I need some time to figure some things out. For now, can you get out of my head?!"

Then just like that, he is gone. I'm sure he could still hear what I'm thinking if he really wanted to, because I know if I really wanted to hear him I most likely could, if I concentrated hard enough. He's just stopped talking to me. At least, for now ...

13

Quintessential

**ow I need to come up with some great
idea to get Mckylee out to the main pool with me.** I
can't tell her that some guy told me to come to the pool in
my head! She'd never believe me anyway.

All of a sudden, we both hear some awesome music
rockin' from over the wall, seeping into our patio paradise.

"I love that song. I wonder what's going on over at the
pool?" Mckylee says. "Do you think there's a party or something? Should we check it out?"

How wonderful is this? I don't even have to entice her or come up with some lie that I might regret later.

"Yeah, sure. Let's go," I say. "I'm going to run inside and put something on over my suit. I'll meet you by the front door."

"I'll be in right behind you after I dry off," she says, getting out of the pool.

Malia greets me as I enter the villa. "Is everything okay Ms. Taylor? Can I get you anything?"

"Everything is great. Mckylee and I are going over to the main pool for a little while. I'm just going to get something on over my suit."

"I will call Mr. Thomas and have him set up a cabaña for you and your sister. You don't want to go to the main pool this late in the morning without a cabaña—there won't be any chairs left, and it gets very crowded. And hot. You will want some shade."

"Really? Thanks, Malia. What would we do without you?"

Malia just smiles at me, "Now go and get dressed and let me take care of the rest."

I head down the hall full of excitement and anticipation. I can't wait to see him again—Dario, that is. I can't believe he is actually here and wants to see me. Why would a guy that beautiful want to see me, *need* to see me? Why is he here, tracking me down? I can't believe this is happening to me.

I pick out one of my cute new sundresses and put it on over my swimsuit. Grabbing a pair of flip-flops, I head back down the hall to find my sister.

"Mckylee, are you ready to get going?" I yell out.

"Just give me a minute. I'll be right there."

"Sounds good. I'll meet you in the kitchen," I say over my shoulder. Then I walk toward the kitchen to catch up with Malia to see if she talked to Kyle—that's Mr. Thomas.

"Ms. Taylor, I got a hold of Mr. Thomas, and he says that everything has been taken care of at the pool for you and your sister. Just check in with the pool desk when you get there and they'll take care of you."

Approaching the pool, Mckylee behind me, I feel an incredible sense of energy and excitement. People are milling around everywhere, taking in the sun's deep rays, sipping frozen fruity drinks and soaking in the fresh cool water of the most exquisite pool I think I've ever seen. We walk up to the pool desk and find Kyle awaiting our arrival.

"Hello ladies. I wanted to personally escort you to your cabaña, which I have had all set up for you."

"You didn't have to do that, but thanks Kyle," I tell him as he leads us through the winding path of lounge chairs. The music is outrageous. It is a party: beautiful girls in sexy bikinis and hot guys in cool swim trunks. It's nothing like the beaches in England, that's for sure. For one, it's too cold there to even think about lying outside.

As we get closer to the cabaña, I notice that it's part of a group of cabañas outlining the pool area. It's as if the entire scene is set inside a colorful picture frame.

Everyone here seems so happy and relaxed. The weather is flawless, and I feel like I am in paradise. Following Kyle, I am completely lost in my daydream. Then, all of a sudden, I feel, I don't know ... maybe a presence of a being filling my body. I'm nervous. I can't breathe. Just like that, there he is—standing in front of a cabaña not far from the entrance to the pool—the most beautiful guy ever: Dario ... and he's staring back at me, deep into my eyes as if he is seeing inside my soul.

I'm beyond mesmerized by his stare. As we look at each other, I feel like I know him, and I know that he feels that he knows me. But how? We've never seen each other before, except in my dreams—and, of course, when we bumped into each other yesterday.

"Taylor! Are you okay?" Mckylee asks, slapping me in the arm.

"Yes, I'm fine. Why?" I manage to wake from my self-induced coma.

"Because you're standing here staring at that guy as if you've seen a ghost or something. Hey, wait a minute. Isn't, that the guy that practically knocked you over yesterday in front of the hotel?"

"Ladies are you coming?" Kyle shouts out at us. He's standing in front of what I'm assuming is our cabaña. Then I realize our cabaña is right next to Dario's. That can't be just a coincidence.

"It's not and I'm so happy you came." Once again, I hear Dario drop into my mind.

Trying to ignore him and listen to Kyle isn't easy. Now I've got two voices trying to get my attention.

I only hear part of what Kyle was saying—something about how the cabaña is stocked with water, other drinks and snacks and if we need anything else, a waitress will be coming around. I need to sit down. I'm all of sudden feeling very hot ...

The cabaña is set up like a living room with a wrap-around couch covered with white cushions and colorful pillows. There's a fridge and a ceiling fan with mist coming out of it and even a flat-screen TV. Four lounge chairs are set up in front for anyone who wants to soak in the rays. Once again, I'm completely blown away.

"Are you for real? It is so cool how excited you are when you look at this place. Seeing this place through your eyes makes me appreciate it again." Dario is in my head again, talking in an amused way.

"You don't look well. Here, have some water," Mckylee says, handing me a cold bottle.

"Thanks. I'm not feeling so well. Maybe it's the heat?"

"I'm sorry. I don't mean to make you upset. Do you want me to stop talking to you?" Dario asks so sweetly.

"No, I just don't understand. I don't understand how you can hear my thoughts and how I can hear yours. Don't you think this is all strange?"

Then silence sits between us as we both think respectively about our situation. It's almost like we know not to try and hear what the other person is thinking right now. Mckylee breaks my thoughts once again.

"Hey, I laid out the towels on our chairs. Want to join me? And by the way, can you believe that that hot guy from yesterday is next door to us with all his cute friends? All I can say is *heaven!*"

"Yeah, heaven ..." I reply as I get up, take off my dress and join her. I feel so uncomfortable lying here in my swimsuit, knowing he's over there with all of his friends, some of them beautiful girls.

It's even funnier that neither one of us knows how to act, so we're just avoiding each other as if we've never met before—which technically, I guess, we haven't. I can't stop looking over there; I just feel so connected to him. What is going on?

Sitting here trying not to pay attention to Dario's cabaña, I can't help but notice all the pool attendants they have going in and out, serving their every need. I thought we had it good over here in our little world, but I'm starting to think that he must be famous or something. How weird is it that I don't even know anything about this guy, except for the fact that if I try really hard, I can hear his thoughts. Other than that, he is a complete stranger.

A big guy walks out of the cabaña, and I suddenly feel a pit in my stomach. I don't know his name, but I recognize him. He's the mean, burly one from my dream, from the airport. It seems 30 degrees cooler out here, from the chill in my bones. Then the other guy from my dream follows him—the one who was with Dario the day he practically ran me over. He doesn't frighten me as much ... but the two of them together? None of this feels right!

I think I'm losing my mind! Needing to re-adjust my thoughts, I decide to jump into the pool.

"Hey, I'm going to cool off. You want to come?" I say to Mckylee.

"Sure. Wait up." She hurries to catch up with me.

We enter the pool via a sandy beach. I've never seen a pool with its own beach before, but I like it. I walk into the water at the shallow end, gradually cooling off and continuing forward until the water reaches my waist. Then I dive down, touch the bottom of the pool and glide back to the surface, where I flip over and begin to float. I love floating in the water. It makes me feel so tranquil, so incredibly free.

"It's you, isn't it?" Dario interrupts my calmness as I blissfully absorb the warmth of the sun.

"It is," I answer.

"I like the way you just glide through the water you, seem to do it so effortlessly."

"I've been swimming since I can remember ... back in England, I swam in the school meets."

So consumed with Dario's voice in my head, I don't notice that I've floated right into Mckylee. She splashes me in the face. "Hello, what's up with you today? I've been talking to you and you're not even listening! Let's get going. Lunch is ready."

Mckylee's voice startles me at first. Not wanting to leave Dario's conversation, I can't let her know that there's another reason why we are here. The thought of lunch is a good diversion ... and I'm starving anyway plus I really need something to drink—water, lots of water! Saying, *"Later ..."* to Dario, I head out of the pool.

What a pleasant surprise when we arrive back to the cabaña to see that Mom and Dad are joining us for lunch.

"How did you know to find us here?" I question them as

I walk in to the cabaña, combing my fingers through my wet hair and grabbing a towel before sitting down.

"Your mother and I came back to the villa to have lunch with our daughters, to find them missing. A little birdie told us they had been lured to the big pool by loud, exciting music," Dad says with a tone that is supposed to be funny, but it never really quite comes across that way.

"So, do you ladies mind if we crash your party and spend the rest of the afternoon with you?"

"Heck no, we are glad you came out. This place is so amazing Dad. We feel like we are on the most awesome vacation." And, I really meant it, and I was kind of happy that both of them are here.

"Well then, let's eat," Mom says, handing us each a salad that looks like it will hit the spot on this hot afternoon.

Our parents tell us that it's not going to take long getting the house ready and that we will be moving in sometime next week. That's good news and bad news. I'm excited to have a home again, but it's fun staying here at the Beauvallon. We have everything two girls could want. I will really miss Malia and her great food. I will miss the excitement of the hotel and all the fabulous things that are happening in my life. Most of all, though, I wonder if I will still hear his voice when we move?

I am happy our parents have decided to hang out with us at the pool. We've barely had any down time together since we left England. Not only that, but they are a good distraction for me from the uncomfortable situation in the cabaña next to us. As Mckylee and my dad swim, my mom and I sit in the cabaña, hiding from the sun, and she talks on and on about house stuff, moving stuff and whatever. She keeps my mind occupied enough that I can't seem to hear anything next door. Not even Dario's thoughts.

"Are you all right Taylor? You're acting strange. Mckylee says you've been acting that way all day," Mom says, probably because I really haven't had much to say during her rambling—not that I could have gotten a word in edgewise.

"Everything is fine. I wish everyone would quit asking me that. It is really starting to get on my nerves."

All of a sudden, I sense panic racing through Dario's mind—nothing with any real clarity. Nothing I really understand. Then, before I know it, I see him and the two frightening guys he's hanging with race off toward the pool area exit. The door slams behind them, and he's out of my sight. I no longer feel his panic.

It's almost as if he were never here.

14

Unexpected

"**D**ario, it just pisses me off that we have to leave the babes at the pool. What's going on anyway?"

Mateo is shouting from behind me as the three of us hurry out the back way to get one of the Escalades so we can meet up with Vincent and his guys at a restaurant Vincent owns downtown.

"I'm not really sure what the heck is going on except that Vincent called and he needs to see us pronto," I answer.

"Something's going down and he needs our help. I guess we'll find out soon enough."

We get in the car, and I start it up. Then we exit out the back gate of the Beauvallon and swing onto Industrial Road toward downtown. I like taking Industrial because it runs behind all the big hotels. The tourists don't really know it exists, so traffic moves quickly. Turning onto Charleston Boulevard toward the restaurant, which is just a few miles off of the Strip, I feel bad that I didn't even say good-bye to Taylor. It seems that we just started to connect and then it's all gone. I know that I'm supposed to be close to her ... I just don't get why and how all this is working. The whole thing is so intense.

As we pull into the back of Vincent's restaurant, we notice that Manny and a couple of the guys are already here, standing out back. Parking quickly, we jump out and head toward them.

"So what's the emergency? Where's Vincent?" I ask, walking toward the restaurant's back door.

"Well ... don't you boys look fashionable in your swim trunks?" Manny says in a mocking tone. The other idiots behind him laugh. Even if they don't think he's funny, they always back up any stupid thing he says.

"Yes, don't we? Seeing as we were so nicely interrupted while we were chillin' at the pool with the ladies," Tony says in our defense.

"Hey Dario," Manny calls to me, "you don't need to go inside. No one is in there. Vincent told us all to wait out here."

"Why are you all standing out in this heat?" I ask. "Why aren't you in the car using the air-conditioning?"

"Because all the morons needed to smoke, and they're not smoking in my car."

"Well, we're going to wait in the car. Call us if you need us," I say as Mateo, Tony and I head back over to the Escalade.

I turn the car back on. The temperature gauge reads 111 degrees outside. I blast the air. Those men are fools for standing out in that heat in all those clothes, especially as out of shape as most of them are.

"What do you think my dad wants? I can't imagine what the big emergency is that he needs all of us here," Tony says, knowing damn well we have zero answers for him.

"I'm just pissed off that I'm sitting in this car waiting for his ass when I could be hanging with that new, hot smokin' friend that Cheryl brought with her," says Mateo. "And what was the deal with you Dario, blowing off Angelina while scoping out the homely chic in the cabaña next to us?"

"Yeah, what was up with that?" Tony chimes in.

"First off, if I've said it once, I've said it a thousand times, I'm not into Angelina anymore; and second, why do either of you care who I scope on?"

"Dario, dude, we have to look out for you bro. And that chick next to us was homely. You're going to sit there and deny it?"

"I don't think she's homely ... she's just doesn't have all the makeup like the other chicks around here. I kind of like her ... she's ... I don't know ... different from the others. She doesn't seem as phony as some of these girls. I think she has potential. And the girl is from England, meaning she's probably just a tourist—like I'm ever going to see her again. So drop it, all right."

Just then, I'm saved by the arrival of Vincent and a few more of his men. We get out of the car and follow him into the back of the restaurant to his office.

"It looks like I interrupted something," Vincent says. I'm assuming he's referring to our swimsuits.

"Kind of ... we were at the pool chillin' with some friends," I say. "No worries though, we can find them later. What's going on?"

"Well, everyone, I got a call from a casino pit-boss down in Laughlin who said he saw the Larsons down there throwing a bunch of cash around about an hour ago. I want you, Dario, Tony and Mateo to go down and grab those pieces of shit and bring them back to Blue Diamond for me. That would be after you get out of those swimsuits and get your pieces, because I have a feeling you're going to need them." His tone implies that this is an order, which he normally saves for his regular men, not us. What gives?

"Why are we going? Why don't you send Manny and his guys or someone else?" I say, hoping to get out of the job.

"The Larsons aren't afraid of you. You boys will have a better chance of getting them. They'll think you're just there to talk again, and they think Dario is soft and won't hurt them anyway, so we'll use that to our advantage."

"What makes you think they think I'm soft?!" I say, anger rising in my voice as I look over at Mateo.

"That's the word out on the street, that's all. You've gone soft, acting weak. So go prove they're wrong and bring those Larson morons back."

Waving his hand, he dismisses us. "Now get out of my sight until you get the job done."

As we walk into the scorching afternoon heat, Mateo tries to convince me he hasn't said anything to anyone about what happened downtown that night. I really don't give a shit if he has or hasn't said anything; I just want to find those assholes and be done with all this and let Vincent take care of the rest. As I speed back to the hotel, again using the back streets to avoid the tourist traffic, I share my plan with Tony and Mateo.

"So, here is the deal. We're going back to the hotel to grab our cars. Then we'll go home and change. Everyone will meet back at my place and we'll head out from there. We have to move fast. It's going to take us at least an hour just to get out to Laughlin. But I'm banking on them being quite liquored up by the time we get there."

"I was thinking the same thing," Tony adds.

"Me too," says Mateo.

"Perfect then we're all on the same page." I pull in the back gate of the Beauvallon.

"Taylor, are you ready to get going? Did you hear me tell your mom and sister we have dinner reservations in a couple of hours?" Dad informs me again, although I heard him the first time.

"Sorry, but yeah, I'm ready to go," I answer.

Walking back to the villa, I find myself unable to stop thinking about Dario. Why did he leave so abruptly and why didn't he come back? I decide I need to take a long shower after being in the sun all day. I'm hoping it will help clear my mind. Why can't I get his face out of my head? When will I see him again? I yearn to see his beautiful eyes and hear his thoughts. One thing I know for sure is that I will see him again. I don't know how or where, just that I will.

My shower lasts twenty minutes—twenty, long fabulous minutes. I'm finally feeling relaxed. Putting on my bathrobe, I lie on the bed to rest for just a few minutes and find myself starting to drift off. Just then, the phone rings, scaring me to death. I barely remember even having a phone in my room. After a few rings, I pull myself together and answer. "Hello."

"Hello ... Hello, Taylor, how's it going over there in America?" asks a familiar voice. It's Vanessa. Life sometimes is so weird. Here I am thinking about how much I'm really enjoying it here and then, just like that, I'm reminded of how much I miss my home and friends in England.

"Oh ... my ... gosh ... I miss all of you so much! It's so lonely here without all of you. This place is crazy, insane and unbelievable. I wish you were all here to share it with me. We would have so much fun!"

"Well, we're all here together—I'm with Alison and Clare as well. Hello ... Taylor!" the other girls shout from thousands of miles away. I feel a broad smile spread across my face as I hear their voices. "You're on a speaker phone," Vanessa continues.

"We're in my dad's office, but we only have five minutes because he says it's expensive. So, are you having fun?"

"I'm having a blast, and so much has changed I can't even describe it, not in five minutes anyway. So how is everything going back there? Any new gossip?"

"No ... everything is great, but it's not as much fun without you. You were always the one dragging us off to do something fun and out of the box. We miss you ... but hey, we have to go. My dad is giving us the evil eye. But really quick: what are the guys like there? Totally hot?"

"Kind of. But they are ... are almost ... pretty ... I feel like they are way out of my league. I wouldn't even know how to act around them, even as friends. It is so different here."

Take pictures for us. We want to see everything, okay Taylor? We have to go. Take care of yourself and, by the way, we sent you an email, so when you get a chance, check it and email all of us back. We love you and miss you."

"I love you all too! Miss you. And when I can get to a computer, I'll email."

"Bye Taylor. Have fun!" they all yell back. Then they're off the line just as quickly as they were on it.

All of a sudden, I feel homesick ... in just those few minutes, I miss them all ... and I know, deep down, I probably will never see any of them again.

Glancing at the clock on the table next to my bed, I realize I've only got a few minutes left before I'm supposed to be ready for dinner. I leap from my bed and run into the bathroom. I pull my hair up in my usual ponytail. I love my new, glowing tan. It makes me look more alive than ever and more like the Vegas crowd. Dad has made dinner reservations at one of his favorite restaurants, and I've been told I have to dress nice. I have no idea what to wear.

Panic strikes as I hear him yell out from the hall, "Fifteen more minutes ladies! We need to get going in order to make our reservation on time. Don't forget to wear comfortable shoes because we are going to be doing a lot of walking."

Walking? What's that all about? One thing that I've learned in this short time in Las Vegas, is that everything seems close at first, but once you leave your hotel, from one block to the next, it seems like a mile!

Luckily all of my new dresses are cute, so it isn't too tough finding one. All I have to do is just open my closet door. I throw on a black dress with cute, fun flowers printed all over it, and then try on every pair of my new, adorable shoes. I decide on the black patent leather ones with the small heels, which make me feel quite elegant. Then I grab my new Louis Vuitton purse and, voilá, the new improved me! I can do this, I think. I can fit in this town, and I can make this place my home or—what's the saying?—at least die trying?

Dad knocks just as I happen to place my hand on the doorknob. "Taylor, we have to get going sweetie. Are you ready?"

I open the door. "I'm ready Dad."

"Well, don't you look beautiful!"

"Dad, don't be so weird," I say, punching him in the arm.

"Okay everyone, let's get going. The restaurant is in Caesars Palace just down the block, so I thought it would be fun to walk down the Strip to get there and play tourist for the evening." He drops this on us in such a way that none of us dare to say no, although my mom was definitely thinking of protesting; I could see it all over her face.

Walking the Las Vegas Strip is an event all in itself. I can't believe how insane one street can be. The blocks go on forever, I swear. I think there's a mile between each one. There is so much to look at; I can see why they put all the crosswalks on skywalks over the streets. There are so many things going on everywhere, people might not watch where they're going and get hit by a car. There's a hotel casino called Circus Circus, and I feel like I'm in the middle of one out here!

This craziness makes me miss the quiet streets of Fenstanton, where people can enjoy the beautiful trees and the sounds of the birds. And now with the phone call, I'm missing Clare, Alison and Vanessa. There are so many people crowded onto the sidewalks. As my feet start to hurt, I'm thankful that Dad is finally directing us off the Strip, leading us to what's called the Forum Shops, which looks like it's part of Caesars Palace. The entryway of the Forum Shops is massive and leads, of course, to another mall. How many malls can one town have?

"I thought we were going to eat at one of your favorite restaurants? Why are we in a mall?" I ask my dad, following him and my mom, with Mckylee trailing behind.

"The restaurant we're eating at is in this mall. You'll see," he answers. My parents walk faster through the never-ending maze of this place. I am stunned at how massive this mall is, not to mention we have passed at least twenty restaurants already, which is making me even hungrier.

"Dad, are we almost there?" Mckylee asks.

"Just around the corner girls," he says as he approaches a restaurant call The Palm.

"I was starting to think we would never get here," I say to my mom in a low voice as Dad checks in with the maitre d'. She confirms that Dad had requested to sit on the patio, which really isn't a patio, seeing as it is inside the building. I guess they consider it a patio because the ceiling is painted blue with clouds, to look like the sky. I hope it doesn't rain! Just joking.

We follow the maitre d' to the table, and as I sit down, exhausted from the "short walk," I tell my dad to order for me because I am starving and don't want to deal with the menu, which is huge.

Everyone follows my lead and hands their menus back to the maitre d'. A server approaches our table and asks if he could start us with something to drink. I so badly want a beer, but that's not going to happen now that I live in America and am too young, so I order a Coke like I am twelve again. At least I can have a cup of coffee when we're done eating.

My dad orders a grand feast for the table: a couple of different salads with strange names like the GiGi Salad and the Slater Salad, a filet mignon for Mckylee and me to share, and lots of side dishes to be served family style.

Dishes started coming to the table one after another, which keeps us all busy stuffing our faces. Everything is absolutely wonderful and filling. From our table, we have a panoramic view of the entire indoor mall of the Forum. I especially enjoy watching the people walking through the Forum shops. I never realized that people could be so different. It is quite entertaining, to say the least. I think "people watching" will become one of my new favorite pastimes.

After dinner, we catch a cab back to the Beauvallon because we are all completely in a food coma and so exhausted that none of us can make the walk back. Whenever my family is full and tired, that's a sure guarantee of silence. Arriving at the villa, I bid my goodnights and head straight to my room.

Worn out beyond comprehension, I get ready for bed. After brushing my hair and teeth, I put on my favorite jammies and, without delay, slip into my nice, soft bed. Sleep is instantaneous.

15

Distress Call

 In my deep slumber, I hear a faint voice yelling … a familiar voice … Dario's, "Taylor I need you! I need your help! Please … help me!"

I listen without being able to see through the darkness. I know I need to find him. He needs my help.

"Where are you Dario? Keep talking to me … Lead me to you … I don't know where you are …" I feel afraid of what is happening and of what I might see when I find him.

"I'm here, down by the river bank ... I know you can come to me. You have to come to me. Just like in all the dreams before ... concentrate Taylor ... please ... I'm hurt, and only you can help me."

Dario's voice is getting louder with each word. Then suddenly, it's as if I emerge through some sort of porthole. I can see things, not just hear his words ...

My feet are taking me along a path that seems to fall beside a riverbank. There are a bunch of hotels and casinos here, which is very peculiar ... I didn't think the Las Vegas Strip was near a river. Where am I?

"You're getting closer. I can see you. Look down toward the riverbank. I'm down here."

"I'm scared Dario. I don't have a good feeling about this. What's wrong?"

"It'll be fine, I just need your help, Please ... come ..."

I look down along the dark riverbed and see a body lying in the bushes. I would never have seen him if he weren't directing me toward him. It looks like he is hiding from something or someone. But who? What's going on?

I run toward him, noticing right away that he is covered in blood and seriously hurt. Kneeling next to him, I want to help, but I'm clueless. This is so surreal. I don't know if I'm dreaming or if I am really here. Not knowing what to do, I reach out to touch him. OMG, my hand flows right through him as if I'm not real. As if he's not real. Yet I know that we can see each other ... like we were actually by each other ...

"Oh my gosh, did you just see that? This is horrible, Dario.

You're hurt, and I can't even help you! What has happened to you ... Why are you covered in blood? Is it your leg? What's wrong? ... Who did this?"

"Taylor, this isn't as bad as it looks. I need you to stay calm. I was shot in the leg, and I have controlled the bleeding. I'll be okay. But I can't go to a hospital and I've lost my cell phone and I need you to find my friends, Mateo and Tony, for me. You know them. They are the two guys that are in your dreams most of the time. The two guys that were at the pool yesterday ... Do you know who I'm talking about?"

I nod my head yes.

"Good. I don't know what's happened to them." Dario speaks so calmly in my mind. Sick to my stomach and not knowing what to say, I just continue to nod.

"Whatever you need, Dario. Just tell me what to do!"

"Okay, I'm only assuming, but I'm pretty sure no one can see you but me, so you can walk anywhere you want and no one is going to be able to see or bother you. The last time I saw the guy who shot me was up there in that parking lot behind us where my black Escalade is parked. Find the truck and see if he is still there. We'll figure out the rest as we go. Just keep talking and we'll get through this. Okay?"

"Okay ... I'll let you know what I find." I run up the hill away from him. I'm afraid for him, knowing he must be in pain.

Running toward the parking lot, I notice a bird—a very large bird—circling over me. It's coming closer and closer, almost as if it's going to fly down on top of me.

"What's wrong Taylor ... what's freaking you out?" Dario asks, sounding so weak in my head.

"It's nothing ... just a bird circling around me. It's big; I think it might be a hawk. This is very strange. Even stranger, I think it wants me to follow it. Dario, now I'm sure of it ... because it's leading me right to your truck. It's sitting on the roof of your truck!"

"Really? It's sitting on my truck?"

"Yes," I respond.

"Do you see Tony or Mateo?"

"Not yet. I just got here, give me a minute."

Walking around the truck, I see no signs of either one of his friends, but I find Dario's cell phone on the ground beneath the back of the truck. Well, I think its Dario's ... who else's would it be? I reach out to pick it up, but my hand goes right through it, in the same way it had passed through Dario.

"Dario, no one is here, but I found a cell phone. I'm assuming it's yours, but I can't pick it up."

The moment I share this with him, the crazy hawk swoops down and grabs the cell phone with its large claws and flies off. I can't believe this. What kind of dream is this anyway? I feel like I'm awake, yet I can't touch anything. I'm having conversations with some guy I don't even know but feel like I've known my whole life. And now I'm being followed by a crazy bird that just stole a cell phone from underneath the car—a cell phone that I know Dario needs in order to save his life.

"Taylor, you need to calm down ... you're freaking out in that little mind of yours and it's not helping matters," Dario says, interrupting my little nervous breakdown.

"You're not going to believe this, Taylor, but turn around and walk back toward me. Do you see the hawk circling over me? I'm assuming it's the one that stole the phone from you! I think it's helping us. I think it's bringing it to me."

As I walk back toward Dario, I can't believe my eyes! I'm so excited, I run to get a better look. "This is unbelievable! I think you're right; it's bringing that phone to you." As I get closer, I see the hawk land right next to Dario, dropping the phone within his reach. Then it hops back away from Dario, keeping its distance, yet it doesn't fly away. It's as if the hawk is watching over him.

"Did you see that Taylor? The hawk?" Dario yells in my head.

"Yes, I saw what it did," I say, walking slowly because I don't want to scare the hawk away. I kneel next to Dario. "I wish I could help you. I wish there was something I could do to take away your pain." I feel tears forming in my eyes, but I can't let them spill ... I have to stay strong.

"You have helped me more than you will ever know. If you hadn't come; if you weren't listening ... who knows what would have happened to me? Then your little hawk friend here bringing me the phone ... well, that's amazing." He slowly picks up the phone and dials a number.

Sitting here next to him, I can feel his pain as though he's conveying it through his thoughts. I look over at the hawk and think how odd it is that it's here. How did it know we needed its help? And how much of what is going on is a dream and how much is real? Still staring at the hawk in wonder, I thank it silently, and I swear it looks straight at me. It tilts its head just a little as if it's saying, "I'm here for you Taylor," and then flies away while I admire its beautiful wings and its graceful flight.

I'm jolted back to Dario. Someone on the other end of the phone must have answered his call.

"Dario is that you? Where the hell are you? Are you all right? What happened to you?" The voice on the other end sounds completely panicked and so loud that I can hear it.

"Tony, I'm okay ... what's going on? Is Mateo with you?" Dario asks calmly. It seems like he's trying not to worry Tony, and I guess me, too, since I can hear everything he's saying.

"Yeah, Mateo's with me and we're inside the Riverbank Hotel staking out some room that we chased one of the Larson brothers into. Dario, what's going on? It sounds like you're breathing really heavy ... are you sure your okay?"

"I do have one small problem ... nothing that can't be fixed. I chased the other brother out into the parking lot and the asshole pulled a gun on me and got me in the leg!"

"What? You're shot! Crap! Where are you? We're on our way ... Let's go Mateo. F-- that asshole. We'll take care of him later," Tony yells to Mateo. "So where are you?"

"Down on the riverbed, right behind the Riverbank Hotel's parking lot. I'm hiding back in some trees that have a bunch of bushes in front of them. Bring the truck down here because we need to get out of here ASAP!" Dario hangs up the phone.

"I wish I could do something for you. I feel so helpless. I can't even touch you," I say, feeling pathetic at how useless I am for Dario.

"*Just you being here helps take my mind off the pain,*" he says.

I sit by him, wishing I could ease his pain; I don't understand this connection we seem to have, but I want to reach out and touch him—for real. Dario closes his eyes, almost as if he's sleeping. Within what seems minutes, the black truck pulls up at the top of the riverbank. Both guys jump out and come running ...

"*What if they see me? I have to get out of here! Now!*" I panick.

"*No ... No, stay. I don't think they can see you. I don't think you're really here. I think you're here through me, through my intentions for you to be here. I know it sounds crazy. But trust me. Don't leave ... please.*" Dario turns his head and yells to Tony and Mateo, directing them toward him.

I see them running down the hill, fear all over their faces. Dario is right. They can't see me. No one mentions my presence. I'm invisible, but I can hear and see everything!

"*I told you they couldn't see you!*" Dario says.

Mateo kneels at Dario's side. "I can't believe this Dario! ... How did this happen? What are we going to do, dude?"

"Just get me the hell out of here, now, back to the house in Blue Diamond. I'll call my dad, and he'll send his doctor out there once we're on the road. I need to get out of here now, so will you two pick me up off of this wet, disgusting ground so we can get moving? I'm freezing!"

Watching them carry Dario up the hill and help him into the truck, I catch sight of the hawk circling overhead once again. Why is it here? What does it want? How did it know to pick up Dario's phone and take it to him? Staring at him up in the sky, I find myself fading out of the current situation—trees are disappearing, the riverbank has become a blur.

"Taylor ... Taylor, are you coming?" I hear Dario faintly in my thoughts as I drift more and more toward the hawk circling above me. It feels as if the bird wants me to be a part of him. I'm intrigued with his glorious beauty. It's as if he is calling to me, pulling me away from Dario and toward him ...

Then all of a sudden, my mind is blank ... like it's filled with darkness of the night once again.

16

Survival

As Mateo races back toward Vegas, with me and Tony in the backseat, I start to feel myself drift out of consciousness. Maybe I've lost more blood than I ...

"Dario! Stay with us! Stay awake! You can't sleep, not in your condition, not yet!" I hear Tony yelling at me from what seems a great distance.

"Yeah, Yeah ... I'm awake ..." I mumble, thinking to

myself how I wish Taylor could have stayed with me instead of these two jerks. She would have kept me awake. She would have been someone to talk to, someone to keep my mind off this excruciating pain. Thinking about this horrible pain reminds me that I need to call my dad, seeing that I'm going to need a doctor to get this damn bullet out of my leg.

"Hey! ... Can one of you pass me a phone? I need to call my dad." I shout as best I can over the loud music they have been playing in their mad attempt to keep me awake.

"Sure, Dario. Here, use mine." Tony hands me his iPhone, already dialing my dad's number. I think about what to say so that I don't completely freak him out.

My dad answers the phone after one ring, which is unusual, seeing as it is 3 o'clock in the morning. "What's up Tony?" he says.

This catches me by surprise. I have forgotten I'm on Tony's phone.

"No ... no Dad. It's Dario."

"Dario? What are you doing on Tony's phone? What's going on?"

"I don't want you to panic, but I need you to call in the doctor. We're on our way to the house out in Blue Diamond."

"What! Dario, what the hell is going on? Who's hurt?"

"Someone's been shot. It's not bad. I don't want you to freak out, but can you just get the doctor to Blue Diamond ASAP?! We're about twenty minutes out." I'm talking as loud as I can, trying to get through to him.

"I'll meet you boys there," he says. Then he quickly hangs up the phone. I swear I heard him leaping out of his bed just before the phone clicked off.

I'm drifting in and out. I want the pain to go away, but it's starting to get worse, and it feels like the bleeding has started again. Lying here, I'm wishing we were at Blue Diamond already.

As I try to block out the pain, I turn to thoughts about how I'm reacting to all of this. I'm calmer than I would have imagined. I never in a million years thought I would be the one with a bullet in me. If I had to bet on it, I would have guessed Mateo would be the one long before the rest of us. Maybe that's why I don't gamble; I don't seem to be very good at it.

Finally, I can feel the tires begin to roll over the Diamond's dirt road. I have a glimpse of hope, anticipating that this blasted pain will soon be gone.

As usual, we pull up to the garage; it's opened for us immediately by one of the guards inside. We pull in, and I see to my surprise that my dad's car is already here, but there's no sign of the doctor's car.

Mateo turns the car off and jumps out quickly. Tony grabs the back door, opening it for me. Together, they help me from the back seat. Right behind them, I see my dad rushing out from behind the secret wall.

"Shit Dario! I can't believe this. I knew it was you when you wouldn't tell me who was shot!" I can hear the fear in his voice.

"Dad, I'm going to be okay. Don't worry." I try to calm

him down, trying to sound strong. I've never seen my dad worried before. It's kind of nice. And then, I feel my pretend strength beginning to drain.

"Where's the doctor? When is he going to be here?" I ask wearily.

"He's downstairs setting up the bedroom for surgery. I picked him up myself." As we enter the elevator, I wish we could just go to the hospital, but that isn't an option. Hospitals ask lots of questions. You have to be able to explain where a gunshot wound came from, and they would have to notify the cops. In my case, that wouldn't go over well.

Tony and Mateo steady me on each side, helping me walk. We keep banging into the walls of the narrow hallway, finally entering the bedroom where the doctor is rushing to get everything ready. Are my eyes seeing right, or is that idiot Vincent helping him? Vincent? Being a nurse? This makes me angry. This entire problem is his fault!

"Hey Doc, how's it going? Glad you could make it with such short notice! Too bad it's not under better circumstances," I greet him with what humor I have in me and feeling I've got to put up some kind of a show for him and my dad. I ignore Vincent totally. Doc looks at my face, and then drops his eyes to the floor, where my blood is dripping.

"Dario, let's take a look at you. You two bring him over and help him on the table." Doc directs us with his voice, hands and eyes at the same time. I know he's feeling some kind of pressure; with me being hurt and my dad hovering over him. Not to mention, it's the middle of the night—not normal "office" hours.

The guys help me up on the table. It's not very comfortable, but at least there's a pillow for my head. The doctor quickly unbuckles the belt on my leg, cuts off my jeans and looks at the bullet wound in my right thigh.

"Well, the bullet is still in there, that's for sure. I can't knock you completely out to remove it without you being in a hospital. I don't have the right equipment here. That was quick thinking on slowing down the bleeding by using your belt, it doesn't seem like you lost too much blood."

"Thanks, Doc. I saw it in some movie and figured it was worth a try."

"Okay. Here's what we're going to do. I'm going to hook up an IV and get some fluids into you and give you a good dose of morphine for the pain. But you're going to have to stay with me while I dig that bullet out of you. Once I'm done, I'll clean you up and give you something that will let you rest for a while. Sound good, Dario?"

"Whatever you have to do, do it Doc. Just get it done. I'm already in so much pain, how bad can it be?"

I close my eyes to prepare myself for the worst. My entire body is beginning to throb with the pain radiating from my thigh.

Everyone around me keeps their silence. It's such a welcome change from the usual yelling that goes on when we're all together, maybe I should get shot more often! On second thought ...

The Doc hooks up my IV, starting the morphine. As the drug sends a relieving sensation, I can feel my body start to relax and drift into an almost twilight-like sleep.

"Dario, are you still with me?" I faintly hear the Doc ask me. I nod my head slowly, letting him know that I am somewhat coherent. I'm feeling very relaxed. To tell the truth, I'm actually feeling pretty good.

"Okay, I'm going to start. This should be pretty quick. I can see the bullet, but I'm going to have the boys hold you down so you can't move, okay? Dario, I need you to acknowledge that you heard me please."

The Doc continues to mumble in my head even as I fade fast. Once again, I nod my head. I feel the doctor poke and prod at my leg but tell my higher-self that it's not happening to me, my way of pushing the pain away from me. Then, just like that, it's over.

"Dario, I'm done. You did great kid. We're going to move you over to the bed now." I know he's talking to me; I'm trying hard to listen. "Then I'm going to give you something to help you sleep and some antibiotics to fight off any infection. Nod if you understand," the Doc tells me.

I nod a slow yes—at least I think I do. And then before I know it, I am laying on the bed. Someone puts a warm blanket over me, and I instantly fade into its comfort and warmth as someone else covers me with another blanket.

I'm so happy that I'm going to live another day. Another day to see Taylor, another day of the ecstasy I feel when I'm with her. Then Doc gives me a dose of something that makes everything go black ...

17

Escalation of Truth

"*T*aylor, hey sweetie, are you going to sleep all day?" I hear my mom softly whisper. As I come out of my deep slumber, I realize she is sitting next to me on the bed.

"Mom? What time is it?" I ask, feeling groggy and beyond tired. I feel like I could sleep all day.

"It's 1 o'clock in the afternoon, honey," she says.

It takes me a few minutes to grasp what she has just said. "1 o'clock?!"

There is no way I slept till 1 o'clock in the afternoon! I feel like I have barely slept at all! Suddenly, I flash back to my strange dream, a dream that doesn't really seem so much like a dream.

"Yeah Mom, I'm going to get up ... just give me a few minutes, okay?" I ask, gently nudging her off of my bed. I need some time alone to think.

"Okay, Ms. Taylor, but if you're not up and moving in fifteen minutes, I'll be back," She says with a grin as she pats my leg.

Rolling over on my back, staring at the ceiling, I contemplate my new life, trying to sort fantasy from reality. Last night was unbelievable. Was I really there with Dario, or was I dreaming? Oh my gosh ... has Dario really been shot?! How will I find out? And the hawk! That strange hawk! What's with me? Why am I so connected to him when I barely know him, or who he is. *Someone, anyone, please explain to me what is happing!*

Then I realize that all that really matters is when I'm going to see Dario again.

I throw on some shorts and head out of my room. The villa is so quiet.

"Hello ... is anyone here?" I shout out.

"In here Taylor!" Mom yells from the master suite at the end of the hall.

I find her sitting on the couch, watching a movie on the telly and sorting through some papers.

"Good afternoon, sleepy head. I'm so glad you finally decided to join me," she says with a hint of sarcasm.

"Where is everyone?"

"Your dad had some things he needed to do, and I really didn't feel like going with him, so your sister decided to go and keep him company." She stands up. "I'm going to make some coffee. Would you like some?"

"Sure, that would be a good start." I follow her into the kitchen, which is unusually quiet. "Where is Malia?" I ask.

"Oh, she had to take her daughter to the dentist. I told her to just take the rest of the day off. The hotel offered to send someone else, but I'm sure we'll manage, don't you think?"

Taking a seat on one of the barstools by the counter, I sit quietly, waiting for my coffee and only half-listening to my mom—until she mentions the house is going to be done early and that we most likely will move by the end of the week. Now she has my attention! I don't want to leave here! I think that this is the only place Dario knows where to find me since I'm always here when I hear him. Suddenly, I am panicked.

"What! That's like only two or three days away ..."

My mother hears the edge in my voice. "I'm a little confused here Taylor. I thought you couldn't wait to move into the house?"

"You're right. But that was before I realized how much fun it is staying here."

"I like this place," I say, trying to convince her while visions of never seeing Dario again fly through my mind. Right now I just see him lying there hurt while he waits for his friends to come and find him.

"Do you want me to put cream and sugar in this for you?" I just love the way Mom so conveniently changes the subject—sometimes she doesn't even realize she's doing it. Coffee, cream and sugar pulls me away from Dario thoughts. It sucks that she is so good at it.

"Yes, please," I say. She hands me my coffee, and it smells amazing. I take my first sip and savor the flavor. Then I decide that I really am looking forward to the new house and having our own home again; in my heart, I know that Dario will always be able to find me.

"Thanks for the coffee Mom. It's exactly what I needed. I think I'm going to go and stick my feet in the pool for a minute. Do you want to come?"

"It's a little too hot out, but thanks for the invite. I'll go back and watch my movie. Come in when you're done, and we can finish talking about the move over to the house."

Stepping outside, I wonder what else would there be to talk about? We're moving to the house at the end of the week, and that's that. Of course we are. We can't live in a hotel forever.

I open the sliding glass door, and a blast of hot air once again hits me in the face. I can't believe I'm still surprised at how incredibly hot it can be outside. Before I let the blazing heat torch me in my clothes, I decide to head back in to get my swimsuit on. I hurry to my room, quickly throw on the first swimsuit I see, and soon, I'm back outside.

The pool's clear blue water calls my name as a wave of heat again blasts my face. Unwilling to suffer another minute in the searing air, I jump in. The water quickly cools my body and forces me to release the air from my lungs as I submerge to the bottom of the pool.

Diving down with my eyes closed, I soon find my hands touching the smooth, tiled surface. In my mind, I relive last night. The fear I had when I saw Dario's wound floods my mind and body, until the lack of air in my lungs forces me back up to the surface. Breaking through the water, I gasp for air. Dario's face fills my mind, and I'm now convinced that last night was not a dream ... I was really there! All I can do is pray for his quick recovery. And safety.

Deep in thought, I float on the water's surface, staring up at the sky. Within moments, I catch sight of a beautiful hawk gliding above me. Admiring its grace, I can't help but wonder: is this my hawk? Mine and Dario's? Is it actually here, or is my vivid mind playing tricks on me? Can other people see it? How can it be here—and in my dreams as well? Was last night a dream?

I can't take my eyes off of the hawk as it descends through layers of air, getting closer and closer until it lands on the back of one of the lounge chairs at the opposite end of the pool. He is watching me. Then it hops off the chair and begins to walk toward the edge of the pool where I am. I'm mesmerized.

Slowly, I move backwards until I reach behind me, finding the stairs of the pool, where I sit down. The hawk stops, turns his head toward the door, then looks at me again as he advances to where I'm now sitting on the step in the pool. I can literally reach out and touch him! I'm amazed by its beauty and intrigued by the power of its presence. We share a strange tranquility—a tranquility that is immediately interrupted when my mom pulls open the sliding glass door.

"Don't move Taylor! If you don't move, he won't hurt you!" she yells at me, panicking.

I already know the hawk won't hurt me. Actually, I'm starting to realize that this bird is here to protect me, maybe even Dario, too. Not allowing my mother's fear to interfere, I hold its stare, even as it slowly lifts off from the pool ledge and flies directly over my head, quickly moving out of sight. Amazed by its beauty and grace, I barely hear my mom standing by the pool's edge, shouting.

"Are you okay Taylor? Where did that hawk come from? You could have been seriously hurt!"

"Wasn't he amazing?" I ask.

"That's not amazing, that was scary. Those birds are predators, killers! You could have been seriously hurt. I think you need to come inside while I call Kyle and report this."

In my heart, I know that I need to convince her not to call anyone—not that anyone would believe her anyway. I jump out of the pool and wrap a towel around me. "Mom, everything is fine. No one is hurt here," I say. "It was just a bird—you seriously need to chill out, please." I know that I need to do what she does so well—change the subject.

"Taylor, you don't understand. That is not normal. I've never seen anything quite like that before."

"Exactly. So if you call Kyle, he won't believe you anyway. Let's just let it go and finish watching your movie.

Better yet, why don't you make me something to eat? I'm starving." I suggest this because cooking always takes her mind off things.

"You're hungry? I guess I could make you something. What are you in the mood for, lunch or breakfast?" she asks.

"Surprise me. I'll be right back. I'm going to go and get out of this wet bathing suit."

Alone in my room, I realize that a new reality is taking over my life. Where is this all going to take me? I need to find and reconnect with Dario more than ever—not because I yearn for him, but because I need to know that he is all right, I need to know he is alive ...

I am startled out of my thoughts about Dario when I hear my dad and sister coming in the front door of the villa. I hurry to greet them. I need to show them that everything is normal and fine before Mom gets to them and starts freaking out again.

"Hey you two, what's up? Where were you today?"

"Well good morning sleepy head. You're finally up? Where's your mother?" Dad asks as he pats me on the head in his passing.

"She's in the kitchen making me something to eat." I turn to Mckylee. "So where did you go? What did you and Dad do?"

Before Mckylee can respond, my mother's excited voice filters in from the kitchen. She's trying to explain to Dad about the hawk sitting on the back of a lounge chair out by the pool. I head in to distract them.

"Would you explain what happened?" says my Dad. "What is your Mom talking about?"

"Dad, seriously it was nothing. I was swimming in the pool and a beautiful hawk was flying overhead and landed on the back of one of the lounge chairs. He was amazing. I wish you had been here. It scared Mom a little, but it was fine. Really, it was nothing."

"Taylor, your Mom's right and has every reason to be concerned. A hawk so close is not natural, but seeing no one was hurt, I guess there was no harm done." He turns to Mom, trying to comfort her.

I sit down on a barstool, taking a deep breath. With the way my life has been going, I can only imagine what might happen next.

18

Transition

"**D**ario, honey, you need to wake up.** The doctor's here to change your bandages, and you also need to eat something."

I hear my mother's soft, sweet voice in my ears as I feel pain shoot through my leg, reminding me that I have been shot. Slowly coming to, I see her sitting in a chair next to me and realizing I'm in my room at home.

"How did I get here?" I ask, groggily. "The last thing I remember was being at the house in Blue Diamond."

"You were at Blue Diamond. But the instant your father told me what had happened, I insisted that he get you home immediately ... I didn't care how he did it. They moved you on a flat emergency board into the back of one of the trucks. You needed to be here in your home, safe with me," she says, reaching out to hold my hand.

"So how are you feeling Dario?" I turn my head and see Doc standing at the end of my bed.

"I've felt better. How long have I been out for?" I notice an IV stuck in my other hand.

"It's been a few days. I've been checking in on you every day. Everything seems to be healing well."

"A couple of days? Are you kidding me? How the hell have I been out that long?!" I struggle to sit up, startling my mother and Doc with my outburst. Then I settle back on my pillow, trying to pull together everything that's happened.

The first thing that comes to my mind is that Taylor must be sick with worry. The last time I saw her, I was lying near a riverbed, shot. Considering that she saved my life, I at least need to let her know I'm okay.

"Dario, how's the pain level? Do you want me to keep the IV in another day so you can continue on the morphine? Or can we go ahead and take it out and I can get you some pills for the pain?"

I barely hear the Doc through my thoughts. But out of the corner of my eye, I notice him staring at me. He seems to be waiting for an answer to a question I barely understood. My mom is no longer holding my hand, where did she go?

"I'm sorry, what did you say?"

"The pain. Do you need more morphine? Or will a pill suffice so we can take out the IV?"

"Yeah, take out the IV. A pill will be fine," I reply as my mother enters the room with a plate of food big enough to serve a king and his court. All that really matters right now is that I get out of here ASAP. I need to find Taylor.

• • • • • • • • • • • •

The anticipation running through my veins is making it difficult to sleep. Today we move into our new house. I am rather excited to see the house all finished, but I'm also sad that we're leaving the Beauvallon. I've had the most incredible time here.

Meanwhile, I can't help but be concerned about Dario. Where is he? I haven't seen or heard from him in days, and it's making me sick with worry. I've heard utterly nothing. What if I never see him or hear him again? Will he know where to find me?

Even though it's early, I might as well get the day started. I take a quick glance around the room, happy that I've already packed all of my belongings, because I'm definitely not in the mood to deal with any packing today. I quickly jump out of bed, put on some denim shorts and a pink Roxy T-shirt, throw my hair into a ponytail and I'm off to seek some seriously needed coffee.

Delighted to find Malia in the kitchen preparing break-fast, I give her a hug and tell her how ecstatic I am that she is going to continue working for us at our new house. Mom gave us this great news last night at dinner.

"Ms. Taylor, I am so happy to be able to work for your family. You all make me feel so appreciated and welcomed," she says, a hint of tears in her eyes.

Soon, I'm out on the patio, where the rest of family is sitting, listening to my Dad give out instructions. "Just to give everyone a heads up about our personal belongings: we won't be moving anything over to the house ourselves. The bellmen are going to pick everything up at 9 a.m. and deliver it later on today. All we have to do is make sure it's all packed and ready to go when they get here to pick it up."

That's so awesome. I really wasn't looking forward to moving all of my crap, and over the last week and a half, I have accumulated a lot of it.

The sun is already quite warm, but it feels nice. Sitting down on the pool's edge, I place my feet in the water and ponder the fabulous time I've had here. Closing my eyes and tilting my face towards the warm sun, I fade off in my mind to try and contact Dario.

"Dario, where are you? Are you okay? I need to talk to you. I'm worried about you ..." I send that message out into the universe over and over again, praying for a response from him—until my dad interrupts, telling me it's time to go.

Sad and in a daze, I head back into the villa. I notice that all of our suitcases, boxes and things are gone. The bellmen must have picked them all up already. I grab my purse and make my way out the door with an empty feeling inside. I still haven't seen or heard from Dario, and this is the only place he knows where to find me. My body aches for him, and my mind can't stop thinking of his beautiful aura.

As usual, the Mercedes is waiting for us at the valet stand. I climb in the back next to Mckylee. All of a sudden, I am experiencing an overwhelming feeling, the feeling I've been waiting for. It's him! Dario's here! Out of the corner of my eye, I catch a glimpse of him—he is here, getting out of his car and heading into the hotel. I can't believe it. He's okay! Still unsure of how our mind connection works, I concentrate frantically, gathering all my intentions. *"Dario, you're all right! I have been so worried about you. Can you hear me? I'm here in the car behind you."*

"Yes, I hear you!" He turns around and looks, quickly spotting me. *"Taylor, where are you going? I need to see you; I need to talk to you. When are you going to be back?"* He sounds worried as our car begins to pull away. I turn and look out the back window.

"We're not coming back."

"What? Where are you going? Back to England?"

"No, no, we live here now. We're moving into our house in some area called Seven Hills. Do you know where that is?" I hope he can still hear me, even though he is no longer in sight and the car is getting farther and farther away from the hotel. After a long pause, I hear him, though his voice in my head is distant.

"I know the place, I'll find you."

I'm so ecstatic; I can't believe how lucky I am that I got to see him before we left the hotel! I thought for sure I was never going to see him again. Trying not to show my burst-ing enthusiasm, I decide to engage in conversation with Mckylee to keep my mind off of the situation and to calm down, and before I know it, we're pulling through the gates of *Bonita Palms* and parking in front of the house. Dad opens the garage door and there sits my mom's awesome Porsche Boxster Spyder that was shipped over from England. Seeing her car reassures me that we're finally home.

I'm excited! I rush to the front door, Mckylee on my heels. We both stop abruptly in the foyer. My mom has done an unbelievable job!

First of all, there's an actual dome overhead that filters in outdoor light when you walk in! The entry is done in a black and white motif creating a large flower designed with alternating marble tiles on the floor of the front door area. It's amazing! The rest of the front room—what Mom calls the formal living room—has a black baby grand piano off in the corner, white marble floors and elegant rugs. The piano is kind of cool, except for the fact that no one in our family really plays the piano.

Walking into the kitchen, decorated in natural colors, I instantly like that it is not so fancy, though it has a nice black countertop and stainless steel appliances. Attached to it is the family room, where I am sure we will be spending most of our time. It has a comfortable-looking tan sectional couch, big enough for all of us to sit on while watching the new big-screen TV that's hanging in the center of a built-in bookshelf monstrosity. This TV is HUGE!

I can honestly say I have never seen a house quite like

this before. Excited to see my room, I run up the back stairs to check out Mom's finished product.

Once there, chills run throughout my whole body ... it's perfect! I have a queen-size bed with the black and pink flowered bedding I picked out and lots of fab throw pillows. I even have my own flat screen TV hanging on the wall. I love it! The bathroom is next—all done in black with pink accents. Opening the other door in the bathroom, I head into the hangout room I share with Mckylee. Mom has created two separate computer areas, each with brand new Apple computers. There is a full entertainment system with a DVD player, stereo, a Wii, and a huge flat screen TV hanging on the wall. We even have a sectional couch and two large beanbag chairs to sit on. This place is insane! I stand there in complete awe when Mckylee enters the room.

"Can you believe this place?" I say. "It's just so mind-boggling that we are actually going to be living here!"

"It's unreal! This house is unbelievable," she answers. Finding our parents in their room, we thank them for everything they have done for us.

"I can't believe this house, our rooms, the hangout room," I say. "I really wish someone would pinch me. Forget that, punch me and wake me up, because this is all too unreal."

In the middle of all our family giddiness, the doorbell rings. The vans from the hotel have arrived and the rest of the unpacking begins.

I can hardly wait to unpack. Grabbing a box and a few loose items, I head back up the stairs. I close my door behind me, sliding down the back of it and placing my bum softly on the floor.

What a day! But the best part of it was finally seeing and talking to Dario. Although he was limping, he looked like he was okay. Maybe a little tired. I'm so relieved that he made it and that he found me before I left. I've never been a big believer in destiny, but lately I'm starting to believe anything is possible.

19

Beyond the Door

"**Thanks for driving me to the hotel, Tony.**"

"I really didn't have a choice Dario. You weren't taking no for an answer—even with your mom begging you to stay in bed. You know, the thing I don't get is why once we got there; you all of a sudden wanted to get back home. What's with you?" Tony asks.

"I'm delirious Tony. Maybe it's the drugs, I know one thing for sure, I need to go and lie down. I don't feel so hot.

I'll catch up with you in a little while," I walk down the hall toward my room with intentions other than sleeping.

Looking back I see my mom and Tony standing there in the living room staring at me, I nod and enter my room, closing the door behind me. I need to figure out what's going on between Taylor and me. What is this connection we have? Why is she here? This thing with her is more than just a coincidence, but what is it?

Lying on my bed, I contemplate my desire for answers and, most of all, my desire for her. I mean, why her? If I wanted a girl, I could have just about any girl in Vegas. What's the attraction? Trying to make sense of all the recent events, I remember a bedtime story my grandmother used to tell Arianna and me when we were younger—back when life was simple and I knew nothing of my father's business.

It was a story, she would share, about finding your true heart's desire—something that happens to everyone only once in a lifetime. When it does, it's their choice to accept it or deny it, but whichever path they choose, there is no turning back. I loved how passionate she was about the legend, but I always thought it was nothing more than a silly little bedtime story. Now, I'm starting to believe differently.

Shit, my leg is killing me. I guess going out wasn't so smart after all. The intense throbbing suddenly takes my thoughts away from everything else. I'm forced once again to take some pain medicine, even though I really don't want to. It makes my mind all fuzzy and drowsy. I decide to take a nap. If I can get a few hours of sleep now, it will be nightfall when I wake ... and then I will work on getting Taylor to come to me in her sleep once again.

· · · · · · · · · · · · · ·

Deep in thought, I jump at the knock on my door.

"Taylor, hey, are you in there? Can I come in?" Mckylee asks from the other side of the door, already turning the doorknob.

"Sure, come on in."

As the door opens, Mckylee greets me with a grin spread across her face.

"What's up?" I ask.

She makes herself comfortable on my bed. "You've been shut up in here for hours and I wanted to see what you're up to. And besides, Mom and Dad wanted me to tell you that dinner will be ready in about 15 minutes."

"Thanks. I just really wanted to get some things organized so I won't have to deal with it later. What have you been up to?"

"Pretty much the same thing—and then throw in a nap on top of all of that. I was tired. Ready to go downstairs?" She asks.

We head to the kitchen, where I'm thrilled to see Malia already here and cooking dinner. I'm pleased, not only because she always makes something really good, but because she brings a certain calmness to our family. Even though we've only known her a little a while, Malia has already become part of our family.

Just as I take a seat on one of the barstools, the doorbell rings.

"I'll get it." Mckylee says. She hurries out of the room.

"I wonder who that could be?" I ask my parents. They look at me, then each other, all of us puzzled. In a moment, Mckylee returns.

"It's two girls from down the block. They wanted to introduce themselves and say hi."

"Really? Did you invite them in?" I ask her.

"No, they're still at the door."

I follow her back to the front door, glad to see that Mckylee at least left it open and didn't shut it on them.

"Hello," I say, studying the two pretty girls standing there.

"Hi, how's it going?" says the one with long hair that's so blonde it's almost white. She has a very soft, sweet voice. "I'm Michaela, but everyone calls me Kayla, and this is my sister Samantha."

"It's nice to meet you. I'm Taylor, and this is my sister Mckylee. Would you like to come in?"

"Sure," Samantha says, stepping into the house with Kayla right behind her.

"We were wondering when someone was going to move into this house," Kayla says. "We've been watching people work on it for the last month."

"We've just moved here from England, and the house wasn't ready so we've been staying at the Beauvallon Hotel on the Strip while we waited for it to be finished," I tell her as we enter the kitchen area. I introduce my parents and Malia. They all greet each other, and Samantha quickly picks up where we left off.

"So you've been living in a hotel room on the Strip? Was it fun?"

"It actually was pretty fun, but we weren't exactly in a hotel room. We stayed in a villa, which is really more like a house," Mckylee says. "When it was time for us to leave, we almost didn't want to."

"They have villas at the hotels on the Strip? I didn't know that." Samantha sounds impressed.

"We didn't know that either, but it was amazing," I say. "Normally the villas are for high-rollers and special guest like celebrities, but our dad is a pilot for the Beauvallon, so his boss let us to stay in one."

They both think that's pretty cool, along with our English accents. I think it's a little peculiar they like our accents, seeing as when I moved to England, no one there thought my American accent was remotely cool.

Kayla tells us that she and Samantha are new to the neighborhood, too. Her family also just moved to Las Vegas—about six weeks ago—from Denver, Colorado. Then it gets even weirder. She goes on to tell us that their dad is also a pilot, but for a major airline.

Samantha is 15 and Kayla just turned 17, around the same ages as Mckylee and me. It's amazing, and a little strange, how much we all have in common.

"Would you ladies like something to drink, maybe some lemonade?" our mother asks.

"Actually, we can't stay," says Kayla. "We just came by to say hi. We are expected home for dinner right about now. She stands up and motions Samantha to follow.

"So, we'll see you around?" Kayla asks me.

"Most definitely," Mckylee answers as we see them out the door.

Returning to the kitchen, we find Malia serving up dinner, which, might I add, smells delicious and makes me realize I'm starving. We all sit at the table, including Malia.

Listening to the small talk around me, I think about Kayla and Samantha. Something tells me we're all going to be good friends.

After dinner, Mom asks us to help Malia clean up, which I don't mind doing—that is, as long as it gets done quickly. I really want to head back upstairs and do some research on the Internet about the weird thing happening between Dario and me. I wish I knew where he was so I could talk to him in person. Who is he? Where does he live? I wonder if I will see him when I start school.

In the middle of cleaning up, the doorbell rings again. Mckylee runs and answers it.

"Taylor, it's Samantha!" Mckylee yells, "She wants to know if we want to meet some of the other kids that live here." I walk to the door, and Mckylee gives me a look that tells me she really wants to go but not without me.

"Okay," I say. "But just for a little while. I have some things I need to take care of." I yell back into the house to whoever is listening that we'll be out front.

Looking up the street, I'm amazed at how many kids our

age are outside, just hanging out. There are guys on bikes and skateboards and others playing a game of basketball in the cul-de-sac at the end of the block.

We follow Samantha to her house, where Kayla sits on the steps with some other girls. Samantha introduces us to Gabby, who lives in the house in between Kayla's and ours. She has the most amazing long, wavy blonde hair. She is 15 and going into the tenth grade, just like Samantha and Mckylee. She then introduces us to Tanya, who lives up the block. She is 17 and going into twelfth grade, just like Kayla and me. She is pretty, too, with long blonde hair. Is there anyone around here besides me that doesn't have beautiful, long, blonde hair? I'm feeling more out of place than ever.

"Nice to meet all of you," I say. Then, trying to break the silence, I ask the dumbest question.

"So who are all the guys over there?" Now they must all think I'm some guy-crazy English girl.

Kayla rattles off all of their names, but I'm so embarrassed that I forget them the instant she says them. One thing is for sure: these girls are nothing like my friends back in England. They—or should I say we—weren't nearly so perfect. We were definitely more on the plain side in the looks department.

They're all tall, with that long, blond hair and wearing savvy-looking clothes. They seem so much older than Mckylee and me. Maybe it's because they all wear makeup and dress like they are going out ... not like the casual sweater and jeans look where we lived in England. These girls are definitely not like my English friends. I wonder if Mckylee feels the same way? Everyone keeps talking about how they love our English accents. I think it's the funniest thing ever, but at the same time, I like it because when I moved to England in the beginning, being an outsider wasn't this easy. These kids seem pretty friendly and accepting.

After the guys finish playing basketball, they come over to introduce themselves, but most of their names go in one ear and out the other. One of the guys, I think his name is Aaron, thinks it's really cool that we've just moved from England. I think it's kind of cool that I used to live in England, too, and right now I'm really starting to miss it and my old friends. I suddenly feel like getting out of here.

"Hey everyone, it was really nice meeting all of you, but it's been a long day and I'm going to head inside. Mckylee, are you coming with me?"

"Yeah, I think I will." She says goodbye to everyone and we start walking back home.

"So … what did you think of everyone?" I ask her.

"I thought everyone was really nice, but the kids here are way more grown up and mature than our friends back home," Mckylee confides.

"I know. Meeting everyone actually made me still really miss England." We walk the rest of the way in silence, nothing left to say.

Our mother stands at the front door as we approach. She wants to know everything about what we did and said.

"Mom, there's nothing to tell you except that there are a lot of kids our age that live here and none of them are like our friends back home. The girls here all wear makeup, even to hang around in the neighborhood." I tell her as I head upstairs. "I'll be online and watching the telly if anyone is looking for me."

20

Serendipitous

*F*rustration, exhaustion and homesickness are the perfect symptoms for convincing yourself it's time to just get in bed, watch a good movie and start over again tomorrow. With this in mind, I throw on something comfortable, brush my teeth, climb into bed and turn on the telly. I have never used this remote before, so I only really understand the "power" button and the channel "up" and "down" buttons. Ugh ... I'm so frustrated!

I discover quite quickly why they call it "channel surfing"—I have never seen so many channels all on one television—It's like an ocean of options and the remote is what I think they would call a surfboard! We didn't have a selection like this back in England, but none of us ever watched a lot of the telly in England either. I always had something better to do, like ride my horse or hang out with my mates. After trying a variety of buttons and combinations on the remote, I find a movie to zone out to. It doesn't take long until I drift off, praying Dario and I cross paths once again tonight. It seems like barely any time has passed when I can tell he is out there ... I hear his voice in the distance calling my name. But I wonder if I'm just hearing it because that's all I've wanted to hear since the night he was shot. His voice seems to be getting closer and closer as my darkness starts to fill with light—light coming from what I can now see is a small lamp on a table in the not-so-far distance. As things start to come into focus, I realize I'm being drawn into a bedroom of sorts, which must be Dario's because now I can see him lying in the bed next to the small table with the lamp.

"Finally! I didn't think you would ever get here. It's taken me hours to finally reach you," the familiar voice greets me.

"*Dario, I was starting to think I would never see you again ... I was so worried until I saw you at the hotel earlier today.*" Sitting in a chair next to his bed, even though I know he wants me next to him on the bed. I know this from reading his thoughts, an ability that is becoming easier now. Nervous and not willing to give in to him, I feel like the chair is the safest place for me to be right now.

"Where am I? I'm assuming this is where you live?" I try to make small talk while taking in his beautiful, perfectly tanned face; his dark, wavy hair; and his gorgeous, hazel eyes—eyes that always make me feel as if they are staring right into my soul.

"It is, actually, and I don't live far from where you live. My house sits up at the top of the hill, just on the outskirts of Seven Hills." Dario explains.

"This is crazy. What's going on? Why is this happening to us? I don't understand this ... this ... madness with the two of us .... but before you say anything, I first need to know that everything is okay with you. How is your leg?"

"Taylor, I don't want you to worry. I'm fine, thanks to you and your friend, the hawk. That night was a whirlwind but at the same time amazing. We have something incredible happening between us, and all I know is that I want more of it." Dario looks at me with such conviction and, I think, passion. Then all of sudden there's a knock on his door.

"Dario is everything all right? Who are you talking too?" The soft voice on the other side of the door sends a panic through me.

"Stay calm Taylor. I need you to stay with me!" Dario directs his voice, his thoughts, into my mind.

"Everything is fine, Mom ... I was just talking on the phone, but I'm off now. Sorry to worry you."

"Okay, Dario, but you really need to get some rest.

When I told Doc that you had gone out this afternoon, he wasn't too happy. If you need anything, let me know sweetie. Good night." We breathe a mutual sigh of relief between us as we hear her slippered feet retreating back down the hall.

"*That was close,*" I convey to him. "*I really had to concentrate to stay here with you. You need to communicate with me without actually talking, seeing as no one else can see me and might think you are losing your mind talking to yourself.*"

"*Well, that wouldn't be so bad, considering everyone thinks I'm losing my mind these days anyway.*" He smiles at me as he answers now only through our thoughts.

"*Taylor, I have been putting a lot of thought into what's happening between us and even doing some research online. In the process of all this, I remembered this crazy story my Grandmother use to share with my sister and me when we were young. At the time, I always thought of it as some fun story any grandmother tells with her grandchildren—until now. I now think differently. I know you're going to think this is totally foolish and maybe unreal, but after you hear it, I think you will agree it may have something to do with what's going on between us.*"

"*What are you talking about?*" I ask. "*What does her story have to do with us?*"

"*I will explain, as long as you promise to just trust me—listen and have an open mind.*"

How could I not give him the chance to try and explain, as I don't have any answers, and the situation is getting weirder by the minute? Not only that, but something inside me tells me to honor his request.

"I'm listening ..."

"Trust me, this is going to sound really crazy, but I remember her telling me that her grandmother had shared this story with her. And she had heard it from her grandmother before her. This story has been passed down for many generations in my family. So, here it goes ...

"Many centuries ago, when humans were put on this earth by the Greek god Zeus, they were created as man and woman in one body, bound together with one soul. They had two torsos, each with their own head and arms, all connected to one set of legs. They were created to perfection.

"These humans were so powerful that the Greek gods were frightened and jealous of their perfect love and the powers they possessed together as one. They wanted Zeus, the King of the Gods and the God of the Sky and Thunder, to destroy this power. Zeus felt he had no choice; he had to do something to satisfy the other gods. But he didn't want to eliminate his creation from existence. So what he chose to do was to split them apart with a thunderbolt.

"The Split-Aparts, as they were called from that moment on, were doomed to roam the earth, alone, separated as a man and woman—no longer connected. But the Gods didn't realize that the Split-Aparts had such strong bonds between them that they would roam the earth endlessly searching for their other halves. Each of them would be drawn toward the other, across the universe, in search of their original wholeness. This search for their other halves sometimes occurs through more than just one lifetime.

"If two Split-Aparts ever actually get close enough to each other, they will begin to get small parts of their powers back. Split-Aparts that become aware of each other's presence are even able to *get glimpses of each other in their dreams, and they begin to hear each other's thoughts, not understanding why. But once their souls are bound together, as Zeus had originally intended, those souls then possess a love only these two hearts can feel, unlike human love with another who isn't their perfect match.*

"*Once these Split-Aparts reconnect, they are finally complete, always by each other's side, with indestructible powers to guide each other through eternity—never aging and never dying ... living as immortals.*"

Dario's explanation leaves me completely astonished, but I know in my heart that what he is saying has to be true. It makes complete sense. It might seem insane to anyone else, but I believe it because this is happening to us.

"*Are you listening?*" Dario's voice brings me out of my reflection. I blink and nod, even though he can read each and every thought of mine now.

"*Anyway, as I was saying,*" he continues, "*she told me that some Split-Aparts have more powers than others, but they all have the power to hear each other's thoughts, see each other in their dreams and, finally, to find each other. The stronger their bond, the more powerful they are and the more powerful they can become. She also told me that if Split-Aparts don't find each other by the time they turn 20 years old, they then spend the rest of that life without their other half. They relive life after life until they meet and reconnect again.*"

Dario looks at me intently for a minute, and then finishes by saying, "*I believe that you and I are Split-Aparts, Taylor. I guess the best way to put this is that I am you and you are me, and we are now one, bonded by our souls. This is why ever since that day we bumped into each other in front of the Beauvallon, we've been drawn to each other more and more, with our powers getting stronger and more intense."*

"So ... what now? With us? How do we handle this...?" I say out loud, the sound of my voice suddenly jarring. I notice the breaking of the dawn through his window and realize I've been here way longer than I thought. Dario and I sit in complete silence, watching the night become day, contemplating inside our heads what all this means.

"I'm tired and I need to get some sleep. I feel myself fading ... almost drifting away ... I can't stay any longer ..."

He fades out of my mind as I'm transported back to the safety of my own bed. I lay here alone, feeling a weird pain in my body that is beginning to feel more familiar. It's as if my body is already aching for him, almost as if I can't survive without him near me.

21

Destiny

I **don't really remember returning from Dario's
house.** I must have been exhausted. But now, I sense he
is waking me, but this time it's different—I have a warm,
caring feeling inside. It's like a gentle nudge from someone
reaching over and touching me, just connecting to see if
I'm okay.

It seems like I'm dreaming, but I'm not—I am becoming
more coherent and alert. Dario must realize I'm awake, as

I hear him say, *"I'm on my way over to see you so we can finish our talk. I'm taking you to lunch, so get dressed."*

The thought of seeing him in person makes me totally nervous. It's like I've had this pretend thing going on. I mean, who would believe me, or him, about what has been happening over the last few weeks?

Quickly jumping out of bed, I push those thoughts out of my head. My only mission now is to get somewhat presentable. What am I going to wear?

"Something cute and nice. You will look great in anything," Dario says. *"We are going to one of my favorite places to eat, and it's casual."*

"Fine," I tell him, a little surprised by the intrusion into my thoughts. I head to my closet, at the same time wondering how he could be on his way over when he doesn't even know where I live.

"I know where you live because I followed you there last night when you directed your thoughts back home."

I know he can hear all of my thoughts, which is kind of cool ... but what if I don't want him to hear me? I jump in the shower for a quick wash, and get out, trying not to think too much, so as not to convey anything to Dario.

I throw my hair into a ponytail, put on a little makeup, and get dressed. Just as I'm putting on my shoes, I can hear his thoughts, telling me he's just around the corner.

"I need a minute. Please don't just show up at my front door before I've had a chance to come up with some sort of story for my parents ..."

"I will give you a minute ... but hurry," he responds.

I grab my purse and head downstairs, finding Mom and Dad in the kitchen.

"Wow, you look nice. What are you doing today?" Dad asks.

"I was wondering if it would be okay if I went to lunch with a friend."

"A friend? I didn't know you had any real friends yet? Do we know this friend?" Mom asks.

"I don't think so, but he will be here in a minute and you can meet him," I say, trying to sound casual.

"I'm a little confused, Taylor. When did you make these plans?" Mom continues her questioning. "I didn't hear the phone ring or anything."

Just then the doorbell rings. I'm saved—at least for a few seconds.

"Dario, I need a few more minutes here." I tell him as I walk to the door. Opening it, I feel so strange seeing him. I've never spent any real time with him face-to-face before, but there he stands ... looking as surreal as ever.

"Hello, come on in, I want you to meet my parents," I tell him. As he follows me down the hall into the kitchen, I notice he's walking normal, his stride smooth and easy.

"I can't believe you're not limping," I say to him.

"I should be. This is very painful, but I don't want to tell your parents some lie the first time I meet them. So I'm suffering through the pain."

"Mom, Dad, this is Dario."

Dario reaches out his hand to my dad. "Hello sir, I'm Dario Mancini, and it's a pleasure to meet you, Mr. Dove."

He shakes my mother's hand, too. "I was just wondering if it would be okay with the two of you if I took Taylor to lunch today?"

My dad gives him permission, but then asks Dario a question I am not at all prepared for.

"Your father doesn't happen to be Stefano Mancini, does he?"

"Who is Stefano Mancini?" I think.

Dario answers me through our thoughts *"My dad,"* he says, telling my father this at the same time.

My parents both look at each other oddly. Things are once again weird around here, and I don't know why. I just want to leave. Immediately.

"I'll explain everything to you in the car," Dario tells me.

Closing the front door behind us, I glimpse at the car waiting in front—a car I've seen before. It's a black town car, just like the one that dropped off the large black duffle bag at our airplane in New York. The windows are so dark that, once again, I can't see the driver inside—that is, until he gets out, opening the back door for Dario and me. I feel my heart begin to race and my head lighten. What is going on?

Entering the car, I see on the seat one of the beautiful orange and red flowers that I had spotted in the desert the night I dreamed about Dario burying that black duffle bag with those two other guys. Oh my god ... that duffle bag in New York... and the one in my dream ... they can't be the same bag, can they?

Trying not to think too much about it, I pick up the flowers and scoot across the seat so Dario can get in.

He smiles at me as the door is closed. Silence. I don't know what to say ... I'm almost afraid to think. Sitting here admiring this unique flower brings back vivid memories.

"It's a desert bird of paradise," he says, interrupting my thoughts.

"I love these strange flowers; they were so beautiful in my dream that night."

"I know. They made you so happy when you were walking through them."

"You knew I was there?"

"Yes, I saw you coming. I didn't know what to do since this has never happened to me, so I just let things be, to try and figure out if all of it was really happening or not, I guess. I now know that no matter what I do or what you do, we will not be able to hide anything from each other, so why bother trying?" Dario's voice trails off as the car starts down the drive.

He has a good point. No matter how hard I try to get him out of my thoughts, it is impossible, and it is obviously the same for him. I can always hear what he is thinking now ... it's kind of nice, but then I realize that none of our thoughts will ever be our own again and I feel a little uneasy.

"So where are we going?" I ask, trying to make small talk, because I'm feeling out of my comfort zone. I've never really been out on a date before.

"*You've never been on a date before?*" Dario jumps into my thoughts.

"*No, is that okay? You can't even drive in England until*

you're eighteen, so I didn't even know anyone old enough to take me on a proper date." I inform him, a little aggravated at his question.

"I'm sorry I don't mean to come across rude. I just think it's cute. If it makes you feel any better, I haven't really been on a true date before either," he shares with me.

"You? You've never been on a date? Now you're just patronizing me!" I burst out laughing at his ridiculous comment.

"What are you laughing at? Really, I've never been on a real date before. I've always felt my life is just too complicated to be with anyone. Usually, I just hang around with a group of friends. I've never been out with anyone I've had feelings for before."

He confides this so seriously.

"Okay ... I believe you. So, you have feelings for me?"

"Now who is patronizing who?" Dario asks as the car pulls up in front of a restaurant. The sign says it's The Mediterranean Café.

Once again, the driver gets out and opens the door for the two us, this time on my side so that I can get out first. These people don't mess around with their proper etiquette. My mom would be pleased.

In the restaurant, a man who seems to know Dario personally greets us and asks if Dario wants his regular table. Dario nods, and we follow the man through the restaurant, out another door and into some sort of atrium. Although the room is indoors, it feels as if we are outside. Plants bloom everywhere, giving it a tropical feeling, and there's a large fountain in the center of the room.

We are seated in a booth in the back corner, and a waiter appears immediately with our menus. After we place our order, Dario turns serious.

"We need to talk about a few things that are really important. And we need to address them right away. Is that okay with you?"

"Okay. Why are you being so serious?"

"Taylor, you know that things are moving really fast. Neither of us knew about the other just a few weeks ago. I know that you feel it's all crazy and weird. So do I. But we've been ... I guess we've been re-connected in some sort of way.

"We both can do amazing things that neither of us knew we could do until the last two weeks started to unfold. You now have the tools to know everything about me and my family, as I do about yours. And because of this, I'm now responsible for you and your safety."

"My safety?" I have no idea what he's talking about.

"What you saw in the desert that night wasn't the burial of my dog. It was exactly what you thought it was." Dario looks at me to see how I am reacting to what he just said.

"Why–? I mean, how–?" I can't seem to put a complete sentence together.

"There is no easy way to say this, so here it goes. My dad is the top Mob boss in Vegas, and no one messes with him or the organization." He looks around, making sure no one is listening—even though they couldn't have heard him anyway, as he is telling me this through his thoughts.

"You are talking completely crazy. The Mob? The Mob doesn't

exist. The Mob is just a scary story people like to tell in movies and books," I say.

"*The Mob does exist, and this isn't just in the movies and books! It is real; it's not a game ... and when it comes to money, the Mob doesn't put up with any shit from anyone or anything! So when I tell you your safety is at risk, I'm talking about your whole family disappearing and no one even noticing!*"

All I can do is stare at him. I'm stunned by what I'm hearing, thinking, feeling. My mouth has gone dry, and I reach for the glass of water in front of me.

"I guess if you put it that way, I'm listening!" I now actually speak out loud, suddenly frightened.

"*You can never, never tell anyone about our special gift, Taylor. I'm not kidding. You can never let on you know anything, no matter how terrifying it may be. Do you understand me? You will be at risk; your family will be at risk; your friends could even be at risk if you do.*

"*I can't keep you out of my head, so you are going to see things that are going to send chills down your body and scare you to death, but you can never let on what you see. Again, do you understand? They could, probably will, kill you if they even suspect for a moment you know anything!*"

Not only can he read my thoughts, I'm feeling that he can now see into my entire being.

"How do you do it, I mean live like this?" I whisper as our lunch is delivered to the table.

"This is my family, and I have never known anything different. I've grown up in it; I didn't have a choice in the matter. Believe me, I hate every bit of it; if I could get out I would, but no one ever gets out of the Mob, unless they're dead."

When he says this extremely quietly under his breath, I feel an incredibly heavy burden, one I know I have become a partner in—and not of my own choosing. A shudder goes through my body.

"Okay, I understand. I will never let on I know anything to anyone. I promise."

Lunch arrives. Although my appetite seemed to disappear when Dario started telling me about his family, it slowly resurfaces. Taking my first bite, I find myself thinking that Dario knows his restaurants; this food is incredible. I notice that he smiles at me as this thought occurs.

Then he continues, "I have never talked to anyone about this. Believe it or not, it's such a relief to finally have someone I can talk to, because I feel that I have been alone my whole life. I'm close to my sister, but the day I bumped into you at the Beauvallon, I knew you were the one I've been looking for to be part of my life. I just knew it—my body, my mind—everything said to pay attention, don't lose her. I haven't even for a second been able to stop thinking about you,"

As Dario says all this, he sounds so sad and alone.

"I know. It's crazy, but it has been the same for me. No matter how hard I try not to think of you, all I do is see your face.

"I was scared the night I saw you in the desert. Did those other two guys see me? At first I was worried you were going to hurt me."

What's happening here? I'm talking like I've accepted all this as real. As if it's my new normal self—my normal life.

"I would never hurt you! Something told me that you were not a threat to me, and no, the other two guys didn't see you. You weren't really there; I brought you there through my thoughts, just like I did the night I got shot and all the other times since. I couldn't stop thinking about you, the girl from my dreams, and it brought you to me through your dream. No, no one can see you when we are connected in dreams."

"Maybe that makes sense. I guess we are just going to have to get used to all of this and how to handle it if anyone is around. Dario, did you have a weird feeling after I left you this morning—something you've never felt before?"

"Yes. I'm assuming you did too?"

"Uh huh. I wonder if that feeling intensifies the closer we get to each other."

"I have a feeling we are going to experience a lot of new changes in our lives; let's just take them one day at a time," Dario says with a small smile, as he reaches out and lightly touches my hand. I never knew someone touching my hand could make me feel so extraordinary inside.

"Agreed," I say, returning his smile.

"The biggest hurdle I have to contend with is explaining you to my family. I have never had a girlfriend, and my parents have a strong desire for me to marry the daughter of another member of the Mob. I have made it clear that I have no desire to ever be with her, let alone marry her. But telling my dad "no" sometimes—well, most of the time— doesn't go over well."

My smile faltered a little at the mention of another girl. But now I feel assured. I really should be feeling overwhelmed right now; but strangely enough I'm not.

I feel safe. I feel like I am finally home with Dario and that I belong by his side. I should be scared to death, especially after what he has told me about his family, but I know the loss of me would also destroy him, so I have to trust that he will never let anything happen to me.

22

Acceptance

We are silent during our drive home from lunch, except for the thoughts going through our minds about how much we are enjoying this new friendship. Why am I not spooked at all about what Dario has just told me? I mean, I watched the Godfather movie with my dad one weekend on the telly, and all the characters seemed to be pretty bad people. How can this great guy come from a family connected with the mob?

Soon, we're pulling into the gate of Bonita Palms, and all of sudden, I feel saddened by the sight of my house.

"Give us a minute, please." Dario tells the driver. Dario takes my hand into his and looks into my eyes. His hand is warm and sends a slight chill through me.

"I need to go home, take some more pain meds and get some rest but I'll see you later on, okay?" He leans in and kisses me on the cheek, although he is thinking about how badly he wants to kiss my lips. He's convincing himself he should wait.

"Sounds good. Take care of yourself," I say, suppressing a giggle as I think about his desire to kiss me.

"We're ready now," Dario directs the driver, who gets out of the car and opens my door for me.

I kiss Dario on his cheek and thank him once again through my thoughts as I get out of the car. As the door closes behind me, I turn to stare at him, but I'm unable to see his beautiful face through the dark-tinted windows as the car drives away. To my surprise, I find Mckylee standing at the door waiting for me.

"Who was that? And when did you get to know someone well enough to go out on a lunch date?" she says.

I realize I can't tell her the truth, and what's worse, my parents may ask me the same question. I have to figure out some sort of lie or at least come up with something that will make some kind of sense to them. What am I going to say?

"He's just some guy I met, no big deal," I respond, then try and divert her with my own question.

"So what's the plan for the rest of the day? You want to lay out at the pool with me?"

"Sure, but don't think you're getting off that easy with the whole lunch date thing, I want some answers," she says as we head upstairs to get our swimsuits on. "Who is he? Where did you meet him? How come he asked you to lunch? ... You know, I want to hear everything ..."

Closing the door to my room behind me, I can't stop thinking about my date with Dario. I wish he had kissed me because now all I can think about is his lips on mine. Okay, I need to snap out of this. My sister is waiting for me. And besides, if he wants to, he can know *everything* I'm thinking.

I find Mckylee out by the pool with our lounge chairs already set up with towels ready to go.

"It's about time you got out here. What took you so long?"

"Nothing. Why are you nagging me lately?" I ask.

"You're just acting so weird and secretive. Why are you being so defensive all of sudden? Are you okay?"

I try to look like I'm seriously considering her question. "You're right," I say. "I am a little on edge. I just have a lot on my mind with all the new changes in our lives ... and I miss England. Don't you?"

We are suddenly interrupted as the back door to the house opens and Kayla and Samantha walk out.

"Hey guys, how's it going? Catching some rays I see," Samantha says.

"You two should go and grab your suits and come hang out with us," Mckylee says.

I'm really not in the mood for any company right now, so I'm a little annoyed when Kayla walks over and sits on the chair next to me.

"Thanks, but we just stopped by to invite you two out with us tonight. We are going to hang out at this place called the District with a bunch of the kids you met last night."

Before I can say a word, I catch a glimpse of Mckylee standing behind Kayla shaking her head yes.

"Sure, sounds like fun. Around what time?"

"Just be at our house around seven o'clock and wear something super cute, okay?" Kayla calls over her shoulder as she and Samantha turn to leave.

"How awesome is this? It's Friday night, and we're going out without Mom and Dad in Las Vegas!" Mckylee says, dancing around with excitement.

"Don't get too excited because we still have to ask Mom and Dad for permission." I don't want to get her hopes up. I mean, this could be a big fat no!

Just then, Mom comes out of the house to tell us that she and Dad are home from running errands.

Mckylee gives me a look like, "Are you going to ask her?" I shake my head no and move my lips to form the words, "not right now."

"Your dad and I are going to work on organizing our things upstairs. We plan on having dinner at six," she informs us before heading back inside.

I'm so glad she didn't ask any questions about my lunch date. I still have absolutely no answers for anyone, especially my mom.

"What are you waiting for, why didn't you ask her about tonight ... ?"

"I'm waiting for the right moment—I'll do it when we

go back inside," I answer her as I shut my eyes for a few minutes. I need to sort all this out ...

I start thinking of all the questions my parents might ask me about my day. Then my mind wanders to what I'm going to wear tonight and how much I hate my hair and how I wish I knew what to do with it besides wear it in a ponytail all the time. Back in England, I always wore it up and it didn't matter because I was always riding my horses, and I really didn't care what it looked like. But I also never had friends who look quite like these Vegas girls do. I feel so out of place here, and I don't know if I'll ever fit in. I wish Dario could give me some answers.

Overheated, I dive into the pool to cool off—not only my body but also my thoughts. And soon, I realize it is almost 4 in the afternoon. I decide it's time to talk to our parents about tonight. I'm not really sure what they're going to say. They can be really cool sometimes but at the same time very protective and strict.

I call to Mckylee to come with me. I figure if she's there, that might distract Mom and Dad from asking me about Dario and lunch today.

We find our parents in their room. Dad is on the phone and Mom asks us to wait a minute. Standing there, I feel anxious. Since I'm the oldest, I'm the one who has to ask if we can get into a car and go out for a night in Vegas with a bunch of teenage girls.

When Dad finally hangs up, they both stare at us expectantly. "So what's up?" Mom asks.

I take a deep breath.

"Kayla and Samantha came over a few hours ago and invited us both to go with them and the other kids in the neighborhood to this place called the District tonight. Can we?" Now let the interrogation begin.

"What time would you leave?" my mother asks. "How would you get there and get back? And what time would you be home?"

This is going to be the hard part, but I can do this. I'm ready. I answer very calmly and simply. "We are leaving at seven o'clock and Kayla is driving. What time do you need us to be home?"

A few seconds of silence go by. Then Mom says she has forgotten about how the kids drive here at 16 and how many of them have cars, unlike in England. And to our surprise she gives us her okay. My parents look at each other like they are talking in parent thinking language or something. "What am I going to do? We live in America now, and kids drive. It's fine with me, as long as it's okay with your dad.

"I just have a few rules when getting into cars with teenagers; first never get in a car with anyone who has been drinking; second, if they're not going to be home in time for your curfew of midnight, you call and ask for a ride and you also call and ask for a ride if anyone has been drinking. If you cannot follow these rules you will be grounded for life!"

Life seems like a really long time but she has threatened that one before. Although last time I messed up I only ended up being grounded for like a week.

We both agree with the terms and can't believe that our

mom is being so awesome but the battle isn't over—now there's Dad.

"So, Dad, what do you say? Can we go?" I ask.

"You can go as long as you understand how important it is to pay attention and look out for each other," he answers. He barely gets the words out, when we jump into action.

"Thanks Mom and Dad!" I shout as we run out of their room to get ready for the night.

"I can't believe they said yes," Mckylee states excitedly as we run into my room to find something to wear.

After trying on multiple outfits, we decide on a couple of cute ones. I'm wearing jeans that I cuffed the bottoms of so they look like Capri pants with a cute black blousy top and little black sandals. Mckylee is wearing a cute little black skirt and a really fun white blouse with red trim and red sandals. I put my hair up as usual but I put on some light makeup including some mascara and lip-gloss.

We are ready.

23

The District

Kayla and Samantha are waiting for us out front. Kayla drives the nicest white, convertible BMW. As we climb into the back seat I ask her why she doesn't have the top down.

"I hardly ever put it down," she says, "because it messes up my hair."

The District is only about 10 or 15 minutes from our house. It's an outdoor mall that sits on streets closed to traffic. Kayla pulls up to valet parking, and then she and Samantha lead the way to a restaurant bar called the *Prickly Blossom Cantina*. I'm amazed at the sight. The restaurant's patio is already packed with kids everywhere. Inside the *Cantina*, we can hardly move through the masses. We push our way through the crowd to where Gabby and Tanya are sitting, saving us seats at a table near the patio. Kayla sits next to me.

"By the way, can I just tell you that I love your purse. It's very cool," she says.

"Thanks, it was a gift from my mom."

"So what's your poison, Taylor?" asks Tanya.

"My what?"

"Your poison. What do you like to drink? This place is famous for their prickly pear margaritas."

"What's a margarita?" I ask.

"This really yummy drink made with tequila."

I have no idea what tequila is, but I am tired of not knowing what this girl is talking about, so I just say, "Oh, that sounds good."

You can barely hear yourself think in this place, it's so loud and crowded! When the waiter comes to our table, all the other girls seem to know him. Tanya orders for everyone, a round of margaritas and appetizers for the table.

"There are so many people here!" I shout to Kayla.

"It's only this crazy on Fridays. The rest of the week gets busy, but not like this. Friday night is when all the cute boys are here—that's what brings all the girls," she says with a grin.

I can relate. That's why we would all go to the rec center back in England. This is a little different though—okay, a lot different. Everyone here is dressed up. They are all teens, but with all the makeup, the girls look like they're in their 20's. I don't understand how they get their hair to look so good, like the girls on TV and in magazines. My hair is all one length, down past my shoulders and super curly, and I never know what to do with it, so I just wear it up in a ponytail. Otherwise, it looks like a rat's nest. I wonder what Mckylee is thinking of all this.

"So do you think that guy over there staring at you is cute?" Samantha asks me.

"What?" I say. I'm completely in my own world and only half hear her talking to me. "I'm sorry. What was the question?"

"Do you think that guy over there staring at you is cute?" she repeats.

I look across the room and see a guy with light brown hair and a nice tan staring at me.

"Isn't that Aaron from last night?" I ask. He really isn't my type, but he is kind of cute, I guess.

"Yeah, that's Aaron. He lives around the corner from us, and he thinks you're cute. He told me last night after you left."

"Really? That's interesting," I say. It's all I can seem to get out of my mouth. I'm feeling a little weird talking to Samantha about some guy I hardly know.

Luckily, our waiter interrupts us as he delivers our drinks along with chips and salsa. The margaritas are frozen like a Slurpee and look quite yummy.

I take a sip. They are as good as they look and taste like the raspberry Kool-Aid I like. Then I realize that I am so stupid. These aren't regular drinks, kids drinks. I think there is alcohol in them. I know you have to be 21 to drink in Nevada, but no one asked me for my ID—no one asked any of us.

I kick Mckylee under the table to get her attention.

"Do you notice anything different about these drinks?" I whisper.

She nods. "It tastes a little weird."

"It has alcohol in it." Neither of us have had any real alcohol before, just beer and wine. "Drink slowly, really slowly, and make it last a long time so she doesn't order us another one."

There is no way we can go home drunk our first night out, unless we never want to go out again.

The place continues to fill up with more and more people, and the more people who squeeze into the *Prickly Blossom*, the louder it gets. The music is so loud it's hard to even hear myself talk, let alone have a conversation with anyone.

"Hey do you want to walk around with me and check out the deck upstairs to see who is here?" Samantha asks me.

I tell Mckylee I'll be right back. I can honestly say I have never seen anything like this before in my life. It's complete mayhem in here.

Following Samantha through the crowd is difficult, but I'm glad I agreed to, because when Samantha sees people she knows, she makes it a point to stop and introduce me. I have never met so many new people at one time. It still surprises me how everyone always looks so incredible in Vegas. I wonder if I will ever have myself put together like they do?

The deck is open to sky, and with the sun setting behind the mountains, it offers quite the view. The DJ is spinning some really good music. Standing here people-watching and enjoying the music, I suddenly feel a presence—I feel him, he's here. And he knows I am here. What is he doing out when he should be home in bed?

"I came to find you," he answers me in my mind.

"How did you know that I was here?" forgetting that he and I are connected with this thought thing. All we really have to do is concentrate on the other and our thoughts do all the communicating.

"I was able to see some of what you were doing, so that's how I found you. How did you end up here? How do you know about this place?" he asks me.

"I am going to make my way back downstairs," I tell Samantha. As I turn to go, Aaron smoothly steps in front of me.

"Hi. Remember me? We kind of met the other day unofficially outside Kayla's house?"

"Yeah, I remember. How are you?" I respond, only because I hate being rude. I am anxious to get downstairs.

We keep walking and chatting, and Aaron follows me, joining our table. I can tell that Mckylee is starting to get a little tipsy from her drink. She is pretty funny when she's been drinking and is making me laugh. Aaron sits next to me, but I'm only getting part of what he is saying because I am wondering where Dario and his friends are.

Mckylee orders another drink, and I give her a look that means, "I don't think so." She then starts pointing at something behind me, and telling me something, but I can't understand what she is saying because she is so excited ... and it's so loud in here!

Then, I nearly fall out of my chair at the sight of him. There he is, as beautiful as he always is, but in a crowd like this, he really stands out.

"Oh ... that's Dario Mancini," says Aaron. "He goes to Vegas Valley High with us. His family is the richest in the valley ... he's actually one of the coolest kids at school. I don't know him personally or anything even though we've been going to school together since the sixth grade."

Aaron just became very useful to me as the boy with the information. I don't want to seem too eager to know about Dario, but I enjoy the info I am getting from him.

Aaron tells me that Dario has his own little entourage and that they have been together since anyone can remember. Then he tells me not to even think about liking him or even dating him because he is way out of my league and doesn't date high school girls anyway. I make it very clear that I have no interest in Dario, all the time thinking, if he only knew ...

"Dario, I think it's best if we keep our distance tonight. We need to formally bump into each other, so I can have some sort of story of how we met. I'm not a very good liar and wouldn't know how to explain you to everyone."

"*I understand and agree with you. I just had to be near you, even if I can't be with you.*"

I can't believe how fast this night is flying by. I'm already two drinks in and not feeling so hot. Before I know it, it's nearing our curfew.

"Kayla, hey are you going home anytime soon? I just realized the time and we have a midnight curfew," I ask her in somewhat of a panic.

"I'm sorry, but we don't have a curfew. And we're having way too much fun to go home right now."

Did I hear right? She's not going to take us home? In England, we always watched out for each other. What's with her?

If Mckylee and I don't get home by curfew, we may never be able to go out with them ever again. I tell her we're going to catch a cab home.

"I can give you a ride," Aaron says.

I thank him, but tell him he should stay. I don't want him giving us a ride because he's been drinking more than the rest of us.

When I try to pay our tab, the server says it has already been taken care of. I know it was Dario who paid it, but I don't have time to think about it, except to note how nice it is to be taken care of in that way. Racing off toward the exit, I pray that we don't have any problems catching a cab. Just as I get to the front door, I notice Dario standing off to the side. I look deep into his eyes as I thank him through my thoughts.

The valet outside tells us the quickest way to catch a cab would be to go to the hotel next door and grab one there.

"We don't have a lot time," I tell Mckylee, as I take her by the arm. "We are going to have to walk fast."

As we make our way toward the Green Valley Ranch Hotel and Casino, a black limo pulls up and the driver puts down his window.

"Excuse me. You ladies look like you need a ride."

"No thank you, we are going to catch a cab over at the hotel."

"Taylor, isn't it? My boss insists that I take you home, so please let me do my job." He points to the front door of the *Prickly Blossom Cantina*, where Dario is standing.

"Taylor take the ride he will get you home safely."

I accept the drivers offer and Mckylee and I get into the car. All I can think about is how I need this man to drive fast, and that we can't hit any red lights and maybe, just maybe, we will get there on time. Please!

As we pull up to the gates of Bonita Palms, I tell the driver we'll get out here. That's when I notice how drunk Mckylee is. I practically have to drag her down the street toward our house.

"Mckylee, you have to pull it together when we go inside, do you understand me? Mom and Dad will kill us if they think you're drunk! They will kill me." I open the front door hoping our parents aren't waiting for us.

"S-A-F-E!" I exclaim in my head. I can't believe we just made it. We're actually a few minutes late, but no one will notice or say anything. I'm sure of it.

"Hello girls. How was your night?"

It's Mom, speaking from the top of the stairs. All I can think is please, please don't come down the stairs.

"It was a lot of fun thanks ... but we're both really tired and we're going to bed."

I give Mckylee a little shove, hoping she doesn't open her mouth, and turn toward the back stairs.

"Alright. I am glad you made it home safe. Have sweet dreams, and I'll see you in the morning." I hear her door close.

Thankfully she didn't ask us to come up; I take Mckylee to her room and tuck her in, then head to my room.

I can't sleep right now, even if I wanted to. My blood is still pumping through my body with excitement. I had the best time tonight and I'm into the most beautiful guy ever.

I change, brush my teeth, then climb into bed and turn on the telly. Sometimes life can be strange, but in the last month it has been utterly unexplainable!

And amazing!

24

Night Caller

*I*n a deep but unsettling slumber, I suddenly hear Dario summoning me, but this time it's different—somehow, he seems so close.

"Taylor wake up, I need to see you. I'm out in front of your house."

The clock says it's 4:20 a.m. Unsure if I'm dreaming or if he's really outside, I get out of bed, open the shutters and look out my window, questioning my sanity the whole time. To my surprise, he really is here—leaning against some black car I haven't seen before.

"Are you alone?" I ask in my thoughts.

"Yes, and by the way, you are really cute when you are awakened from a dead sleep."

"You shouldn't be driving in your condition. You shouldn't even be out; do you even realize what time it is?"

"Does it matter what time it is? I needed to see you in person, and I couldn't wait. I can't get you off of my mind. Please, come down here and talk to me."

"Dario, you need to go home. How can I come down there and talk to you? Are you out of your mind? Do you want me to get in trouble?"

"No ... No ... You won't get in trouble. Just come down here. Please."

"Give me a minute."

I'm starting to panic ... I don't know about all this: what if I get caught? How do I talk myself out of this one? What if Mckylee sees me? What if she hears me moving around?

I can't go outside in my underwear and a T-shirt, so I throw on some clothes while trying to come up with an idea on how to get out of the house without being caught.

"You are so adorable. Are you for real? I have never met anyone so innocent." Dario drops into my thoughts in the midst of my panic.

Slowly, I open my door and tiptoe out, closing it behind

me by turning the handle first, pulling the door and slowly releasing the knob into the closed position.

My heart feels like it's going to burst out of my chest. I can hear myself breathe. I need to steady myself. Standing here in the hallway, I listen closely to make sure no one has woken up. So far, so good.

I can hear Dario's amusement at my cautiousness.

"Dario, stop laughing at me. I have been a perfect citizen in my house, and I haven't spent a lot of time defying my parents until you came along," I tell him as I slowly walk down the dark and still unfamiliar hallway. You never realize how much you don't know a place until you are walking through it in the pitch black.

The moonlight becomes my friend as it shines in through the windows. Feeling surer of myself with its light, I begin to relax a little as I head out the back door and around the side of the house.

Suddenly, I come face-to-face with Dario. I should have guessed he would easily find me, seeing as he is able to read all of my thoughts.

"You are so funny," he says. "I can't believe how nervous you are. It's not like you're doing anything you wouldn't do during the day. Do you ask your parents for permission every time you leave the house?" His voice makes me feel extraordinary inside.

"No, I don't ask permission every time I leave the house, but I always tell them where I'm going so they don't worry," I say. "And, if we are going to talk, we've got to whisper..."

"I really do think it's sweet. Most of the girls I know are very independent—but not nearly as real as you. That's all."

I think he's concerned that he has hurt my feelings.

"It's fine Dario. Don't worry. But what are you doing here?"

"I told you, I needed to see you in person. Who were those girls you were with at the Prickly Blossom? They didn't look familiar. I'm sorry if it seems like I'm prying, but I've never felt like this for anyone ever before, and I just really feel protective of you."

Dario is sounding so sweet. If this were any other situation, I might think he's a little overbearing, but this isn't any ordinary situation, and I actually like the way he is fussing over me.

"The girls that were with us tonight live right here. Gabby lives in the house next door. Then next to her house is where Kayla and Samantha live. They just moved here from Denver about six weeks ago. I really like them. We actually have a lot in common."

Dario sits down on the front steps of my house and reaches for my hand.

Sitting next to each other, our bodies slightly touch—just enough that I feel a warm tingling sensation run through my body. I'm trying not to think about how much I want him to kiss me, how much I want him to hold me. *Focus Taylor*, I'm telling myself, forgetting that he knows what I'm thinking. I've got to do something to get myself focused.

"Aren't you tired?" I blurt out. "How is your leg feeling?"

"My leg is feeling better, and the Doc says it looks great. It's healing quite nicely."

"Dario, I really need to get back inside and you need to get some rest."

"I will only go if you promise me you will hang out with me tomorrow. I want to take you somewhere, I want to share something with you."

"Okay, as long as you get some serious rest tonight. Well, what's left of tonight anyway. Where are we going?"

"It's a surprise. Trust me, you are going to love it!" I try to figure out what the surprise will be through his thoughts, but he's doing a good job not thinking about it.

"You're trying to cheat Taylor, that's not fair! Stay out of my head!" he teases as he leans into me and takes hold of my face with his warm hands.

This is it ... I can feel my heart flutter, and I think he is going to kiss me. I close my eyes, and he turns my head slightly and places his lips on my cheek and says goodnight.

That's it? That's all? I think to myself, again forgetting he can hear every thought. Is that a slight smile I see on his face as I open my eyes?

"Have sweet dreams Taylor, and I will see you in the morning." He is laughing softly as he heads to his car.

I sit back down on the step, watching him get in his car and drive away down the street. As his car disappears from view, I suddenly feel overwhelmed. What is this sad, weird pain in my body that aches for him?

25

Transformation

Waking up abruptly, my mind is already **racing.** What is going on in my life? How come everything is changing so fast? A few weeks ago, I was living in a quiet village thousands of miles away. Now, I feel like I've stepped into another world. I hear voices ... well, I hear his voice. I never sensed anyone being around me like I do now. But now ... but now ... I feel him as soon as he's anywhere in the same location as I am. It's like ... he's becoming part of me ... and me, him. Was he really here in the night, or did I imagine it? What is going on in my life?

These are my first thoughts as I wake up, but then I remember the feeling of Dario's hand in mine and I know it happened. He *was* here last night. I don't have long to consider this, though, because as I glance at the clock, I realize I have about thirty minutes before Dario gets here. I bolt into the bathroom to get ready and soon I'm dressed and downstairs. I find Mom and Dad drinking coffee and deep in conversation.

"What are you so dressed up for?" Dad asks. "Where are you off to today?"

I take a deep breath, gathering my courage. "I was wondering if it would be okay if I went to lunch with Dario again?" I pray they don't give me a hard time and just let me go.

They both look at each other for what seems like the longest time. Then Dad turns to me with concern on his face. "I don't know Taylor. Didn't you just see him yesterday? This is starting to go pretty fast. You just went to lunch with him and you've only met him, what, two days ago?"

Just then the doorbell rings. "He's already here?" Dad asks. "Taylor, why don't you go and tell him you'll be out in a minute? We need a few minutes here, please."

My dad isn't asking, but telling me. I've never seen this side of him before.

"*I didn't mean to get you in trouble,*" Dario tells me.

"*You didn't. This is all new to my parents, that's all.*"

"I'll be right back Dad. Let me get the door."

I find Dario standing on the front step with the cutest grin on his face.

"Stop smiling, you're going to make me laugh. Just wait in the car ... I'll be right there." I try not to laugh while closing the door on him.

"Who's that?" Mckylee asks as she comes down the stairs. I can't believe this. How many more people do I need to explain myself to?

"No one!" I snap as I walk back into the kitchen.

"Okay," I say to my parents, "What do you want to talk about?"

"Who's outside?" Mckylee interrupts again.

"Why does it matter to you Mckylee?" I practically yell at her.

My mom tries to calm me down. "Taylor, don't be so upset. We just want to talk to you for a few minutes, and then you can go. Your dad just has a few concerns he wants to share with you."

"I'm not sure how I feel about you being friends with, let alone dating, my boss's son," Dad says. "Although he seems like a very nice young man, and I do want you to be happy, I just want you to understand this boy is no ordinary boy," Dad adds. Is that a kind of a warning I hear in his voice?

"His father is one of the wealthiest and most powerful men in Las Vegas. I am worried this boy is going to break your heart. Do you understand what I am saying to you?"

"I do, but it's not like I'm asking you if I can marry him

or anything," I add. "It's just lunch. You do want me to have friends here, don't you?"

"Of course we do honey. But I just want you to be careful and take it slow, okay?"

I nod. Then I say goodbye to everyone and quickly hurry outside to find Dario. This time he's driving a beautiful black ZR1 Corvette. I only know the model because it says so on the back of the car. It's the same one I saw him driving before at the hotel. He gets out of the car as he sees me approach.

"Dario, stay in the car, I can let myself in."

"No Taylor," he says, "I'm fine. I'm feeling much better."

As he puts his hand behind my elbow, guiding me to my door, I notice he is limping. I slide in and once again see a beautiful, orange and red desert birds of paradise flower on the seat. He smiles at me as he closes my door and walks around the car.

"Are you hungry?" he asks as he sits behind the wheel.

"Yes, actually starving. Where are we going?"

"It's a surprise. So how did you sleep last night—or should I say this morning? I was so glad I got to see you."

"It was a little weird sneaking out of the house, especially that late ... but it was exciting, too."

"I'm going to be such a bad influence on you. I guess we will have to be careful."

I become aware that we're driving toward the Strip. Tapping into Dario's inner thoughts, I know that he is taking me to a restaurant in the Beauvallon—his dad's hotel. That makes me a little nervous. I wonder if his dad will be there. Bypassing the valet service, Dario parks in a spot right in front.

"Must be nice to have your own special front row parking," I think to myself, and he answers, *"It is."*

I will have to try not to think so much.

"Good luck with that." Dario laughs out loud. *"Let me know how that works out for you."*

He once again opens my door for me and I climb out of the car—literally, because it sits so low to the ground. I didn't know that getting out of a Corvette could be so difficult.

As we walk to the front doors, I feel as if everyone is looking at me—at us—wondering what Dario could possibly be doing with me. If I didn't know better, I would be wondering the same thing.

The doorman opens the door for us and greets the two of us. "Good afternoon, Mr. Mancini and guest." We both say at the same time, "Hello," and enter the hotel, the hotel I'm all too familiar with. Dario stops abruptly once inside with me following his lead and stopping right next to him. He leans over to me and gently whispers in my ear, "Are you ready for this?"

Dario takes hold of my hand, which, of course, sends warm chills through my body. I can feel myself shudder. I wonder if he can as well? Then we walk together, as a couple, through his dad's casino, as if we've been doing this our whole lives.

The restaurant sits in the back of the hotel. I had never noticed it before, even though Mckylee and I had explored the whole hotel—at least I thought we had. Instantly, we are greeted by a maître d'.

"Good afternoon Mr. Mancini. Your table is ready. Please come this way."

Dario gently directs me in front of him with that same elbow move he used earlier, and we follow the maître d', who leads us to a table set for two by the window. Looking out, I notice a lovely pond with a beautiful fountain in the middle. Gliding gracefully across the water are the most extraordinary black swans. I never knew black swans even existed! They are absolutely breathtaking.

Dario is laughing at me because he gets such a kick out of my innocence. It's not my fault I have lived such a sheltered life—but I can tell he's enjoying seeing things through my eyes. Sharing my excitement with him just increases my joy.

"I hope you don't mind, but I took the liberty to call ahead and order lunch for us. I wanted us to just be able to sit and enjoy each other's company," he says. "First, I need to warn you about my dad. I'm sure he will be showing up, and I don't want you to be surprised."

"What do you mean? Did you tell him we were coming? I'm not ready to meet your dad," I say, panicked at the thought.

"No, I would never do that, but the cameras in the sky will," he says as he moves his eyes upwards as he talks to me. "In every casino, there are always high tech cameras that observe whoever is in the hotel. It's for security, and the occasional theft. The cameras will let him know we're here, and trust me, he will grace us with his presence. I've never brought a girl here before—well not alone on a date anyway. So I just want you to be prepared, that's all. You know, my dad knowing about us wouldn't be so bad. Then I wouldn't have to run around hiding you from him," he says.

Suddenly, he seems nervous and distracted. Following his eyes, I see a handsome, well-dressed man walking toward us. Some of the diners greet him as he approaches our table. I know it's Mr. Mancini from reading Dario's mind.

"It's going to be difficult for my dad to accept you as my girl-friend, but I need to get the news of us out on the table as soon a possible—you are just too big of a secret to hide."

"Why would it be hard for him to accept me as your girlfriend?"

"Just trust me ... he's had plans for me and my future for a long time ..."

His dad is a very powerful man and, from what I gather, doesn't like not knowing what's going on. Standing at the edge of our table, he looks me over—actually, it feels more like a stare down. "So Dario, who do we have here?" Mr. Mancini asks.

"This is Taylor, Dad. My girlfriend."

"Well Taylor, it's a pleasure to meet you. Do you have a last name?"

"The pleasure is all mine Mr. Mancini. And yes, my last name is Dove."

"What an adorable accent you have. English, I am presuming?"

Before his father can ask me any more questions, Dario changes the subject by inquiring about where his mother is today. I realize he is worried his father will put two and two together about my dad.

Mr. Mancini informs us his wife is at a charity luncheon and will be around later. Then, completely throwing Dario off guard, he invites us to join them for dinner.

"Your mother would love to meet Taylor," he insists.

Can I just say that the way he says my name creeps me out? I don't know what it is, but it's like there is something sinister about him. Dario tells his dad that he will call him later to let him know whether or not we will be joining them for dinner. But Mr. Mancini tells us he will be looking forward to seeing us for dinner at 7:30 at Piero's. Whatever Piero's is. With a final hard look at the two of us, he says goodbye and leaves suddenly, almost like a poof of smoke.

Dario sits quietly for a moment, his mind blank. He then thinks to himself that it could have been worse, way worse, and leaves it at that for now.

We continue eating our lunch—a scrumptiously, delicious blackened ahi tuna steak sandwich, a new and yet tasty delight for me—and go back to enjoying each other's company as if his father hadn't even stopped by.

After lunch, Dario gets up from the table and takes my hand. "I want to share something with you, a very special place to me." I can tell that he is trying his hardest not to think of it, so he won't give away the surprise as I tune into his thoughts.

He leads me out of the restaurant, down a short hallway, then out a door by the pool.

"Where are we going?" I ask.

"You will see ... be patient, it's not far."

We continue down a path that leads us around the back of the villas where my family had stayed. When we reach a gate that says "Restricted Area—Stay Out," Dario brings out a key from his jeans pocket. I keep trying to figure out where we're going, but I can't seem to get a clear vision from Dario's mind. All I can see is butterflies. How peculiar—and neat—is that?

We walk down a narrow, hedged-lined path toward what looks like a greenhouse.

"What is this place? Where are we?" I think to myself that this spot is too lovely to be hidden in the back of the hotel's property.

"I agree. You'll see why in a minute ... just be patient a little more."

We stop in front of beautiful, stain-glassed doors. My heart is fluttering with anticipation. Dario once again uses his key to open the doors, which allows us to enter an elegant sunroom furnished like some of the old parlor rooms that we would see when our parents took us to visit some of their friends in England, or in old movies.

"This place is amazing! I feel as if we have stepped back into time. I love it here."

"Here let me take your purse for you." He sets it down on a chair. "Now, I need you to do me a favor and close your eyes. Totally trust me, and take my hand."

"Dario, what are you doing? Where are you taking me now?"

Dario gently takes my hand in his and guides me through another door. The new room feels airy and humid, yet warm and relaxing.

"Taylor, keep your eyes closed or you'll ruin the surprise."

The anticipation is killing me, but it's so exciting just to be here with him. Then I feel him slowly turn toward me, taking hold of my other hand. The gesture sends chills through my entire body. His touch is so warm. In a sweet, gentle voice I hear, "Open your eyes."

I open them to a wonderful—actually spectacular—sight of beautiful butterflies fluttering all around us, amid the most exquisite flowers, plants and trees. I'm stunned.

"Dario, this is so extraordinary! I can't believe it."

"I knew you would love it."

"I do. I absolutely do!"

"I have never shared this place with anyone. I come here to get away from all the insanity in my life and to prove to myself that there is still peace and beauty in my world. Now that I've found you, there will always be peace and beauty around me."

He gently pulls me closer to him and places his hands on my cheeks, leaning in slowly. Our lips melt together and feeling silk caressing my skin ... as he gives me the softest kiss while we're surrounded in this special paradise. I know, I just know, that this will be our special place ... always.

As he slowly pulls away, I'm not sure what comes over me. I throw my arms around his neck and my lips onto his, passionately kissing him with all my heart! I don't want to ever stop. My body is full of feelings that I don't even know how to describe. I feel alive, truly alive, as if we are one.

"I feel the same way," he shares with me. "This is the most wonderful thing that has ever happened to me. I will always be here, right next to you, I promise you that forever."

26

Complications

*O*ur drive home is silent, except for the amazing thoughts flying through our minds. Our incredible kiss. How much we enjoy each other's company. How we can't wait to see each other again. I'm feeling almost breathless as the events from the past few days swirl in my head.

Dario takes my hand, reassuring me that everything will work out. He knows how worried I am about my dad's job ... What if his father disapproves of me, and therefore doesn't like, or want my dad working for him? And what about my family? How I'm going to keep this giant secret from everyone?

"So I'll see you later ... after I play tennis with Kayla?"

"Yes and I'll try to get out of dinner tonight with my parents." He enlightens me as he gets out of the car to open my door for me. As the car door opens, my heart fills with sadness.

Walking into the house, I pray that I don't have to deal with anyone's personal issues about Dario and me.

"Taylor? Is that you? Come see me. I'm in the kitchen," I hear my mom yell out to me as I close the front door.

"Yes, it's me Mom."

"How was lunch?" she asks as I enter the kitchen, where my Mom and Malia are busy. "Did you have a nice time?"

Hoping to avoid any unwanted questions, I quickly change the subject.

"What are you two cooking?" I know that when my mom is asked anything about cooking, everything else is forgotten.

"I'm teaching Malia how to make crêpes. I thought it would be fun to teach Malia a few French techniques."

"Sounds like fun. I'm going upstairs to change. Kayla and I have a tennis game."

"That reminds me. Kayla called and wants you to call her the second you get home."

"You didn't tell her where I was did you?" I don't want

anyone knowing about Dario and me right now.

"No I didn't tell her anything. She left it on the voice-mail while we were out shopping. I wrote down her phone number for you and put it on your bed."

"Sounds good, Mom. Thanks."

Mckylee catches me as I walk down the hall. "How was lunch with Prince Charming?" she asks sarcastically, but quickly forgets her own question. "Hey, you're not going to believe this ... you have a gift from Mom and Dad on your bed. You're going to love it! And I want to thank you because if it wasn't for you and your new boyfriend, we would never of gotten them. I got one too!"

She follows me into my room, where I find a small black box sitting on my bed next to the note with Kayla's phone number.

"Is this what I think it is? Mom and Dad actually got us iPhones? No way! Why? How?" I take the phone out of the box and turn it on.

"Dad felt that he needs to be able to find you and know where we are, now that were living life in the fast-lane. That's the way he basically said it."

Now that she puts it that way, I'm not sure how happy I am that our parents can monitor our—my—every move. But at least I now have my own phone.

"It has some power, but you need to plug it in before you go anywhere. It doesn't take long to charge." Mckylee informs me as I turn on the phone and dial Kayla's number.

"Hi Kayla. It's Taylor. My mom said I needed to call you right away," I say as Kayla answers.

"Well ... yeah, we have a tennis game ... what phone are you calling me from? This isn't your house phone because I have that number programmed into my phone."

"I know. This is my new iPhone. How awesome is that? My dad bought it for me today!"

"That's really cool. You're moving up in the world. So are you ready to play some tennis?"

"Well, I'm ready to try, I guess. I did tell you that I've only hit a few balls over the net with my sister ... and that I've never really played before, didn't I?"

"Don't worry ... I just started playing a little while ago ... you'll catch on quickly ..."

"Don't forget to bring me a racket, okay?" I ask her as I hang up.

Before I know it, I hear the doorbell ringing and Malia yelling up at me that Kayla is here. Kayla comes running up to my room, looking perfect as always. I don't understand how she does it.

"You ready? We need to get going to make our court time."

"I'm as ready as I'll ever be let's go, I guess."

I yell goodbye to Malia and my mom, telling them I will be at the club if they're looking for me. As I exit out the front door, I jump into Kayla's golf cart, and we're off. I really don't understand how she ever got her driver's license. She's a horrible driver!

"Why are you driving so fast?" I ask.

"We need to get there. We're late."

"Late for what?"

"You'll see."

What could she be up to? We pull up to the tennis courts and park the cart—barely. Not only is Kayla an awful driver, it's like she didn't know that she should stop it by the curb, instead of just leaving it several feet away. Kayla jumps out and walks to the court before I even have a chance to get out.

"Are you coming?" she yells over her shoulder.

She is acting a little weird, and I have a nervous feeling about all this. That feeling is doubled when I notice *him* playing tennis on the court next to the one Kayla is standing on. He's playing with some guy I've never seen before. What is he doing here? Why didn't I sense his presence? It's probably because Kayla was driving and acting so crazy.

I duck my head and hide behind my sunglasses and proceed to walk faster before he notices me. Like I can hide from him ... he knows I'm here.

Entering our court, I see that things are definitely not getting any better. Aaron and Mike have joined Kayla, and they're all waiting for me. I think I am going to die! What is she thinking?

"We have a few other players joining us," she says with a grin. "I hope you don't mind?"

I smile and say "hi" to the guys.

"So Taylor, you want to be my partner?" Aaron asks. I knew that was coming. Of course, I say, "yes," because I always say yes. But all I can think is that I am going to kill Kayla, as I give her a look letting her know I'm not happy! Actually, all I can really think about is Dario, hitting balls on the court next to us. I hope he doesn't get the wrong idea about Aaron and me—especially since I told him I was playing tennis with Kayla and didn't mention anyone else.

"*An interesting change of events ...*" Dario drops into to my mind.

"*Isn't it? All of it. What are you doing here?*" I ask as I turn to my tennis partners. "I just want to let you all know I have never played tennis before," I blurt out.

"We know. That's why I brought Aaron to play with you," Kayla says. "He's one of the best players around and he offered to teach you."

"*How sweet. Aaron is going to teach you how to play tennis,*" Dario adds, just as Mike and Kayla walk to the other side of the net and Mike gets ready to serve the little yellow ball right in my direction.

What am I doing here? I can't concentrate. I don't even care if I play well or not. To my surprise, this attitude seems to be helping, as I hit the ball back over the net!

Aaron is trying to give me pointers, but I really don't want to hear what he has to say. I mean, he's not my type ... not only does he bore me, he just, well, he just bugs me. I don't know why. I want this game to be so over. As if Dario is coming to my rescue, he says, "*Taylor, something has come up and I need to talk to you. I need you to come with me. Now!*" His words have an urgency ... different from the ones I heard when he called to me when he was shot.

"*What? How am I supposed to get out of all this? I can't just go with you. How would I explain leaving with you to everyone over here?*"

"Tell them you have to go to the ladies room and meet me inside by the restrooms."

"Really? You want me to lie? I'm not good at lying Dario."

"Taylor, now! Meet me, please. It's important."

"Fine, I'll be there in a minute." I try to think of something to tell the others.

"Hey everyone," I say, coming up with a story even as I speak. "I'm not feeling very well. I think it's the heat. I'm going to head inside to get some water. I'll be right back."

"Do you want me to come with you?" Kayla offers.

"I'll be okay. Stay with the others. I'm just thirsty and feeling hot. I'll be right back. Just play without me."

Moving quickly while hoping that no one is following me, I look back, double-checking, as I enter the clubhouse.

"Dario where are you? I'm here ... what's so important?"

"I'm right behind you," he answers as he wraps his arms around me and kisses me on the neck, practically scaring me to death.

"Dario what are you doing? You frightened me! What is going on? What is so important that it couldn't wait until I was done playing?"

"Come with me Taylor," he whispers as he grabs my hand and leads me quickly into a small room at the end of the hall.

"What is going on Dario? You're freaking me out!"

"You need to read this."

He pulls his cell phone out of his pocket and shows me the text message on the screen:

Dario who's your cute little friend you've been spending a lot

of time with? You better keep her close to you. What is her name? Taylor? We're watching you, and we're especially watching her....

"What does this mean? Who sent this to you? How do they know about me?" I ask frantically.

"It came from an unknown source, but I think it's these guys, they're the ones who shot me. They owe my dad a lot of money, and now they are on the run. I've got it taken care of. I just wanted you to be aware, and I promise I won't let anything happen to you. You've got to trust me. It's me they want."

I know that he's trying to make it sound like no big deal. He's acting so casual, yet I know, I can feel, that he is really worried, and this isn't anything small. It is a big deal ... a really big deal. Why would someone want to threaten him ... and me? Who sent it?

"So what now? What do you want me to do?" I can hear a quiver in my voice. It doesn't matter if he knows I'm afraid. I can't hide how I feel from him anyway. He can read every thought and feeling that's rushing through my body right now.

"I need you to go back out to the court and tell Kayla that you really don't feel well and you need to go home. Then wait for me there," he says. He is now completely calm, acting like this is just another day for him.

"Okay, I'll be waiting for you."

He hugs me, gently kissing the top of my head. Then he quickly leaves the room.

I stay there for a few more minutes, feeling as if time is

standing still. Finally, I gather my thoughts and head into the hallway, where I bump right into Kayla.

"Taylor! What are you doing? That's not the ladies room." I glance up and down the hall, wondering if she saw Dario come out of the room before me. Unsure of what to say, I blurt out, "I'm still looking for the restroom."

"You passed it right by the front door. Are you sure you are all right? You don't look very well. Actually, you look a bit pale."

"You're right. I don't feel very well. Would it be okay with you if you took me home?" I'm trying to play the role of a sick person, not of a scared, witless one, but given my state of mind, it's hard to tell how I'm coming across to Kayla.

"Sure. No problem. Let's get you home now. I already brought the cart up to the front of the club."

I can't get home quickly enough. I actually am starting to feel kind of sick. As we walk out the front doors, I look for Dario. But he is nowhere in sight.

"Are you all right?" Aaron asks as we approach Kayla's cart, where he and Mike are waiting.

"I'll be fine. I just need to get home and cool off. I think the heat is just getting to me, that's all."

Sitting next to Kayla on the cart, I wave as we start off toward home.

"Hey Taylor, we're all going to a concert tonight at the Mandalay Bay Hotel out by the pool. If you feel better and want to go with us, let me know, okay? We have a few extra tickets, and Mckylee is welcome, too."

"That would be fun. I'll see how I feel and call you later," I tell her as we pull up to my house.

"Feel better and I hope to see you later." Kayla says as she heads home.

I head directly inside, closing the door behind me and leaning heavily against it as I take a deep breath, so happy I am home safe.

27

Vita, Amore e Felicità

Leaning against the door, catching my breath,
**I realize that some of what my dad said earlier about
Dario may be true.** He could break my heart. I mean,
I've never met anyone like him and I literally feel like I'm
floating when he's near. This connection we have is both
fabulous and let's face it, a little bit scary.

I know Dad didn't say it, but Dario is definitely out of
my league, and I most likely would never be dating a guy

with such a high profile. I mean, everyone knows who he is. And Dad knows that his father is loaded with money.

Think about it ... the huge hotel he owns, private jets and treating us like we were the Royal Family when we first arrived from England. Now that I'm thinking about all this, I wonder, though, if Dad knows that Dario's dad is actually running the Mob here in Las Vegas?

The Mob! Can you believe it? I'm not even sure what being a Mob boss really means. Honestly, I didn't even believe the Mob existed until we moved here and I met Dario.

My mom enters the front hall, startling me in my confused state. "Taylor, what are you doing here? That was a quick tennis game. You're looking a little pale. Are you okay?"

"I'm okay. The heat, it just got to me, that's all. I'm going to get a glass of water and go upstairs to lie down." It's a little scary how good I'm getting at this lying stuff. I mean, I never used to lie.

"Hey Taylor, how was your tennis game with Kayla?" Mckylee asks as I enter the kitchen where she's hanging out watching the telly.

"It was okay, a little too hot for me ..."

"By the way, Dario called looking for you while you were gone and asked if you could call him when you got home. I wrote his number down for you. It's on the counter."

"Thanks. I'll catch up with you in a little while."

I grab Dario's number and a glass of water and head up

to my room. Shutting the blinds, I eliminate most of the light, then fall face first onto my bed, trying to make sense of everything that is happening in my life while holding the piece of paper with Dario's number on it tightly.

How crazy is all this? If I understand what Dario was saying, my life is possibly being threatened by some crazy guys who have some death wish with the Mob—Dario's father's Mob. To top it all off, I'm hopelessly and completely in love with my perfect other half—my soul mate—a guy who just happens to be completely out of my league.

Tears come to my eyes when I think of how easy my life was in England and how there is no way I will ever be back there. My life was so uncomplicated just a month ago, yet I wouldn't trade being with Dario for anything in this whole, entire world.

Brushing the unexpected tears from my eyes, I roll over and reach for my phone, dialing the number on the paper.

Dario answers, his voice filled with reassurance. "Hey Taylor, I want you to know everything is going to be okay. Do you understand me?"

I'm quiet for a moment, then say, "Why did you want me to call you? And how did you get my number?"

"Taylor I can get anything I need, anything we need, at any given moment. But that's not important. What's important is that now you have my number. There may be a time when we may not be able to communicate through our minds; we need a back-up plan in case something happens with our telepathy and we need to get in touch with each other."

"What do you mean 'we may not be able to communicate through our minds?' ..."

"Please, don't worry ... it's just my nature to have back up plans with everything I do. Now that you are in my life, I don't want to lose you ... you are that important ... that special ..."

Smiling at his words, I feel myself relax. He sounds so reasonable, and I *do* know that he will keep me safe from whoever sent him that text message.

"Okay. Sounds good. So, what's going on tonight? Did you get us out of dinner with your family?" I ask, even though I already know the answer by reading his thoughts.

"You already know. I'll pick you up at 6:30, and, yes, you can bring your sister if you want. Wear something nice. This will be a special night, I can feel it ... I sense that my father knows that you are special to me—I've never told him that anyone was my girlfriend before ... okay?"

"I'll see you soon. Bye."

"And Taylor, smile for me so I can feel it in your voice. I promise you everything will be all right. I give you my word."

Turning over on my bed, I find myself staring up at the ceiling. What am I going to wear tonight? Special, he said ... then I remember I haven't talked to my sister yet. I drag myself out of bed and head downstairs. Where I find Mckylee lounging out on the couch.

"Hey Mckylee, do you want to go to dinner tonight with me and Dario? His dad invited me to join them, and I don't want to go alone."

"Really? You want me to go to dinner tonight with the two of you ... with his family?" she says excitedly.

I know, I know, I'm not really going to be alone, since I am going to be with Dario, but I don't have to point that out to Mckylee though. I really do need her there for moral support, if nothing else. And let's face it; Mom might be more open to it if Mckylee were coming too.

"Are you kidding? Where are we going and what should I wear?"

"We're going to some restaurant called Piero's, and I'm sure it's really fancy because Dario told me to wear something nice. Oh, and before I forget, he's picking us up at 6:30. That is in about an hour and a half, so be ready. I'll go get Mom's okay."

Mckylee jumps off the couch, happy at the prospect of another night out. But when I ask my mom about the plan, she frowns. For sure, her enthusiasm doesn't match Mckylee's.

"Taylor, you just went to lunch with Dario, and I was hoping you and your sister would have dinner with Malia and me tonight and stay in, maybe watch a movie. And weren't you not feeling so well just a bit ago?"

"I know Mom, but we really want to go. Please? And I feel fine now—it was just the heat."

"I don't know Taylor. Your dad isn't very comfortable with you spending so much time with Dario."

"What are you going to do? Forbid me to see him? I don't understand—he's like the best guy any girl could ever have as a boyfriend. Everybody says so." I hope my face is not turning red as that little lie falls out of my mouth.

"I didn't say that, Taylor. This is all just a little new to us, that's all. It is a little strange how close the two of you have become in just a few dates."

"We can't help the way we feel about each other. I remember you telling me you fell in love with dad on your first date."

"But that was different Taylor. We were in college—not 16 and in high school."

"Whatever Mom," I say, trying to sound unconcerned, but holding back tears. It seems like she won't be giving us permission to go.

Then she surprises me. "Okay, you both can go. But you really need to change your attitude. I don't like it, and if this is how you're going to act dating Dario, then maybe you shouldn't be seeing him."

The silence is heavy in the room. Mom looks at me as if she feels wounded. I don't want to hurt her; we've always been close.

"I'm sorry Mom, but you've been giving me such a hard time about him."

"I understand. Let's just try and talk to each other without the attitude. Deal?"

"Okay. I'm really sorry and I love you, and if it means anything, thanks for letting us go tonight."

Mom smiles and I feel better about the situation as I leave to talk to Mckylee in her room.

"Mckylee, get your party dress on ... were going out!"

"I'm so excited, I can't believe you're letting me go with you and Dario. Does he have any cute friends?"

Mckylee's question takes me by surprise. I wish I could share how I really feel about Dario's friends—people I don't think I want to spend much time with.

Changing the subject quickly, I ask her, "What have you decided to wear? I have no idea what to put on."

"I'm going to wear the dress I wore to our going-away party in England."

"That's perfect, you're brilliant! That's what I'll wear too, the black dress that everyone thought was fabulous. You know what is so weird? When Mom bought me that dress, I thought it was way too nice and that I would never wear it again. Now here we are."

Jumping in the shower, the hot water runs over my face and down my body, the soothing comfort of the waters tranquility glides over me. Closing my eyes, I try to focus on this whole situation I'm in. The Mob, Dario and this whole Split-Aparts thing ... really ... Split-Aparts, who ever heard of such a thing. All of it is just a little unreal, and if I weren't living it, I wouldn't think any of it was possible.

Is it possible? Is it real? Am I just dreaming it all?

Getting out of the shower, I begin to towel dry and realize that I should do some research on the mythology of Split-Aparts when I get a free moment. And while I'm at it, I might as well research the Mob as well ... and Dario's dad.

I need to be beautiful. I need to do something with my hair besides the ponytail thing. What I really need is to call in reinforcements—my mother. She is going to have a heart attack just hearing I want help with my looks, but sometimes a girl's got to do what a girl's got to do.

"Mom!" I yell, "Can you come here for a minute?"

"What do you need now, Taylor?" she asks.

"I just need your help. Can you please come here and bring your curling iron, please?"

I can hear her coming down the hall toward my room.

"Did I hear you just say 'bring my curling iron'?" Mom looks at me in shock. "Look at you ... you said you would never ever wear that dress again."

"I know Mom—you were right, I was wrong. It was Mckylee's idea to wear our England dresses and I need your help with my hair ... please," I plead.

"I never thought I would hear those words come out of your mouth, but I would love to. I'll be right back." She has an amused smile on her face as she heads back to her room to get her hair tools.

She's right. I have never cared about what I look like, and now all I want to do is look beautiful for Dario. I've always heard being in love makes you do crazy things.

It's official. My life is out of control.

• • • • • • • • • • • •

The ringing of the doorbell makes me jump; I'm not really sure why, seeing Dario had warned me he was around the corner. I'm a little nervous about tonight I guess—I'm not really sure what to expect.

"Hurry up Mom!" I frantically demand. "We need to finish ... he's here!"

"Taylor ... for heaven's sake, calm down ... Why are you so nervous?" she asks, with a hint of concern in her voice.

"I don't know ... maybe because I hope he likes the way I look? How do I look?" I ask her as I make some finishing touches to my make-up. I grab my purse and phone as I make my way downstairs to answer the door.

Opening the door there he stands, as handsome as always with his shoulder-length brown wavy hair, green dusky eyes and amazingly tanned skin. His presence makes me feel warm and nervous all at the same time, yet so complete and full of life.

"Wow! You look incredible," he says. "I really like your hair down and all curled ... are you and your sister about ready to go?"

"Thank you, and you don't look too bad yourself. I love the suit jacket."

Mckylee and Mom join us, and Mom asks Dario when we will be home.

"Well, I have a surprise for them after dinner, so I was hoping you could make an exception and allow me to bring them home by 2 a.m.? Would that be all right?" Dario asks.

"What kind of surprise?" she inquires, I knew she couldn't just let it go.

Smiling, he says, "Would it be okay if Taylor called you

after dinner to let you know, so we don't ruin it for them now?"

A moment of silence passes. As she looks at him, then the two of us, she finally speaks.

"I guess that'll be all right," she says hesitantly, "as long as you will be somewhere I approve of. Taylor, you make sure you call me before you go anywhere. Do you understand me?"

"Yes Mom. I understand." Suddenly, I hate my new phone. For the first time in my life, I have to account my every breathing moment.

"Taylor, she just cares about you, you don't need to get so upset," Dario relays to me.

Walking out the front door, I notice once again that Dario has a different black car. How many cars can one guy have?

"A lot!" He shares sarcastically as he opens our doors for us.

Driving away from the house, Dario turns to Mckylee and me. "I want to prepare you both for tonight. I'm not really sure how many people are going to be there, but usually it's never just my immediate family. Dad has a lot of friends and work associates who join us often. It personally gets on my nerves, but he's busy and feels his work needs to be taken care of at all times."

"We don't have to meet them—we can do it another time if you want, Dario."

"No, we have to go. He is expecting us and no one says no to him. I rarely get that pleasure, and I am his son."

I wonder what Mckylee is thinking in the back seat. I

can tell by her silence that she isn't really sure what she's in for tonight. Neither am I, considering I am about to have dinner with a man who scares me to death. After one short meeting over lunch, I know that I never want to be alone with him.

I feel bad because at least I know who Mr. Mancini really is, but Mckylee knows nothing, and I can't tell her, even if I wanted to. What am I getting us into?

"Stop thinking so much. You're hurting my head!" Dario says.

He's right. I'm even hurting my own head.

All of sudden my phone starts to ring. I see Kayla's name on the caller ID.

"It's Kayla. What should I tell her?"

"Don't tell her anything. Don't answer. Just call her later after dinner. Or text her right now and tell her you're at dinner and you'll call her later," Dario suggests.

"I don't know how to text, you'll have to show me. What do you have planned for us after dinner that is such a secret anyway?" I ask.

"I have something in mind that I thought the three of us could do if you're interested, and I'll show you how to text when we get to the restaurant," he answers as he drives quickly through the streets of Vegas.

"Why can't you just tell us? And how come we aren't telling Kayla that we are with you ... ?" Mckylee asks.

"Just wait and see. Let's first see how late we're at dinner and go from there. Okay?" he asks the two of us.

"Okay ... it's just that everyone is going to some concert

tonight at the Mandalay Bay. And we've never been to a concert before and really want to go," I explain to Dario, at the same time ignoring Mckylee's question about Kayla

I can tell she is wondering as much as I am what Dario has up his sleeve. He's right, I really want to get through dinner first then go from there. Silence surrounds us for the rest of the ride to the restaurant.

As we pass the Convention Center, I catch sight of the restaurant. We pull into the valet, where all of our doors are opened at once. The man who opened Dario's door asks him how he is doing this evening and tells him that his father is already inside.

"Take a deep breath ... I promise everything will be fine," Dario shares with me as he takes my hand and leads the way.

Stopping abruptly, he says, "Hand me your phone, I almost forgot we need to text Kayla. I'll do it for you."

"What are you going to say?"

"I'm just going to tell her you're at dinner and you'll call her later," he says as he's texting her.

"I'll show you how to text later, okay?"

Walking past the hostess stand, Dario greets several pretty girls and continues toward the back, walking as if he owns the place. Obviously, he's been here before.

We come to a small dining room where two meaty-looking guys sit at a small table outside. I feel as if my heart is going to jump out of my chest as we walk past them. In the room, at least 10 people sit around a large table, with Dario's father at the head and a beautiful woman at his side. She must be Dario's mother.

"Look who is here everyone—Dario with his new friends! Come in ladies and let me introduce you to our family," Mr. Mancini says in an overly loud voice.

"Oh yes, our family," Dario is thinking. *"My family of vicious, malicious and inexcusable men who will do anything it takes to get whatever they want! My family!"*

Startled with what I just heard, I look over at Dario. His expression doesn't change, but he does squeeze my hand a little tighter.

We walk over to Mr. Mancini, who introduces himself to Mckylee and then begins introducing everyone else at the table, starting with Mrs. Mancini, who insists we call her Madeline. With her long blonde hair and blue eyes, her beauty lights up the room, especially compared to all of these overpowering men.

Dario's sister Arianna—"Air," as he calls her—sits next to her. She is stunning, too, with long, dark hair and Dario's green eyes. I would have thought she was at least 18 years old if Dario hadn't already told me she's only 14.

Mr. Mancini continues to rattle off all the men's names so quickly that I know I won't remember any of them later. There are two familiar faces at the table, though: Tony and Mateo.

"Please, sit," Mr. Mancini says—or rather directs us.

Dario sits to the left of his father with me on his other side. Mckylee sits between Mateo and me. The energy in this room is tight and powerful in a way I've never experienced before, but once the introductions are over, everyone goes back to talking, and the mood lightens.

Dario's mom is fascinated with the fact that we have just

moved from England. She says she loves London, especially Harrods department store. Mckylee and I both agree with her (we both love Harrods as well, even though it was way out of our price range when we lived there).

Huge platters of cold seafood are delivered to the table, each laden with crab legs, stone crabs, shrimp and oysters. This is just the appetizer! Mckylee's eyes open wide, in disbelief. Dario's dad then holds up his wine glass and toasts everyone.

"La Vita, l'amore e la felicità," he says with a grin on his face as he looks at Dario. Everyone holds up their wine glasses and replies, *"Salute."* I know they are all speaking Italian, but I have no idea what they just said. I just join in, holding up my wine glass.

"Dario, what did your dad just say?" Mckylee asks, as if she could read my mind.

"My dad always says this at our gatherings. It means—to life, love and happiness."

Dinner goes smoothly, better than I had thought it would, and the Italian gourmet cuisine is marvelous. I am definitely ready to be out of here though. One thing for sure, I don't think I will ever need to eat again; I'm not even sure if I can walk ... I'm so full.

"This wasn't as bad as I thought it would be," I share with Dario.

Soon, Dario pushes back his chair. "So, are you ladies ready to get out of here?" he says. "Hey, I hope you two don't mind but Arianna is going to join us tonight, along with Mateo and Tony. "

"Sure, but you still haven't told us what we're doing. And I have to call my Mom and get her okay," I remind him.

I tell myself that I'm glad that Arianna is coming with us but definitely not thrilled about Mateo and Tony.

Dario immediately picks up on my thoughts.

"I'm not going out without Tony and Mateo with everything that has been going on ... we need them in case something goes down ..."

With so much noise at the table, it's hard to pick up everything Dario is telling me ... but at least I have the opportunity to get to know Arianna better—I think I will like her.

As we wait for his car to arrive from the valet, Dario and his friends stand apart, deep in a private chat—although it really isn't that private, seeing as I know everything that is being said through Dario's thoughts.

"Taylor, stop listening in. You are just going to ruin your own surprise," he tells me ... I know he's still not use to the fact that I can hear every little word that goes through his mind.

The car finally arrives, and the valet helps Arianna, Mckylee and me, while Dario, Mateo and Tony finish their discussion. While they were talking, I heard Dario mention a show, so I'm pretty sure I know where we're going, but I don't want to ruin it for the other two, so I keep quiet and just play along. Dario finally comes to the car and soon we are on our way, with Mateo and Tony following behind us.

Dario knows all the back streets, and he drives down them like a maniac. For some odd reason, I love it. It's thrilling and dangerous and completely irresponsible. Kind of like what my life is beginning to feel like ...

28

Reality

$\mathcal{A}$s we drive up to the **Mandalay Bay Hotel and Casino, Mckylee and Arianna are buzzing with excitement in the back seat.**

"I knew you were going to take us to the concert tonight," Arianna says, poking Dario's shoulder. "Why didn't you tell me when I asked you earlier and you said you didn't feel like going?"

"If I would have told you, then it wouldn't have been a surprise now, would it, Air?"

"I hope they still have tickets available for all of us," I say. "Kayla said they had a few extra if we wanted them when I was at the club this afternoon."

"Already taken care of," Dario says as he pulls up to the valet. We all start to pile out, and I notice that Dario nods at the guy who opens my door. I am starting to wonder if there isn't anyone in Vegas who doesn't know him. Can someone really know this many people?

"*Yes*," he informs me. "*This is a very small town when you have lived here your whole life. Everyone knows everyone.*"

Walking through the Mandalay Bay is like walking through all of the other hotels and casinos in Vegas—absolutely incredible, but in its own special unique way.

As we all move across the casino floor, I'm amazed at how crowded it is and how many people are sitting at what looks like miles of tables. I know I'm exaggerating a bit, but there must be hundreds of them. Dario says that the men and women standing behind the semi-circular tables are the dealers and the casino "guests" are all sitting on chairs around the blackjack "21" tables, each waiting for cards to be dealt. It looks like the dealer is pulling them out of some sort of box ... Dario says it's called a "shoe."

To the right of all the blackjack tables are several large tables that are long ovals. Few are sitting here, and I think I can tell who the dealers are—they are the ones in uniforms. One is holding a long stick and there are piles of different color chips in front of lots of people and on several numbers in different boxes on the table. There's a third dealer at the end of the table. As if reading my eyes as they scan the room, Dario says, "*Those guys are playing craps.*"

I don't hear anyone saying crap, but what I do hear is an amazing amount of noise and excitement coming from those tables. A couple of the women are jumping up and down while one man is yelling out, "C'mon baby" as he asks the woman next to him to blow on the dice he has in his hands. In contrast, the blackjack tables seem so much quieter.

My eyes jump from one scene to another, trying to take it all in. My ears are being pounded by the noise of all the slot machines. Different bells, songs, and music, all pouring out in a symphony of dissonance. How does anyone think in this place? It seems like people are throwing their money away. I don't think very many people walk away winners, which I guess is how all these big, beautiful casinos exist.

"You are right. There's glamour attached to being here, and the casinos make huge amounts of money—far more money is lost here than you could ever imagine," Dario shares.

All of us girls are so thrilled that we're actually going to the concert? Especially Mckylee and me, seeing as we've never been to one before. I'm beginning to learn that with Dario, just about anything can happen!

He leads us through the never-ending, winding path of this massive hotel toward the main box office. The woman behind the window hands him a slip of paper that he signs. She then hands him a pile of badge-looking things that we put around our necks.

"These are weird tickets," I comment.

"These aren't tickets; they're passes. We are guests at this show, not ticket buyers like the others. This show is sold out," Tony says impatiently.

"What does that mean? What is a 'pass?'" Mckylee asks.

"It means that these are comp tickets and that we are allowed to walk anywhere we want, including backstage," Arianna says. "Haven't the two of you ever been to a concert before?"

"No, where we lived, there were never any near us, and our parents would never have taken us to London to see one. It's not their style ... so can anyone go backstage? What happens backstage? Does that mean we'll get to meet the band?" I rattle off a bunch of questions in my excitement.

"You really are just the cutest girl," says Arianna. "I can see why Dario is so into you; you're not like other girls. And yes, you get to meet the band. Dario obviously didn't tell you that he knows them."

I look at Dario with amazement. He squeezes my hand and asks, "Are you ladies ready to go into the show?"

"Oh my God, I forgot to call Mom," I blurt out, looking at Mckylee.

"I already took care of it," Dario says.

"What? When?"

"Taylor, do you trust me? I took care of it. You and Mckylee are good til 2 a.m. So let's get going. The show is starting." He grabs my hand and leads our group out the doors entering the pool area into a swarm of people.

Mckylee is ecstatic and can't wait to see a band live in concert, especially since it's one of her favorites. And the thought of meeting them is just unreal to her ... and to me. We walk in right as the music starts playing.

Immediately, Mckylee starts jumping around and

dancing, she is so excited. The place is packed. The stage is built over the pool, right in front of the beach—sand, water and all! Some people are actually standing in the water watching the show. It seems to be a standing-room-only, or grab-a-seat-where-you-can, kind of situation. I just assume that's what we will be doing, which is fine. But no, Dario has a cabaña waiting for us, stocked with the works! This just can't be my new reality; I feel like I am living someone else's life.

Arianna and Mckylee dance away while the rest of us take a seat. I get my phone out and try to figure out how to text Kayla to let her know where we are. Dario grabs my hand and pulls me over to him, motioning for me to sit between his legs.

"Just a minute. I'm trying to text Kayla to let her know that we're here," I shout at him because it's so crazy loud.

"Are you sure you want to do that? I mean she and the others have no idea about us and maybe we should keep it that way for a while." Dario wraps his arms around me.

"Maybe, but I'd rather just get it over with than have them run into us sitting here by some weird chance. That would be way more uncomfortable, don't you think?" I lay back against him, placing my head on his shoulder. He leans his head into mine and kisses my cheek.

"I guess I just have never been friends with any of those guys, even though I've known of them since the sixth grade. Actually, now that I'm thinking about it, I've never been friends with anyone other than Tony and Mateo."

"Well, Kayla is the only new girlfriend I have and I would like

to keep her around, so I guess you will have some new friends in your life. It will be good for you, anyway."

"Fine, Taylor. If it will make you happy, invite them over. I'll show you how to text her, but let's wait a little while. We just got here."

"It will make me happy—and thanks for understanding, Dario."

Dario shows me how to text Kayla. I tell her where we are and to look for us at intermission.

"Dario, I am having the most incredible time, I think someone should pinch me because none of this can possibly be real." What does he do? Pinches me right on my butt!

"Taylor this is all real, and you better get used to it, because this is how my life is, and I'm not going to live it another day without you right by my side."

I turn my head to face him, placing my lips on his. I swear when my lips are touching his, I feel as if I'm dreaming. The connection between us brings tears of joy to my eyes.

At intermission, we all talk at once. Mckylee comes over and hugs me, "You are the best sister Taylor! I love being here!"

Dario then pulls me closer ... another one of his amazing kisses. Out of the corner of my eye, I catch Kayla and a group of kids approaching the cabaña. Looking more closely, I see that she's with her sister and her friends from the neighborhood—Gabby, Tanya, Mike, Aaron and some others I've never met. The look on her face is one I'll never forget, but certainly not as astonished as the look on everyone else's faces. I wish I could read *their* minds. Jumping up, I give her a hug and tell her that I can't believe how awesome this concert is. She remains speechless as she looks from me to Dario and back to me—I can only imagine what she is thinking.

Smiling, I turn to everyone else and introduce them to Dario, Tony, Mateo, and Arianna. The look on Aaron's face is ... well ... weird ...

"Yeah, we know everyone, Taylor, but my question for you is how do you know these guys?" he says.

"Aaron ... didn't I mention that I met Dario when we were living at the Beauvallon when we first arrived from England? His father owns the hotel ... but I think you know that ... don't you?" I comment sarcastically.

Before he can really respond, I smile at him in my best "be nice" smile as the band begins to play again. I head off to join the girls for a little bit of dancing, not wanting to deal with him right now.

Seeing Dario's stare as he watches me dance is so strange. I don't think anyone has ever looked at me this way.

"Taylor I love watching you ... you look so beautiful dancing."

I feel myself blushing, glad that it's now dark outside and no one can actually see my red face.

In the back of my mind I feel Dario getting a text from the band's assistant asking him where he is and when he is going to come backstage. This is different ... now I can sense him moving his thumbs and fingers as he texts. That must mean that he can do the same with me. Maybe the longer we are together, we will be able to expand are connecting skills ... I mean how cool would it be if we could actually see what the other sees ...?

I hear him ask Mateo and Tony if they're going to come backstage with us. Of course they are ... I don't think those two can breathe without Dario. Dario tells them that we're going in about ten minutes and to be ready.

"Do you and Mckylee want to head backstage and say hi to the band with us?" he asks me even though I already know the plan. This whole idea of being able to hear each others thoughts is beyond extraordinary and is something I don't think I'll ever get use to.

"Yes of course ... who wouldn't want to go backstage and meet the band?!" I reply excitedly.

"Then your in charge of getting the girls together and meeting us by the backstage entrance in about ten."

I yell out to Mckylee and Arianna, "Hey, we're going to go backstage in a few minutse, but first I need to go let Kayla know what's going on, I'll be right back."

Spotting Kayla nearby, I make my way through the crowd over to her and give her the 411. As I head back I grab my sister and Arianna. We meet up with Dario and the guys at the entrance to the backstage area. Where a large man checks our badges, granting us access to continue down the corridor.

This place is anything but empty. From the front of the stage, all we saw was the band. Back here, there must be a hundred people that no one knows about. Each ready to respond to the band's needs in some way. Several are hooked up to headsets and mics; I'm not really sure who they are talking to. At least a dozen are holding clipboards, and as I look closer, they also have on headsets. Uniforms are everywhere—security must be pretty important.

Two dozen people dressed in non-concert clothing, almost like suits—I'm guessing that they have something to do with the Mandalay and the band's business. I wonder who keeps track of all this. All I know is that it's amazing how many different people it takes to bring a show together.

The band's manager seems to be glad to see Dario, Mateo and Tony, and he shares some kind of a special handshake with each of them. He gives Arianna a big hug and introduces himself to Mckylee and me.

I'm mesmerized with all the activity and Dario leans over and whispers in my ear to stay right where I'm standing ... and that I will meet the guys in the band after this is over.

Being backstage is pretty awesome—even though we really can't see the performance anymore, just the sides of the band's heads. But we can move around and Mckylee and I are dancing up a storm on the sidelines.

After it's over and the band exits the stage, they stop and talk to a few different people and then see Dario. The lead singer gives Dario a hard time about finally coming to see him.

Dario just laughs. "It's great to see you my friend. Let me introduce you to my girlfriend Taylor and her sister Mckylee. It's their first concert ever."

"Wow, that's intense. You've really never been to a concert before? I hope you enjoyed the show ladies."

He immediately turns his attention back to Dario and asks what he's been up to lately. He tells Dario that they won't be hanging out tonight, because they're hitting the road right after the show—heading to their next gig in L.A.

It's really bizarre to think that I just met the lead singer to a rock band and he's just like all of us—just doing something that he loves. How cool is that?

Dario, Mateo and Tony finish their conversation and we go back to the cabaña, where we find everyone is waiting. Well almost everyone.

"Where are the guys?" I ask.

"Oh ... they got tired of waiting and went inside to check out some club and see if Tad's friend is working there. They thought he might get us in after this is over," Samantha says.

"Who is Tad?" I ask. "I've never met him before." Then I turn to the girl I hadn't recognized earlier. "I apologize for not introducing myself earlier. I'm Taylor."

"It's nice to finally meet you Taylor, I'm Skyler. I live in the neighborhood—at the other end from you, by the back gate. I've heard a lot about you and your sister the last couple of days."

"It's nice to meet you too Skyler and may I add, I love your name. It's very cool."

When that came out of my mouth, I am realizing that I'm starting to fade. And fade fast. Doesn't anyone around here ever get tired? It is amazing to me how much energy the people in this city put out! They seem to be able to go 24/7. After barely getting any sleep last night, thanks to my late-night rendezvous with Dario, I'm exhausted. It's midnight. I hear Dario ask Samantha if she happened to catch the name of the club the guys went off to.

"Some club that is on the top floor somewhere or something—but I really don't know. Sorry."

"That's okay. This hotel has a lot of clubs. It would be a waste of time trying to find them, so we'll just hang out and wait for them here I guess. I don't want to leave you girls alone."

I realize, again, what a gentleman Dario is. I decide to take a seat over in a lounge chair away from everyone else to get a few moments of peace, and Dario soon joins me.

"Are you all right Taylor? What's up? Why are you sitting over here by yourself?"

"I'm fine, just a little tired that's all. Since I met you, my sleep hasn't been what it used to be."

It's only a few minutes before the guys are back, asking us if we want to go with them to some club in the hotel. They inform us that their buddy can set it up. Not surprisingly, everyone wants to go, but Arianna looks upset. She knows she can't go, for a few reasons. One, she is way too young. And the other is that her father and Dario are very protective of her.

I really don't want to go, either. I'm tired and could really care less about it.

"So, what are we doing?" I ask Dario out loud because I'm unable to completely understand what's going through his mind right now—there seems to be a lot of ... I don't know what ... words ... going on. Maybe it's like noise—I just can't get a clear sense of what he's thinking right now.

He speaks up quickly, directing his answer toward Aaron and the others, "Hey guys, thanks for setting things up for us at the club, but we already have plans. You are all welcome to join us, but we are going over to a club at the Beauvallon called Unity."

Turning to Taylor, Dario says, "I've wanted to show you this club, but if you are too tired, it can wait ..."

Before I can respond, Kayla shouts out, "I want to come with you Taylor! Don't you, girls?

"Why don't you all text Taylor when you figure it out. If you want to come, just let her know and we'll meet you outside Unity's entrance. Let's go."

Dario starts to walk briskly toward the exit. Watching him, I realize how powerful he really is. He says 'jump' and we all do just that.

"Stop thinking, Taylor, and let's get going. I know you are tired. I promise I'll get you home soon. Right now, we're running late."

Late? Late for what is all I can think as I quickly try to catch up

29

Vegas Nights-Mob Style

*T*railing slightly behind with Arianna and Mckylee, I hear Dario telling Mateo and Tony to drive Arianna home and then join us at Unity. He appears to be rushed and agitated.

"Dario what's going on? Why are you so frustrated? Why the rush to get to this club?"

"Taylor, don't worry about it, and stay out of my head ... you don't need to know everything. You and your friends will be

entertained, and the view from up there is unbelievable. Trust
me."

"View? Where is Unity?"

I try to learn more through Dario's thoughts, but for
some odd reason his stress makes it hard to listen in.

The valet opens each of our doors and swiftly closes
them behind us as we get in. Before we have a chance to put
our seat belts on, Dario accelerates down the drive. I really
don't want to go to the club, particularly with Dario's new
attitude.

"*Taylor, let it go okay? Please. There is a lot going on right
now that is out of my control, and it would be nice if you would
just chill out!*"

"*Fine. I'll leave you alone. Let me know when you're able to
be yourself again.*"

I'm so frustrated that I have no say in this matter and
that I'm being dragged off to some club when I'd rather
be going home. Why doesn't he know how I feel? I sit in
silence, staring out of the dark tinted windows as he darts
through the streets. I'm unfamiliar with Dario's route to
the Beauvallon, but quickly we're at the back of the hotel,
entering through a guarded gate. Dario doesn't stop, not
even for a second, and the gate opens with no questions
asked. The parking lot is dim and not as glamorous as the
guest lots. He pulls into a spot directly behind a building. If
I'm guessing right, we're back behind the villas somewhere.

"Why are we parked back here?" I ask, hoping to break
the eerie silence.

"It's closer to the club, and I don't want to walk through

the whole hotel and announce our presence. We're keeping somewhat of a low profile. Let's go," he says to Mckylee and me.

I'm amazed at how quiet Mckylee has remained this whole time. I just hope she isn't too freaked out by all of this craziness and the way we are being rushed. Dario slides his keycard into a door and we dart through some back hallway.

Walking a few feet in front us, he approaches an elevator, a service elevator I'm assuming. He stops abruptly, waiting for us to catch up.

"Taylor, have you received a text from Kayla yet?" he asks sternly.

"I don't know. I haven't even been paying attention." I reach into my purse to check. "Yeah. They're here parking the car, planning to meet us at the club's entrance."

"Fine, then we'll need to go another way. Follow me." Dario once again has us winding in and out of long, never-ending hallways trying to keep up with him.

"Taylor, is everything okay with Dario? What's going on with him ... with you two?" Mckylee asks me as we scurry behind.

"I think we're okay. He just wants to make sure we don't miss Kayla and everyone."

I'm trying not to show how unsure I am myself, and it's easy to lie to her. What's with me? I've so easily slipped into doing this, when I would have never lied before we moved here.

When we finally come to a set of double doors, Dario

slams his way through them, and without wasting a minute, we continue down a walkway along the edge of the casino. We must be close to the club, as we pass a long line of people dressed to impress and looking like they are ready to do some dancing.

"Dario, are all these people actually in line to get into Unity? Why aren't we getting in line? This is crazy! Why would anyone want to stand in a line this long to get into a club? That's just foolish to me!"

"It's like this all the time; you'll see why in a minute. And no, I never stand in line in Vegas for anything. Actually I don't think anyone from Vegas stands in line, ever."

We walk into a large marble-lined hallway where Dario heads directly over to a desk marked VIP.

"Taylor!" I hear Kayla shout my name and, glancing over my shoulder, see her off to the side with everyone. Relieved, I feel like I'm in friendly territory again. I don't know what's going on with Dario, but I definitely don't like it.

"I'm so glad you all decided to join us," I tell them as we walk up. "It wouldn't have been the same without—"

"Everyone ready?' Dario interrupts. "Let's go in."

We follow him to the front of the VIP line, where a nice-looking guy in a dark suit greets him.

"Hey Dario, how's it going? The club is off the hook tonight." He then calls and informs someone that Dario Mancini and his party are on their way up.

"They're ready for you." He takes down the red–velvet rope, allowing us to pass, and we follow him to an elevator door that opens. Holding out his arm, he directs us onto our own personal elevator.

"If you need anything else, please let me know. Everyone have a great time." The doors close, and inside the elevator there's another attendant.

"Hey Dario how's it going tonight? New friends? Where are Tony and Mateo?" the guy asks as he pushes the one and only button.

Turning around, I realize the elevators made of glass. We're in a glass elevator like in Charlie and the Chocolate factory. This is so wild!

"This is amazing, so awesome! Taylor do you see this?" Mckylee is literally bubbling over, shouting at me.

The elevator takes off with great speed; heading up to what I think is the top of the building. The phenomenal panoramic view of the Las Vegas strip leaves all of us awestruck and speechless. I'm glad that Dario has chilled out enough to allow all of us to entertain him with our amazement. I see that he has a slight smile on his face.

The elevator comes to a stop, and the doors open. Another nice-looking guy greets us.

"I was surprised to hear you were here on a Saturday night with such a large party, Dario. What's the special occasion?" he asks, giving him what looks like some kind of a special handshake. At least, it's not the regular hand clasping hand one that is normally used when someone is introduced to another. I'll have to ask Dario about it.

"No special occasion, just hanging out," Dario answers nonchalantly.

"We have your table ready for you. Right this way."

As we walk through the crowded room, I notice that the whole club is encased with floor-to-ceiling glass windows. It's fantastic! There isn't one bad view from up here. We walk out onto a patio, to private areas all sectioned off, each with inviting couches and their own large tables nicely stocked with what looks like all the necessities for the preparation of the ultimate drink.

I am mesmerized watching all the unusual-looking people, all dressed to kill—and the dancing is off the hook,. Everyone is rocking to the DJ's awesome mix of the latest hits. I've never heard music mixed quite like this. It's awesome—a mix of music that even has the people who are sitting down moving and grooving to the beat! Suddenly, I'm not so tired anymore.

"This DJ is unbelievable!" I shout out to our group.

"This is one of the best DJ's in town. People come just to see and hear her mix," Tad says as the waitress approaches our table and starts making drinks for everyone. I've never actually seen inside a nightclub before—this is unreal.

"Did I hear you say *her*? This is a girl! That's so cool!"

Kayla directs the waitress to make all of us girls screwdrivers—whatever that is—with a splash of cranberry juice.

Dario sits silently by my side. He, again, seems put out by the situation, though I don't know why.

"Dario, if you don't want to be here, why did you insist on all of us coming here?"

"I'm fine. Don't worry about it, Taylor." I decide to leave it alone and turn to see Tony and Mateo now standing by our table. Dario gets up abruptly.

"I'll be right back. We have to take care of something. Have fun with your friends. Also, I would suggest trying to block out what's going on in my mind, if that's at all possible. I know it's hard. Be good." He kisses me on the forehead, and then quickly walks away with Mateo and Tony.

Dario's weird behavior is something I'm going to have to get used to, but I'm not sure what this all involves. What could he possibly have to take care of 45 floors above the ground? I know Dario gave me very specific directions not to listen, but I'm not sure how to turn it all off, and being told not to do something just makes me want to do it even more.

I see Mckylee enjoying her drink, and I don't want her getting the way she was the other night. Neither of us should be drinking, and if Mom finds out, who knows what she will do besides the "grounding us for life" promise.

"Hey do all of you want to join me out on the dance floor?" I ask.

I pull Mckylee away from the drink she is just about to sip, and we move to the dance floor. I'm hoping the loud music and dancing will help me drown out Dario's thoughts. I'm not really feeling good about things right now, at least in my own little world. Then all of sudden I'm stopped by this amazing-looking guy who seems to come out of nowhere.

"Hi there ... are you all right?" he asks me with this beautiful accent, Italian I think. His teal–blue eyes look at me so intently. There's something about him ...

"I'm fine, thank you," I answer. I look behind me for someone. Anyone.

"That's good to hear. You look a little upset." He sounds genuinely concerned.

"No, I'm okay …"

"Hey Taylor, are you ready to dance with us?" Skyler asks, coming up behind me. She has startled me. Forgetting the man, I look around, realizing I've lost track of Mckylee. Where is she? Then I find her around on the dance floor with the others.

"Yeah, I'm ready, let's go." I follow Skyler out on to the floor, glimpsing back through the crowd for another peek at the intriguing stranger, only to find he has vanished just as quickly and bizarrely as he had appeared.

The DJ mixes music unlike anything I've ever heard before. Her sound has stirred up the crowd of dancers across the floor like a wave roaring up from an ocean's floor. This place is jumping!

I love dancing. I love the way the music seems to move my body with its rhythm, as if it's fully in control. Back in England, dancing was the way I would always express myself. Sometimes I would find answers to things I was trying to figure out as I moved with the music. I guess music is to me like meditation is to others.

"No! Please Dario tell them to stop!" Someone is shouting into Dario's mind. I can see someone being hung off the top of the club's rooftop by Mateo and Tony.

"My brother's crazy, and I told him to stop! I told him he was messing with the wrong people! No one messes with the Mancinis, everyone knows that, Dario, everyone!" What was that? Did I really just see someone on the roof … or am I imagining

this? I try to continue dancing, blocking whatever my mind thinks it's seeing out of my head. It only lasts for a few minutes—until Mateo almost drops whoever he is holding from the rooftop. To say that this vision completely disturbs me is an understatement. This is real, I am seeing the roof ... and I must be seeing it through Dario's eyes ... what else could it be?

"Oh ... my ... God!" I blurt out on the dance floor.

"What's wrong?" Kayla asks.

"Nothing, it's nothing," I say, regaining my composure. I'm going to go to the ladies room. I'll be right back."

"I'll come with you," she offers.

"No, no, stay here. I'm fine. Stay and dance. I'll be right back. I insist!"

I walk quickly to the ladies room. I can't get there fast enough. I feel like it's the only place I can escape the craziness in my head. I can't believe that Tony and Mateo are hanging some guy off the top of the roof, while Dario is threatening him. I heard Dario tell the guy that if he doesn't pay off the debt and tell them where his brother is, then he will be dropped to his death! The guy yelling, screaming and pleading for his life has my stomach tied in knots. My heart is racing and I feel as if I'm going to puke!

I enter a stall, lock myself in and stand against the wall with my eyes closed, trying to breathe. I feel tears well up in my eyes ... Dario has got to stop this madness ...

"Dario, please don't kill him! Please! Just give him a couple of days to get it together, to find his brother, whatever!"

"Taylor, stay out of it!"

He's yelling back at me! How can I stay out of it when there's a guy's life at stake? I don't care how much that person owes someone or what his brother has done. What kind of insanity is Dario caught up in?

All of a sudden I see the hawk, my hawk, circling around them. Dario and his friends are amazed and startled, allowing for the unthinkable to nearly happen: Tony and Mateo almost drop the guy again. I scream from my stall.

"Are you all right in there? Hello ..." Someone is knocking on the stall door.

"Taylor, pull it together right now. Tell the person on the outside of the door that you're all right and get out of there. I'll meet you back at the table."

"I'm fine ... Thank you ... I just saw this big spider ..." I say to whoever is knocking on the door. At the same time, I hear Dario give the guy until Monday to pay up and deliver his brother or he will have Mateo and Tony finish what they've started! Gathering myself, I make my way out of the ladies room—and bump right into the mysterious Italian guy again.

"Whoa, slow down there tiger. You okay? You look like you just saw a ghost."

"I'm fine. Really." I snap at him and push past. Why does he keep appearing and talking to me as if he knows me? Approaching the table, I see Dario standing there like he's been waiting for my arrival.

He's silent for a few seconds, and then says, "Who's that guy you were talking to a minute ago?"

"I don't know ... just some guy I saw on the dance floor and I bumped into coming out of the ladies room."

"Well, it seemed like he knew you." Dario is stern, unsmiling.

"Dario, I don't know him. He said hello when Mckylee and I went out to the dance floor ... Just drop it."

"Fine, we need to go. I promised your mom that I would have you home by two. Get your sister off the dance floor and meet me by the elevators. And tell all your friends everything has been taken care of," he says. Then he walks away with Mateo and Tony.

I can't believe this night! I scurry off to find Mckylee.

30

Fortitude

"**I** know you're mad and disappointed with me, but this isn't my fault.** I'm just a normal girl who's been living a very simple life up to this point. I'm sorry. I'm really sorry!" I share with Dario as we ride down the elevator.

"First of all, I'm not mad at you or upset, so let me make that clear. We just need to come to an understanding with each other. I need to be honest with you on what your life is going to be like with me in it, that's all. I never realized how detrimental my life *would be to someone else's, especially someone who can read my mind!"*

He puts his arm around me, pulling me into his shoulder to comfort me. The elevator doors open to a ridiculously crowded corridor.

As we're walking through the crowd, Dario informs the guys that he'll call them after he takes me and Mckylee home. Mckylee and I follow behind him silently. We come to a side door and once again enter into the stale, empty back hallway. He's freaking me out. I can't decide if I'm more freaked out about the whole club incident or Dario's weirdness ... what have I gotten myself into?

"What's going on? Why are you and Dario acting so strange? Are you okay?" Mckylee whispers to me.

"I'm fine, just so incredibly tired. It's been a long two days, and I really need to get some sleep. I don't know what's up with Dario," I reply.

"You just seem a little distant, that's all," she says as we approach the car. Dario gets in. He seems distant from the rest of us, as if we aren't with him. Mckylee and I let ourselves in, close the doors, and not a second later, Dario quickly drives out of the parking lot. I'm praying he's heading to our house and not the desert, where I've seen him dispose of other things that were no longer useful to him.

His mind is completely blank. I don't understand. Did something happen that isn't allowing me to hear his thoughts? What have I done? ...

Still completely freaked out, I want to replay the whole

rooftop incident in my head, but I know it's in my best interest not to ever think about it again! I can never allow Dario to think that I'm more of a hazard than an asset. Trying to keep my mind blank is a next-to-impossible feat! It's racing completely out of control. He's not responding to me, so I guess what I'm thinking doesn't matter to him, or he is off somewhere else.

Luckily, Mckylee is tired and not speaking in the back-seat—at least, I think that's why she is so quiet. And before I know it, we're pulling up to the gates of Bonita Palms. The guard waves Dario through. I don't think there has ever been a time in my life where I've been so completely ecstatic to see my house. Dario doesn't even have time to turn the car off before Mckylee hops out, gives a big thanks to Dario and tells me that she'll see me inside. Her door closes, and a certain fear comes over me.

"Are you going to kill me?" I ask, not wanting to beat around the bush.

"What! Why would you even think that? Why would you even say that? I would never hurt you! Do you under-stand me?" There's a little fear in his voice, too.

"You just seemed so upset with me at the club. You still seem upset with me now. What am I to think?"

"Taylor, I wasn't upset with you. I was mad at myself, at this whole situation. This is why I've never dated anyone ever before. I just don't know how to handle all of this."

"I can't believe you've never had a girlfriend before."

"I haven't. Can't you see why? If anyone knew who I really am because of my family—if anyone saw the monster side of me—they would never want to be with me. I'm not even sure why you want to be with me. Hell, I don't want to be with me at times."

"You're not a monster! You're a considerate person who is forced to live a life you were born into—a life that was not chosen *by* you but *for* you. And you know I am with you because I belong with you. We are whole together—you are my soul mate, my Split-Apart. I don't know how many lives we have lived looking for each other, but we are together now. I'm never going to be without you, and we will find a way to free you from all of this craziness, I promise."

Dario leans in and places his beautiful lips on mine, taking away all of my fears.

"Thank you for being so understanding," he shares softly.

Pulling away, I feel completely exhausted. "Dario, I will always be here for you. Please don't ever forget that. Promise me."

"I promise, Taylor."

"I'm really sorry, but this night has wiped me out, and I am in desperate need of my bed. I really need to go inside. I can't go without sleep like you seem to—"

"I understand, but I don't want to leave you upset. Are we okay now?" He touches my hair and pulls it away from my face, looking deep into my eyes.

"We're good, Dario. I don't want to leave you either, but I do need to get to bed. I'm worn out, and this night has just drained me."

"I get it," he says as he gently strokes my face. He takes my hand and walks me to the door. Holding me for a few seconds, he nestles my neck, then gives me a quick kiss goodnight, wishing me "sweet dreams." I watch him slowly walk back to his car and wait for him to get in, and then I head inside.

I can hear Mckylee upstairs, excitedly telling Mom about the evening. I follow their voices up and pop my head into Mom's room, where I see Mckylee sitting on the edge of the bed. "I'm in," I say, smiling. "I'll catch up with everyone in the morning." I head to my room.

• • • • • • • • • • • •

Lying in bed, staring up into complete darkness, I realize I don't even know who I am anymore. All I know for sure is that my life will never be what it was when I lived in England and that I belong with Dario now. Everything else is a complete mess—one that I'm apparently not fixing tonight. Needing some serious sleep, I roll over and shut my eyes.

Of course, the first thing that creeps into my mind is the vision I saw through Dario's eyes of the guy hanging off the top of the Unity nightclub, pleading for his life. Then there was the hawk. What was it doing there? My last thoughts are on the hawk as sleep overtakes my body and mind.

Whenever I fall into a deep sleep, my mind is usually completely at rest, without dreams. Or at least, I'm not aware of any dreaming—that is, until Dario came into my life. Now, he has decided to once again bring me to him during my sleep.

Hesitantly, I'm walking through a dark, unfamiliar hallway toward a beam of light that's seeping through a crack in a door in the distance. A chill rushes through my bones as I find myself propelled to walk toward it.

Knowing in my heart that Dario is on the other side of the door, I pray he isn't involved in some kind of torturing or in any of the other awful deeds he seems to get himself drawn into. I really need some time to process what I saw when I was at the Unity club. Is this just what Tony and Mateo like to do, and Dario feels pressured to go along? Or does Dario want to do it? It seems to be the way he and his posse handle things.

I feel as if I can't breathe. Cautiously peeking through the crack in the door, I'm both uncertain and anxious to see what's on the other side.

To my surprise, it's a beautiful bedroom with a grand, four-poster bed. The room is lit by candlelight, the floor and bed sprinkled with deep-red rose petals. I slowly push the door open, suddenly wondering whether this has anything at all to do with Dario or if I'm really just dreaming.

"Dario, are you here?"

"*I'm here, Taylor ... come in. I've been waiting for you. Tonight, it took longer than it has in the past for me to summon you. You must have really been out,*" he says, sitting in a chair in the far corner of the room.

"*I think I was trying to fight you off at first, but I quickly realized it's not possible to say no to you or to us being together ...*"

"I'm sorry. I wasn't able to sleep. I couldn't stop thinking about you—the incident at the club ... my family ... everything. So I decided to bring you to me instead of sitting here alone dwelling on it all."

Dario stands up and walks toward me, reaching out to touch my cheeks with both of his hands. The contact isn't quite what we thought it would be. His hands touch me, but not my physical body—they touch my inner–body ... OMG! It's crazy, almost like I'm a hologram! His hands drift through me, the same way my hands touched him when he was shot. But now he's touching me, and I'm able to feel him. It's like I'm on some higher level of consciousness. It's like he's inside of me, but not like sex. Not that I've ever actually had sex before, but I know instinctively that this is different. Could it be better than sex?

I need more; I want to feel all of him. Standing there face-to-face with him, I step into his whole body with mine, not knowing what will happen. The force sends him collapsing to the ground, leaving me standing over him. For the short amount of time I was in him, the feeling was explosive. It's something I want to experience again!

"Are you all right?" I ask, looking down at him lying on the floor.

"Wow! I'm incredible! ... What was that? How did you do that?" he asks, laughing.

"I don't know. It just felt so incredible to have your hands go into me that I felt the urge to step into you. But that was way better than I could have ever anticipated! It was amazing ... By

the way, where are we? This isn't the same bedroom I was in before?"

"Nope, it isn't. This is my bedroom, just not the one in my parents' house. This is my bedroom at a house I hide out in when I don't want anyone to bother me. We're out in Blue Diamond, a small town about 30 minutes out of Las Vegas, but worlds apart. This old house has been in my family for years, but it's just a decoy for what's really on this property. No one ever uses it but me, and no one even knows that I stay here.

"Once I was old enough to drive, I started coming here to clear my head and get away from the madness of what my family does. When I first started coming here, there wasn't any furniture in the house, so I slowly started bringing stuff out here to make it my own. It was my luck that there were already blackout curtains on the windows to keep nosey people from looking in, so no one has ever noticed that I have put furniture and stuff in here."

"This is so cool; you have your own hideout. I can't believe no one knows about this place. Not even Mateo and Tony? They don't even know?"

"No way! They're my friends, but Tony's dad is my dad's right-hand man, and you can't trust anyone in this line of business. No one! They'll turn on you in a second if they feel they have any sort of cause. I have learned to play their game until I find a way to get out alive. Do you understand what I am saying to you? You're going to have to trust me and know that together; we are going to find a way to free ourselves from these people who like to call themselves my family!"

He offers this overwhelming information as he sits down

on the bed. Then he taps the spot next to him, indicating that he wants me to join him.

I sit next to him, "*You should try and get some sleep, Dario. You're rambling on and not making any sense ... you seem really tired.*"

Shaking his head, he lays down on the bed, and I lay next to him. Before I know it, he's sleeping peacefully, and I drift back to my blissfully sleeping body, where I'm safe in my bed.

• • • • • • • • • • • • •

The next morning, while feeling a little disoriented and still tired, I recall my dream with Dario and how awesome he makes me feel, especially when our bodies connect. I can't believe how incredible he is. Right now, I feel like I'm the luckiest girl in the world. I wasn't so sure last night when I thought he was going to kill me. Then, I really was frightened for my life.

Somehow, I'm going to have to learn how to disconnect Dario with what his family makes him do. In a way, it sounds like he's almost imprisoned by them. He's been around it a lot longer than me, so I'm going to have to trust him to help me work through it.

Maybe not, but luckily I don't have to have all the answers today. Glancing at the clock, I see that it's 12:30 in the afternoon. I can't believe it—I need to get out of bed and face reality.

"She's alive!" my mom states sarcastically, as I enter the kitchen.

"Like what else would I be? I just needed some serious sleep!" I kiss my mom on her cheek; grab a glass of water and head out to the pool for some fresh air, where I find Mckylee and Skyler sunbathing.

"Wow! You're finally awake. You must have really been tired!" Mckylee says, while putting on suntan lotion.

"I was. I still am, actually. I think I'm going to grab some food and go get some more shuteye. I'll catch up with you two later." As I walk away, I think about how interesting it is that I didn't even notice that those two hit it off last night.

I go back to the kitchen to prepare myself a peanut butter and jelly sandwich and find Malia there.

"You have been a very busy girl lately," she says, after offering to make the sandwich for me.

"A little too busy, if you ask me," I say. "This town is crazy."

"This town has been known for getting the best of people. You have to be careful out there. Here is your sandwich. Would you like some chips with it?"

"No, that's okay. This is good, thanks. I'm going to head back up to my room. I'll see you later."

As I walk away, I wonder what she meant by this town getting the best of people? Anyway, I head straight to my laptop before climbing back into bed. I desperately need to check my e-mail before I do another thing. I'm sure my friends back in Fenstanton think I've either completely forgotten about them or I'm dead—which, by the way things have been going these days, could be possible. I also want to do a little research on the Vegas Mob and all this Split-Apart stuff.

Picking up the peanut butter and jelly sandwich Malia made downstairs, I sink my teeth into it. I don't know what it is with a PB&J sandwich but with each bite it just gets better and better. They are my personal favorite ... I just love them.

Anyway, back to Google ... first, the "Split-Aparts." I need to see if there's any real truth behind the story Dario shared with me the other night. I find one very interesting piece—a philosophical text Plato wrote that gives me facts that confirms some of Dario's grandmother's story. Could all this be true? Can Dario and I really have been searching for each other our whole lives? How many lives?

All I know is that I definitely belong with him. He makes me feel complete, and I think about him every minute of the day, even when I'm sleeping. Then there's the fact that we are able to hear each other's thoughts, connect through our dreams and are learning new inner powers everyday. It all proves to me that I belong with him. Right?

Continuing my searches, I Google "Las Vegas Mob," and many results pop up. Most of the articles tell about the Mob's history in Vegas, almost giving the impression that it no longer exists, which is most likely what everyone wants to think. Who wants to believe such a powerful organization still exists? I find a book and movie, made by the same person, called Casino, which is based on the real Las Vegas Mob. I order both online and decide to leave it at that for now.

I really just want to see what I'm up against, so that I can learn how to handle the reality of Dario's life and how to control my emotions during extreme situations. I need to become stronger. I need to be someone Dario doesn't have to worry about. I need to be someone who stands by him—a person he can trust and believe in.

31

Freedom

"What are you doing? I miss you. When can
I see you?" Dario asks, interrupting my napping.

"I don't know, but I haven't really spent any time with my
family. I've been in bed all day."

"Well, get out of bed. I have somewhere I want to take you. I
have something I want to share with you, and I need some alone
time with you."

"Give me a few minutes. I need to see what's going on with

everyone else around here," I inform him as I drag myself out of bed, slip on a sundress and head downstairs to check things out.

To my surprise, there's no one around. Instead, I find a note on the kitchen counter telling me everyone went out for the afternoon, and they didn't want to wake me. If I need them, I'm to call one of their cell phones. It's already 3:30 p.m. I can't believe I've wasted the whole day.

I'm contemplating my next move when the doorbell rings, making me jump. What is it with our doorbell that spooks me all the time? I can't imagine who could possibly be at the door, seeing as I'm not expecting anyone. I look through the peephole, and to my surprise, Aaron is on the other side. I open the door a crack and greet him. "Hey what's up? What are you doing here?"

"Can I talk to you for a minute?" He sounds determined.

"Sure ... I guess so," I say hesitantly, opening the door to let him in.

"Did you just get up?"

"Yeah. This town wears me out! All of you wear me out! I would go back to sleep, if I didn't feel so guilty about it. So what's up? Why are you here?"

"I don't want you to get upset or mad," he says as we walk into the family room, "but I'm just a little worried about you."

"Why would you be worried about me?" Now, I'm utterly intrigued.

"First off, I want to tell you how glad I am that you moved to Las Vegas. I like you, and I think you're sweet.

I'm going to be blunt here, but I don't think you understand what you are getting into by hanging out with Dario Mancini. How did you meet him anyway?"

I try to come up with some crazy lie, and then decide not to lie at all but maybe just change the truth a little bit. "We met at the Beauvallon pool when I was staying there. But I don't understand ... what is your concern?"

"Taylor, I don't want you to think that I don't think he's a nice guy or anything, but there are things I've heard about him that aren't so nice." Aaron pauses to see if I'm paying attention.

"Okay, I'm listening. Like what?" I play along, even though I already know way more about Dario than he'll ever know.

"Well, I've heard that Dario, Mateo and Tony are mixed up in some bad stuff. I've heard that they once beat up a guy from school so badly they almost killed him. They also supposedly killed a homeless guy one night just for the thrill of it, and Dario's dad got them all off." I can tell by the look on Aaron's face that he's very concerned.

"What is he doing there, telling you all this crap? I'm going to kill him!" Dario shouts in my head.

"Give me a break, Dario. He's just concerned. Get over it! It's not like I don't already know about your extracurricular activities. And you'd better not touch him or any of my friends for that matter," I reply.

"Wow! That's crazy Aaron," I say. "I will be careful. Trust me; I am taking things very slow with Dario."

"Well, from what I've seen, you have been pretty

sheltered. Vegas is a fast town—it can all look fantastic, but there are some things that aren't so good. I just don't want you to get hurt. I like you. I just felt like you should know what I've heard about him, that's all."

There's an uncomfortable silence. Then Aaron gets up to leave. "So what are you up to for the rest of the day? Have you talked to Kayla? I think we're all going to be hanging out later and maybe go swimming over at the Club. Do you want to join us?"

I follow him to the front door. "Sounds good. Most likely, I'll see you later. And hey, thanks for stopping by—it means a lot to me."

Watching him go, I think about how cute it is that Aaron cares about my well-being. I mean, that took guts to come over here. Realizing I've made friends with some really good people around here, I'm suddenly a little disappointed that I've wasted the whole day sleeping. I could have been over at Kayla's just hanging out.

I head upstairs to take a shower. Walking into my room, I almost have a heart attack—Dario's sitting on my bed!

"Whoa ... what are you doing here?" I shout, practically jumping out of my skin. "You scared the crap out of me! How did you get up here anyway—I mean without me knowing? And where's your car? I didn't see it out front."

"You weren't giving me any straight answers on us hanging out today, and I was beyond frustrated with Mr. Information's visit, so I decided to just come over. I came in the back when you were saying your goodbyes to Mr. Wants to be Romeo, and I left my car parked by the front gate."

The adrenaline starts to wear off, and I can feel my heartbeat slow down. I manage to internalize most of his explanation.

"Dario, I didn't mean to blow you off. I had a lot of things I had to deal with today, stuff I wasn't going to put off another day. And one of those things was sleep, something that I'm losing a lot of since I've met you." I walk over to him and kiss him, trying to appease the frustration in his eyes.

"I understand you had things to do. I'm sorry. I just missed you. I can take you where I wanted to go another time," Dario says and then takes me in his arms. "Where is everybody anyway?" he asks.

His hug has made a lot of things start to feel right again. "I don't know. They left a note saying they went out and to call them if I needed them.

"Hey, I'm going to jump into the shower, I'm assuming you're staying for awhile?"

"Yep, if that's okay with you? I'll be here waiting."

I grab some clothes from my closet and head into the bathroom to shower. The hot water running over my tense muscles feels soothing. As the water flows over me, I realize I need to stop fighting the changes in my life and embrace them. I need to jump in with both feet and enjoy the ride that my new life is offering me.

Believe it or not, I enjoy danger and excitement. For goodness sake, I did find a dead body in the river one time back in England! The man hadn't been murdered or anything like that. He just happened to fall in the river during a drunken stupor and drown. But a dead body is a dead body! Surprisingly, it didn't freak me out—I guess I'm a little stronger than I look in handling something like that. I'm just going to have to develop tougher skin for all of these new adventures, that's all.

I know Dario is listening to me, but he's keeping his thoughts to himself, which is nice. I don't mind him listening in, as long as he leaves me some of my own thinking time. I finish my shower and dress quickly. Since he's waiting for me, I throw on some light makeup, brush my teeth, and quickly towel-dry my hair. Then I go back into my bedroom, where I find him lying on my bed reading one of my magazines, laughing.

"Do you really believe in some of this crap?" he asks me.

"I don't know. It is kind of interesting, I guess."

I climb on the bed next to him and snuggle into his warm body as he puts his arms around me. Lying with Dario feels so scrumptious and makes my whole body tingle with anticipation.

"Can you bring your beautiful lips closer so I can have one of your wonderful kisses?" he asks seductively.

I slowly stretch to place my soft lips on his, instantly feeling the sensational bond between our bodies. Kissing Dario gets better with each and every one of our encounters. From what I'm hearing in his thoughts, his kissing experience is the same. It is very strange to be able to hear how someone really feels about you, but at the same time it's pretty awesome! I believe it makes our kisses that much better.

We are so involved in each other that we don't hear anyone coming home. When my bedroom door starts to open, it scares us both. Luckily for us, it's just Mckylee checking in on me.

"You are so busted!" she says, grinning.

"No I'm not, because you aren't going to say anything—we're sisters, and we have to look out for each other, right?"

"You're right, but you are so lucky I came to check in on you and not Mom or Dad!"

"Thanks, I owe you. Did I hear you say Dad? When did he get home? ... We'd better move into the hangout room and turn on a movie and pretend we've been there the whole time. You want to join us?" I ask her.

"Yeah sure. I'll meet you in there in a minute. I'm going downstairs to cover for you and grab something to drink. Do you want anything?" she asks.

"Thanks Mckylee. Can you grab me a large glass of water while you're down there please? Dario and I will share it."

Mckylee heads downstairs as Dario and I go to the other room to find a movie we can watch that's already started on the telly.

"That was close! We got so lucky. I can't believe how deeply involved I am when I kiss you—it's like nothing else matters."

"I know. I feel like I'm in a trance or something. It's incredible!" he answers.

Mckylee comes back. "Mom and Dad are cool with the movie-watching up here with Dario. And look who came over to join us," Mckylee says as Kayla, Samantha and Skyler enter the room.

"Hey girls, what's up?" I ask.

"That's what we were wondering. I see you finally decided to get out of bed," Kayla jokes.

"I know. I was beat—you all wore me out the last couple of days. I'm sorry I haven't called you back yet ... do you want to join us? We're watching a movie."

"We actually came down to ask you if you and Mckylee—and now Dario, since he's here—would like to come with all of us over to the Club for pizza and swimming?" Skyler asks.

I take the liberty of answering for all of us, seeing as pizza sounds so good right now—and I've decided that I'm going whether Dario and Mckylee are or not!

"That sounds great! We would love to come."

"Well, let's go then. The guys are already over at the Club."

"Sounds good. We'll meet you down at your house in a minute."

After the girls leave, I get up to grab my suit when I hear negative ramblings in Dario's head.

"Are you two okay with going over to the Club?" I now ask.

"Yeah, I want to go as long as you two are going," Mckylee says as we both look at Dario. I know that the pressure of us both wanting to go leaves him without much of a choice.

"What! Why are you both staring at me? I don't understand why we have to go with them. I thought we we're fine just hanging out here."

"Really, that's all you have to say?" I ask, bothered.

"Fine, I'll go. But I'm calling Mateo and Tony to meet us there."

Mckylee and I go to grab our stuff. Then we all head downstairs.

"Hi Mom and Dad, how's it going?" I ask. "Dad, how was your trip?"

"My trip was uneventful—unlike you and Mckylee's lives this weekend." My dad has that tone in his voice that makes me feel like I've done something wrong. I decide to just ignore it.

"Yeah, we had a great weekend, and I'm glad you're home. We missed you."

"Hello, Dario. How are you doing today?" Mom asks trying to ease the tension that's building in the room.

"I'm good, thank you."

"Yes, hello, Dario," Dad says. "So what are you three up to with the bags on your arms?"

I had almost forgotten about the bags.

"Oh, we're going to the Club for swimming and pizza with all the kids in the neighborhood," Mckylee speaks up, knowing it will be better if the information comes from her at this point, rather than me. "Kayla and the other girls are waiting for us down at their house."

"Sounds good," Mom says quickly, as if trying to convince Dad this is a good idea. "We are having dinner with some friends tonight so we won't have to worry about you and dinner then. Right, Robert?"

I don't understand why he is acting so irritated about everything I do lately. It's really starting to get on my nerves!

"Okay, but don't be home late," he says, then adds with a look in his eye and tone in his voice that literally excludes everyone else in the room, "and Taylor ... when you get back, we need to sit down and talk. I mean it ..."

As if silently communicating with him, I nod my head, and then Mckylee saves the day. "C'mon ... we'll be late for the others," she warms the room up with her energy and urgency. I know she can't read my mind, but I'm sending her "thank you for bailing me out" thoughts just the same.

We both thank Mom and Dad, giving them a hug as we head out the front door. Was it my imagination ... did Dad feel a little stiff, then give me an extra squeeze when he hugged me back? I have to remind myself, he's not bad ... he just wants the best for me ...

I'm really looking forward to a mellow, no-craziness kind of night, if that's at all possible. Dario goes to get his car and meets us at the Club, while we pick up Kayla, Skyler and Samantha.

• • • • • • • • • • • •

The night is everything I anticipated—low key. The only drama is when Dario catches sight of Aaron, and it's clear that he's pissed. Luckily, I had told him earlier that if he wasn't anything but nice to Aaron, I wouldn't talk to him for a week! He let it go and was cool—or at least he acted like he was cool. We all hung out talking, swimming, and eating, for the rest of the night.

I feel like I've known these people forever, and I couldn't have asked for better new friends. Mckylee and I are fortunate girls. I am so happy that I've decided to free myself from my hesitations and live my Vegas life with the freedom of spirit it deserves.

Love is definitely in the air, I think—not sure—Kayla and Mike have something going on between them. Summer love—how cute is that?!

Vegas summer nights are perfectly warm! I love how the heat lingers in the air after the scorching hot days. I don't miss the dampness and dreariness that we had in England all the time. I've heard several of the kids here say that there is no place like Vegas ... I'm beginning to think they are right. And I live here.

How awesome is that?!

32

Created Paradise

Convincing Dario to go home and sleep in his own bed instead of sneaking into my house and sleeping in mine was a challenge. But I came up with an idea: couldn't we both be sleeping at our own houses yet meet in a dream—a dream we create together in our minds at the same time? I mean, if Dario's able to bring me to him by controlling my dreams, then it would only make sense that I could do the same to him. And what would happen if we both decided to come together in a dream at the same time? I really want to give it a try. Dario is a little skeptical about all of this and is giving me a hard time.

"*I don't understand why you won't let me just come over?*" he keeps insisting.

"*Dario, trust me this is going to be so cool. I just know it ... Don't you trust me?*"

"*You know I trust you. I just want to be there with you. I want you in my arms.*"

"*Dario, remember how I stepped into you? Remember how incredible that felt? I know it can be so much more, but you need to focus. I need you to be in on this with me 110 percent; please ... can you just give it a try?*" I'm practically begging him.

"*Fine, but if it doesn't work, I'm coming over. Do we have a deal?*"

"*Sure. We have a deal.*"

I only agree with him because I *know* it's going to work. I'm so excited. This is going to be an incredible out-of-body experience. And we'll get to hang out with each other all night without sneaking around and no one will ever know.

Lying in bed, I begin to visualize a beautiful place—a sanctuary. It's a cave surrounded by red stonewalls lined with the most beautiful orange and red flowering plants— my favorite, the Desert Birds of Paradise that Dario brought to me the first time he picked me up. I can see him with me and he is what I am seeing; he's there with me on the other side. The moonlight is gleaming down through gaps at the top of the cave. The ground is covered with silky white sand, and there is a tranquil pool of mesmerizing aqua-blue water with a delicate-looking steam floating over its surface. We see complete and total paradise as we doze off into a deep, unconscious state of sleep. I love how our souls are connected to each other, even though we aren't together or even talking to each other. I can see him with me, and as we slowly come together on the other side, we are standing face to face inside the cave.

"Wow! That was so awesome! I knew we could do it! This place is unbelievable!" I whisper to Dario, forgetting for a moment that we are in our dreams, not where others can hear what we say. It's absolutely perfect. Just the way we visualized it. I'm beyond thrilled with myself.

"I really wasn't sure if it was possible," he says as he looks around. "This place is so real. I can't believe we did it either! This is unimaginable!"

"Apparently, it is imaginable," I say, laughing.

My laughter echoes around the cave, and I glance up at the moonlight shining down on us. I spin around with excitement, feeling the sand flow through my toes and plopping myself down on it. I reach up and grab Dario's hand, but my hand goes right through his. I have forgotten that holding hands isn't possible.

"Come lie here with me," I say, stretching out on the sand. "This sand feels so weird on my body. You need to feel this."

Dario lies beside me and reaches his hand into mine, sending his warm energy throughout my entire body. Silently, we look up at the breathtaking moon surrounded with bright stars shining in the dark sky directly above us.

"Isn't it magical, Dario? Look at the stars ... they're so perfect. Look over there! It's the Little Dipper!" I point to it.

Just then, out of nowhere, a hawk flies directly over the cave. But it isn't just any hawk; it's our hawk. I can feel the hawk's power connect with ours; it is absolutely breathtaking, and it's as if we are one with the universe. The sounds around us are mesmerizing, and they are putting me into a completely tranquil state. Then the hawk flies down into the cave and perches on the ledge near us.

"Dario, this is going to sound really weird, but I think I know why the hawk's been following us and keeps appearing when we're together. I think it belongs with us, to us. I'm getting this really strange feeling, like I've been here before and—even more bizarre—that I've been here—with you and that hawk."

"What are you talking about Taylor? I've never been here before, and this isn't even real. We're in a dream."

"How awesome would it be if we've actually been here before? Like in another time or another life, together in this cave."

"Taylor, you're not making any sense. I've never been here before ... *We've* never been here before ..."

"You're right. It doesn't make any sense. I'm not really sure if I even know what I'm talking about. I just have this sixth sense that I've been here before with you. Then the hawk acts like it knows us, and I feel ... I know it sounds weird, but I feel like it's familiar to me, not just because it came to us when you were shot; it came to me when I was in the pool in our villa one afternoon just before we moved to the house; and then it appeared on the rooftop the other night at the club. And how do you explain it being here with us in a dream? I think it has a message for us. You have to admit it's all very coincidental."

Dario's speechless, just taking it all in. I know that he is trying to make sense of my ramblings. I just lay here and relish the silence, while admiring the hawk sitting on the ledge before me. I take pleasure in the fact that one of the best things about being with Dario is that we don't even have to converse with each other to enjoy each other's company.

Glancing at my body, I realize I'm practically wearing nothing, just the underwear and tank top that I wore to bed. A little embarrassed, I check out Dario's nicely tanned, carved, muscular body, covered only by a pair of sexy black boxers. I should totally be weirded out by this, but when I'm with him, nothing seems weird or uncomfortable.

With the tranquility of the water nearby, my mind starts to yearn for the water on my body. Listening to its soothing whirl, I quickly realize that my visualization actually places me in the pool, floating, with the water flowing through me. Its warmth is soothing; I imagine it against my skin.

Sensing Dario joining me in the water, I turn and find him close behind me. It amazes me how our minds are on this unbelievable level of synchronicity. Closing my eyes, I feel him bringing his body closer to mine. Slowly opening them again, I see his face right next to mine. He tries to kiss me, but a kiss is impossible; we both knew it would be, but he felt it was worth a try!

With our intense energy needing and wanting each other, my body moves up against the smooth rocks along the sides of the pool. I allow my whole spirit to rest and wait for his arrival. Slowly his body's spirit enters mine. We both experience the most powerful encounter ever! As our energy passes through each other with a pure intensity, our souls become as one.

This is the most wonderful experience I've ever felt, and I don't want him to ever leave me. My breathing is faint, and yet I'm full of life. This must be what the freedom of truly sharing life with another human being, your soul-mate, feels like. Experiencing pure ecstasy is absolutely, positively, a mind-altering state.

Suddenly, I feel fear rush through Dario. He tells me that his dad is waking him. Before I can say anything, he quickly leaves my body. The sudden emptiness I'm feeling freaks me out enough to awaken me—safe at home in my own bed. Taking a deep breath, I clear my mind and bring myself fully back to reality.

Worried about Dario, I tune into his conversation with his father. His dad seems to be upset with him. Really upset. Even though Dario is trying to stay calm, he is very intimidated by his dad. It seems that he was supposed to meet up with one of his dad's guys, Frankie. They were to go together to sort things out with some other guy who is trying to screw Dario's dad over. Dario tells his father that he had called Frankie and told him he didn't feel right about it; he told him not to go and that they would take care of it tomorrow. Frankie ignored what Dario had told him and went ahead by himself and was ambushed, killed and then dumped at the back door of one of the Mancini restaurants.

I hear voices rising. Dario is trying his hardest to explain to his dad that he told Frankie not to go because he had heard from an inside source what the other guy was up to; he had warned Frankie not to go, so it's not his fault. And he's glad he wasn't there, because he would have been killed and dumped along with Frankie.

His dad starts to cool down as Dario's explanation sinks in. Dario's dad doesn't understand why Dario didn't inform him of the so-called inside source. It seems that he wants Dario to understand the consequences of not communicating with him.

I don't know all the names they are talking about. Now his dad is telling Dario that he will talk with Anthony and insists that Dario help take care of the issue tomorrow, because if Bruno thinks he can pull this kind of shit off, then he has his coming. Dario's beyond upset but doesn't let it show.

Dario's dad leaves the room.

"*I'm so sorry, Taylor. I'm sorry I left you there alone. Are you all right?*" Dario asks.

"*I'm okay. The sudden interruption sent me right back as well.*"

"*I'll make it up to you, I promise. But right now, I have to take care of this. Try and get some sleep. I'll catch up with you later. Okay?*"

I hear his frustrations. He can't believe his bullshit life, a life he has no control over. Why does his dad expect him to do his dirty work? Doesn't he have a bunch of guys who work for him that can do it? Dario loves his dad, but the things he is asked to do are absolutely inexcusable. He's tired of it. He just wants to live the life of a normal teenager, not a Mobster!

I can't help worrying about him and his safety. He loves telling me that everything will be fine, but how can everything be fine when there is murdering going on? How can I sleep? I'm too worried. Trying to distract myself, I turn on the TV. But quickly, my tired body gets the best of me. I fall asleep, despite fighting to stay awake.

Not sure how long I've been out; I'm awakened by Dario as he wraps his arms around me, cuddling up to me in my bed. It's as if I'm dreaming, but I know I'm not. With him next to me, I am assured that he's safe, safe with me.

"I missed you," he whispers in my ear.

"Me too. How did you get in here?" I ask deliriously.

"Don't worry about it. No one knows I'm here. Your never going to believe what happened earlier in the pool, the pool in our dream."

"What?" I ask quietly.

"I don't know if it was the water or us connecting together, but my gun shot wound has completely vanished."

"That's impossible!" I state sitting up. Determined to see for myself, I turn on the lamp next to my bed and pull back the covers. I am left speachless. He's right, it's completely gone. "That's amazing ... unbelievable ... I don't understand?"

"Neither do I, but I never have to worry about it again. It's like it never happened." Dario states as he turns out the light and whispers in my ear. "Go back to sleep."

Both exhausted from our intense night, we hold each other in silence, blissful to be together as we doze off.

33

Ingenuous Indulgence

Dario had planned it perfectly: after waking-up, he'd sneak out before anyone else was up. The alarm was set on his cell phone and put under the pillows so no one else would hear it. He had hoped it wouldn't scare me to death when it went off. When the faint buzzing vibration came from under the pillow, it was a calm way to be woken.

"Hey, sorry for the alarm," he says, "but I wanted to

wake up with you peacefully and get out in time to avoid any hassles." He speaks softly into my ear, pulling me closer into his hold. Waking up in his arms is definitely a sign that today has the potential of being extraordinary.

My time with him is sweet yet too short, as he whispers in my ear that he has to get going before we get caught. As he sneaks out unnoticed, I'm left lying here wide-awake. Unable to fall back asleep, I decide to surprise the family by making breakfast. Getting out of bed and throwing on a pair of shorts, I head downstairs.

As I start the coffee, Malia comes in.

"What are you doing up so early, Ms. Taylor? Is every-thing all right?" She is concerned. Granted, it is a little strange for me to be in the kitchen before seven in the morning.

"I don't know. I just woke up and couldn't go back to sleep, and I'm a little hungry, so I thought I would just start a little breakfast for everyone," I say, hoping she doesn't suspect anything.

After I finish making the coffee, I sit down at the counter to enjoy my first cup. Malia, rarely missing a beat in her kitchen domain, steps in to get breakfast started, despite the fact that I had told her I was going to do it. Within minutes, my dad joins us and is astonished that I'm already up.

"This is a surprise!

"I woke up and couldn't go back to sleep, so I thought I would surprise you all and make French toast. But Malia so kindly took over." I smile at him as I pour myself another cup of coffee.

"Well, it's nice to see you up bright and early Taylor. While you are over there, can I put in an order for a cup of that?" he asks.

"Sure, it would be my pleasure." I think to myself that it's nice to finally be having a normal conversation with him.

As I return to my seat, my mom now joins us.

"Why is everyone up so early?" she asks, taking a seat next to me. Dad fills her in as he gets her a cup of coffee.

The smell of bacon must be waking everyone up. Now even Mckylee has joined the breakfast party. She's as surprised as the rest of us and has an "I-know-you've-been-up-to something" look on her cute little face. I plead the fifth by sipping my coffee—the best answer to her look that I can think of—as I wait for breakfast.

"So, are you ladies still going to the pool at the club today with the girls?" Mom asks.

"I think so. I don't know, but I really didn't set this up—it's Mckylee's deal."

I'm trying to sway my parents into believing that this whole day is Mckylee's plan. Thankfully, all the girls are covering for me—Dario and I had planned to spend a real day and night with each other, not in our dreams.

"I think the plan is to hit the pool at the club, then go over to Skyler's house for a sleep-over," Mckylee says. "We're having a girl's beauty night supposedly—whatever that is. But she made it sound like fun, don't you think, Taylor?"

"Yeah. Sounds great to me. I'm looking forward to it,"

I say to everyone, while thinking to myself that I can't wait for what I'm really up to tonight.

After some enjoyable family time, and if I may say, a delightfully yummy breakfast, Mckylee and I gather our things for our day at the pool with our friends.

"What time do I need to be ready by? Is there enough time for me to catch a quick nap before we take off? I've been awake since 6," I ask Mckylee as we both head toward our rooms.

"Not really. Kayla and Samantha are picking us up in like half an hour or so ... so you really need to get ready."

"I'm so tired, and I know there is no way I will get any shut-eye at the pool today."

"What's going on with you? What were you doing last night that you didn't get any sleep, and why were you up so early this morning?" she says as she stands by my door.

"I've been having these weird dreams since we moved here, that's all. Haven't you ever had any? And sometimes I wake up and just can't go back to sleep. You've got to admit it, lots has happened since we moved here a few weeks ago."

She just looks at me, as if she knows that I'm lying, and then disappears into her room.

Gosh, she's right. I really shouldn't be complaining. I did bring this on myself, and last night was so unbelievable, and today is going to be an incredible day ... so who needs sleep anyway?

As I'm gathering my things, the doorbell rings. I run downstairs to answer the door, guessing it's Kayla and Samantha picking us up. I'm right. On the other side of the door, I'm greeted with Kayla's smiling face.

"Bonjour Kayla, how are you today?" I say.

"Well, aren't we in a good mood, Miss I'm-Always-With-My-Hot-New-Boyfriend-Dario? Are you guys ready for a hot, fantastic day at the pool?" she says, a bit of sarcasm in her voice.

"Well, yes we are, Ms. Smarty Pants! I just need to grab a few more things and we'll be right out. Do you want to come inside while you wait?"

"No, that's okay. Samantha is out here so I will just wait with her. But hurry up, it's starting to heat up," she says.

I close the door and run back upstairs to grab the rest of my things.

"Mckylee, hurry up! The girls are outside waiting for us. We need to get going!" I shout while running into my room to finish getting it together. In a few minutes, we meet back in the hall.

"We need to find Mom and Dad to say goodbye," Mckylee advises as we head down the stairs.

"It was in my plans. What did you think? That I wasn't going to tell them we were leaving?" I ask.

"No. Just stating the obvious, that's all. What's with the attitude, Taylor?"

"Sorry, nothing. I guess I'm tired and excited at the same time. Does that equal irritable? I'll shake the attitude, promise." I try to sound as convincing as I can as we approach our parents in the family room. They are reading the morning paper and sipping coffee, which I wouldn't mind having another cup of ...

"We're leaving. The girls are outside waiting, and we

just wanted to say bye and remind you that we'll see you tomorrow," Mckylee says.

"Have fun and be good ... Don't get out of control over at the Club, and I mean both of you. And please call me when you get to Skyler's house so I know you get there safely," Mom says, with that parent look in her eyes.

"Yes, you girls be safe and have a good time. Call us if you need anything," Dad says, looking up from the paper and holding his eyes on me, as if saying, "I'm keeping my eyes and ears on you, Taylor."

"We will. Love you," I call out we head toward the front door.

"Love you, too, and we'll call you later!" Mckylee shouts as she closes the door behind her. We find Samantha and Kayla impatiently waiting for us in the golf cart.

"Finally! What took you two so long? It's frigging hot out here, and I'm ready to get in the pool already," Samantha says. "Not only that, Skyler called and said that everyone else is already there and to hurry it up!"

We get into the cart, and Kayla instantly takes off. We all quickly grab our things and hold on for our lives.

"Why do you have to drive so crazy?" I ask her.

"I don't drive crazy, and we're late," Kayla answers, as she puts a lead foot on the pedal and pushes it even faster. It amazes me how fast these little things can go.

When we pull up to the Club, we find Skyler sitting in front waiting for us.

"You will never believe what Dario did!" she shares excitedly as we all pile out of the cart.

"What?" we all ask at once.

"He got one of the cabañas for us and has it totally set up rock-star style! You are like one of the luckiest girls I know Taylor! I can't believe you're dating Dario Mancini ... he is like the coolest guy!"

"I guess I am pretty lucky," I reply, but I'm thinking to myself how my luck with Dario has a few drawbacks, like dealing with his father. Walking through the club, listening to the girls ramble on about the cabaña and other less important things, all I can think about is how my life has changed so much and so quickly. I wish I didn't miss England as much as I do. I miss the simpleness of my life there, and I can't help but wonder what my friends are up to. Las Vegas is a whole different world, that's for sure.

Dario interrupts my thoughts with a thought of his own, *"Are you sorry you met me?"*

"Of course not!" I reply as we approach the pool area. Skyler leads us straight to the cabaña, where we find everyone hanging out. Now, when I say "everyone," I really mean it. There are people here I haven't even met before. I thought it was going to be a quiet day at the pool with a few friends. Not that I am complaining. Well, I guess I'm complaining a little bit—does everything have to be such a big event?

Dario approaches the cabaña.

"Sorry about all the people. Tony and Mateo got a little carried away with the guest list. I did save you all some chairs though."

He looks at me with concern. "I know you didn't expect

all these people; I can see it in your face." Of course, we both know he heard me think it before he saw any disappointment on my face.

"I'm just glad you saved us some chairs," Kayla chimes in, trying to break the tension.

"That I did, my ladies … right this way." Dario leads us over to our own area. It's a little away from the party but still close enough to catch everything that is going on. I guess I'll forgive him.

After we all get our towels laid out on our chairs and the rest of our stuff situated, Dario drags us off to introduce us to his friends. I'm barely paying any attention as he rattles off names, until he comes to one girl, a beautiful girl I might add, who's staring at Dario as if she wants to eat him. I make sure to catch her name as he introduces her, for the mere fact that she's making me uneasy. She even has a name that suits her luring beauty: Angelina. Wait, I know that name … I've heard it before … She's the girl Dario's dad wants him to be with. What is she doing here? Why did he invite her?

Feeling totally ill, I decide to go swimming. It's really hot out here, and cooling down in the water is just what I need. Not hesitating for a second, I dive into the refreshing water, submerging myself below the surface. It's so peaceful being caressed by the sensuous water as it flows over my skin. I gracefully swim down toward the other end of the pool, enjoying every stroke—even the lack of air in my lungs—as I push myself to make it all the way down to the deep end.

Meanwhile, I see Dario walking along the side to meet me. Surfacing, I take a deep breath of fresh air and open my eyes to his intriguing smile, as he has knelt down to greet me. How can I resist that beautiful face? I smile back at him as he suddenly dives in right over the top of me. He quickly swims over to me, placing his arms around me and holding on to the edge of the wall to support us from falling into the depths of the pool.

"Don't be mad at me," he says, adding, "even though I think you are really cute when you're mad." He shares another one of his amazing, luring smiles.

"I'm not mad. I just feel awkward with her here. That's all."

"Don't let her make you feel anything. She is nothing to me. I thought I made that very clear to you?"

"You did. I just don't understand why she has to be here."

"You have to remember: Angelina's family has been part of our larger family since we've both been alive. She's not only my friend but Mateo and Tony's, as well. Maybe you should get to know her and not make all of this a bigger deal than it is."

"I never said it was a big deal. I just feel a little weird that's all. Isn't she the girl your dad wants you to be with? I can tell by the way she looks at you that she is totally in love with you. Can't you see that?"

"Well, I think that has a lot to do with the fact that our parents have been talking about us being together and getting married ever since we could walk."

"Why aren't you with her then? Why haven't you taken that next step? She's beautiful and seems to understand your life with the Mob much better than me or anyone else here for that matter. I mean, she knows what your family is all about ..."

"Not really. All the women in the family know some things, but nothing compared to what you now know. I'm done talking about this; let's just enjoy the day. When we get back to the cabaña, you can formally meet her, and that will be that," he declares as he takes off swimming toward the other end of the pool.

Here alone, I contemplate the situation and my own insecurities. I'm unable to get over how pretty she is. Knowing I just need to let it go for now and not wanting to fight with Dario over the matter, I swim to the other end of the pool to join him. He gives me a quick peck on the lips, gets out of the pool and heads toward the guys. Following him, I make my way over to the girls, where I sink my body into my chair next to Kayla to soak in the sun and catch up on the conversation with Mckylee, Skyler and Samantha.

"Who is that Angelina chick? She can't keep her eyes off of Dario," Kayla asks me.

"Is it that obvious? It *is* that obvious, isn't it?" I say. "Funny you should ask. Angelina is Dario's family friend. Both of their parents always thought they would get together and be married some day. How fun is that?"

"Wow, that must be kind of weird to deal with. Have you ever met her before today?"

"No, but Dario swears that she is really nice and has asked me to give her a chance."

Just then, I notice Dario walking over to Angelina, apparently getting ready to bring her over to me so that we can get better acquainted. Yeah! Lucky me ...

As they approach, I'm glad I have my moral support surrounding me. She's giving me a look that says she isn't happy with all of this either. What's Dario up to? I don't know why he insists on forcing us on each other. I take a deep breath and pray. I'm not really sure what I'm praying for or why, but I have to deal with this situation, so I guess I'm praying for the strength to understand it and deal with it.

"Taylor, this is Angelina. Angelina, this is Taylor, the girl I told you about. I felt that you two should formally meet, seeing as you're going to be spending time around each other once in awhile."

I sit up and greet her with a sincere smile. "It is nice to meet you. I have heard a lot about you from the guys."

"You too. It is so nice to finally put a face with the girl who seems to have stolen our little Dario's heart," she says with a haughty tone in her voice. Then she turns and walks away.

I'm a little taken aback, but I also understand where her remark came from. I just smile as I watch her leave.

"See, that didn't go so bad, now did it?" Dario says.

It's clear that Dario is going to see what he wants to see. I just shake my head, pretending to agree with him, knowing it isn't worth getting into.

I decide to blow the whole thing off and make the best of my day, enjoying my time with my friends and Dario.

I can't believe how many people have showed up to our little pool get-together. Actually, our little pool get-together has become a big pool get-together, which I have to say, is quite entertaining. I'm especially enjoying watching Kayla and Mike flirt with each other. I'm excited that they are into each other; it kind of takes some of the pressure off of Dario and me dating so quickly. Aaron, of course, is still not happy with the whole Dario-and-me thing ... but that's his problem, not mine.

Angelina has obviously decided to avoid Dario and me at all costs, which is fine by me. A relief, in fact. She isn't the type of girl I would ever be friends with anyway. I realize that I might have said that about Kayla and the other girls, too, before I got to know them. But this is different—I have taken her man, and I have a feeling she isn't going to let me forget it. Whatever. She can give me all the dirty looks she wants; it isn't going to change anything. Dario and I are meant to be together, and that fact is way bigger than any of us. There's nothing anyone can do about it.

Aaron interrupts my thoughts. "Do you girls want to get a game of volleyball on in the pool?" he asks. "The girls against the boys!"

"I'm in," I tell him.

"So am I," Skyler says as she heads to the pool, followed by everyone else but Kayla, who hates getting her hair wet.

Playing water volleyball is going to be so awesome! Even though the guys are going to kick our butts, we are definitely going to have fun trying not to let them! Of course, Angelina decides not to play with us either; obviously she is too good to be on our team. Or maybe she doesn't want to get her hair wet either.

Anyway, I'm kind of surprised that some of her friends decide to join us. She is making cutting remarks to those who are sitting with her—to the point that it's very apparent that she is seriously bothered that her friends are playing with us. That gets Dario's attention. He actually tells her to chill out and get over it!

I've never played volleyball in the water before, but how hard can it be? After two games of the guys whopping us, I come to the conclusion it's not that easy. But it's a blast, even though we suck! We all decide to play another game, this time mixing up the teams. Dario ends up on the opposite team as me, and Aaron's on my team. Aaron finds it impossible not flirt with me, which Dario seems to find quite amusing. He seems to be encouraging him with his comments. At least it's better than Dario being mad at Aaron for liking me, I think to myself.

"Dario, stop telling Aaron to help me with my form and to get my back!" I yell at him through my thoughts.

"You are so cute when you get frustrated."

"Whatever. You better be careful or Aaron might just steal me away from you," I tell him, laughing out loud.

"What are you laughing at?" Skyler asks me.

"Nothing. Just Dario's faces. He entertains me." All of a sudden, an eerie feeling comes over me. Glancing up in the sky, I notice black storm clouds rolling in quickly over the horizon. I can honestly say I have never seen a storm roll in like this before. It is mesmerizing how quickly it comes upon us, gusts of wind blowing up the sand from the desert floor and amazing bolts of lightning followed by large bangs of thunder not far off in the distance. We all jump out of the pool, gather our things and run inside just as large raindrops start to plummet.

Everyone is excited with the rush of the storm, and we all gather in the lobby area, all talking at the same time. I glance over at Dario.

"I'm going to take a shower and get ready in the ladies locker room," I tell him. Turning to the girls, I say, "Hey, I'm going to the locker room to shower and get changed. Anyone with me?"

Everyone joins me in the locker room to get ready for whatever we will stumble upon next to do with our day. Originally, Dario and I were supposed to take off for Blue Diamond later, but we weren't planning on the storm rolling in. I don't know if we should go now or hang out for a while and go as planned later?

While getting ready, we all decide we're starving and went to look for the guys to see if they want to grab a bite to eat somewhere. Skyler really wants to go to some restaurant called the Roadrunner. She says they have awesome food and bowling, which would be perfect for a rainy afternoon. We find the guys hanging out in the game room, playing pool and shuffleboard.

"So, what's the plan?" Skyler asks as we enter the room. "We were thinking of grabbing a bite somewhere ... maybe at the Roadrunner," she continues.

"Good idea!" Mateo says. "We were trying to think of

a place we could all go hang out, and that is a great place."

"Well then, it is settled. Let's all meet at the Roadrunner on Eastern," says Dario.

"Kayla, are you going to ride with us or Mike?" I ask her as we head out into the parking lot.

"I am going to ride with the guys. I'll see you there." She hands the golf cart keys to the valet out front to store it for her.

"So Samantha and Skyler, I'm assuming you are riding with Mckylee and me in Dario's car?" Whatever car he has with him today, I think to myself.

Luckily, Dario is driving a big car and not the Corvette. We all pile in quickly and drive down the hill toward the Roadrunner restaurant.

I can't believe this rain—it's fascinating in the desert. That storm came on so fast, yet it still feels tranquil here. Everything that seemed so dry and boring moments before now seems to blossom and feel fresh and alive. Even the non-living things, like the buildings, seem new from their washing.

We arrive at the Roadrunner, and Skyler was right—this place is great. We grab a few tables by the cute bowling alley. It's like a miniature alley with only two lanes and instead of using the large deadly balls one would usually use bowling, you use these small little wooden balls. How fun! Surprisingly, even Angelina and her friends decide to join us. I am sure she came just to torture me and make it clear that she isn't backing down anytime soon.

After a few hours of food and fun games of bowling, I

start to become bored with the whole group thing and want some serious alone time with Dario.

"Can we go? I'm tired of being here and want to be alone with you," I relay to him.

"Yeah, I'm ready if you are."

"Then let's go. I'll see if the girls need a ride and we'll get going either way."

"Sounds good." he answers as he walks toward the guys to let them know we are leaving.

Thankfully, no one says they need a ride. They're going to hang out for a while. I really can't get out of here fast enough, for the mere fact that I don't want to be around Angelina another second—that girl is really starting to bother me.

I'm not sure, but I think Angelina's determined to make me as uncomfortable as possible. Her flirting and carrying on with Dario, then him being completely oblivious to it all, is just way too much.

34

Secret Hideway

Dario can't drive away from the Roadrunner quick enough for me—I definitely need to get away from everyone for a while. I'm ready for some Dario and Taylor alone time.

We jump on the 215 Freeway, head west, and after a few miles, we get off at Windmill Road, which then continues west toward the town of Blue Diamond. I'm not sure what to expect, but from what Dario has told me, Blue Diamond is out in the middle of the desert off a two-lane highway about 30 minutes from Las Vegas. He promises there's a surprise waiting there for me.

After about 10 minutes, we're into the open desert, where the rain has caused a light fog on the road in front of us. Now knowing some of the things that go on out here in the open desert, it feels almost creepy. My body seems to react to my thoughts as it shivers. Dario reaches over and grabs my hand, attempting to relay that all is okay.

The farther we drive, the closer we get to the mountains. They are absolutely peaceful, their peaks covered with scattered gray and white clouds and it looks like there is a fresh hint of green showing in the color of the leaves and flowers that have been freshly doused by the rains. The scenery is quite magical, and even Dario is amazed by how mysterious the atmosphere is around us. He tells me he has never seen the area quite like this before. It is almost as if our presence here is transferring the energy of our two beings creating this unique setting.

Originally, we had planned to see a play at Spring Mountain Ranch, a ranch out near Blue Diamond where some famous man named Howard Hughes used to live. When Dario suggested driving to Spring Mountain, he told me that Hughes was the one who really put Las Vegas on the map.

The rain and dark skies have changed those plans seeing as the theater is outside, so he drives us straight to what he calls his "secret hideaway."

Blue Diamond is nothing like I expected. It is a small

town with very few homes. We have to take it slow to avoid the wild burros that have a tendency to place themselves directly in the middle of the road. Heading up a hill, we pass a park, a church and a small store. Then Dario turns down a street and goes quickly down a drive that ends at a dirt road. Off in the distance, a house comes into view as we continue along the desolate, unpaved, bumpy road. As we approach, Dario opens the garage to the house and quickly pulls in—closing the garage door behind us before the car even stops.

"That was a little odd," I say.

"I like to keep things as discreet as possible. You never know who is watching, and I rarely come up here when there is any bit of daylight. By the way, you can breathe now ... I don't think anyone is going to hear you breathing," Dario says with grin on his face.

"Are you laughing at me? I can't help it. Coming to your secret hideout is a little intimidating. But hey, thanks for all the support!" I laugh with him, feeling silly about my initial fear of the place.

We get out of the car and head inside. I'm completely amazed at how he has decorated the interior of this house. The house looks worn down and deserted from the outside. The inside is another story.

"You did this yourself? I can't believe you did this—it's amazing!" I say as Dario turns on the lights. The room I'm in is what someone would call "tastefully done," meaning that there's a strong sense that Dario has created a room that has just the right amount of furniture and accessories in it—there's no hint of garage sale castoffs.

Everything looks like it belongs together, even the paintings I see on the wall, to the throw pillows on the couch. Slowly turning in the room, I realize that it's completely dark from the blackout curtains on the windows.

"I know. Sometimes I can't believe I did this either. It took me about eight months to finish it all, seeing as it's kind of hard to slip in and out of here without anyone noticing me, especially with furniture. But it has been so worth it. Having a place to come to and pretend that the rest of the world outside doesn't exist is invigorating but also calming for me. And now having you here to share it with ties it all together."

Dario gives me a tour of the house. It seems so much bigger than the night I was here in my dream. He only has furniture in the rooms he uses. There is a rich black granite counter in the kitchen with a few bar stools. The living room has a large sectional couch and a couple of side tables with these elegant lamps on them that reflect light that isn't glaring, but has a glow that makes you want to curl up and watch a movie.

Of course, there's a large flat screen TV over the fireplace. The house has four bedrooms, but only the master has been furnished for Dario's use. He apparently doesn't plan to ever have houseguests. Rugs lay on wood floors that look like they could be cherry—I only know this because my mother had pointed what looks like the same type out to me one time when we were looking at a magazine together in England.

"So what is the deal with this house?" I ask, remembering that he had said it was a cover for something else.

"This is my great grandfather's house. He ran the Mob in Vegas at one point. This is where he would come to clear his head and escape the craziness of Vegas, from what my grandmother told me. When my dad stepped up to take over his dad's role as leader of the Mob, he used this land to build an underground lair on the back of the lot under a large warehouse-garage. All I can say is that he hides many different things here ... or has them taken care of," Dario shares.

"Really?" is all I can manage to say.

As Dario talks about the house, I can see the lair through his thoughts: it sits below a large, second garage at the back of the property. Lots of cash is hidden down there in a big vault. There are many tools and a lot of guns. I see flashes of scenes where people are being tortured—people who obviously didn't see things the same way the Mob does or had done the Mob wrong in some way. My body responds with another shiver ...

Suddenly distracted by the intensity of the rain as it beats on the roof, Dario and I both have a strong feeling that something isn't right. Even though we aren't really sure why we feel this way, another quiver runs through my body.

As I move closer to him, he seems to be a little calmer. Then I realize why I'm feeling uneasy.

"Someone is at the door."

He knows it, too.

"Don't panic, it will be fine; I'll take care of it." He is trying to calm me.

As Dario approaches the door to take a look through

the peephole, someone places a key into the lock and tries to enter the house. He jumps back. Luckily, he had recently changed the locks—not that that is going to keep the person on the other side from coming in eventually, but it might buy us just enough time to figure out who is on the other side and what they want.

Dario steps back up to the peephole. To his surprise, it's his father on the other side. Now he's as panicked as I am.

"Listen to me closely. You need to go into my bedroom. Inside my closet, there is a special room—a panic room—on the back wall. Get into it quickly and lock the door behind you. Don't come out until I come for you."

Listening to someone in a panicked state tell you how to do something isn't necessarily the best way to get information. But I manage to find my way into the panic room through the false wall in the closet and close the door behind me. I feel a rush of terror going through both of our bodies. I can't breathe; my heart is pounding so fast, and my entire body is shaking.

Repressing my fearful state for a minute, I begin to worry about Dario. Unable to move, I stand against the wall paying close attention to every detail of what Dario is doing at the front door. Dario's dad is pounding on the door, furiously demanding that Dario open it. He is yelling that he knows Dario's in the house.

Dario, having waited to open the door until he knew I was safe, finally slowly opens the door.

"Dad, what's going on?" he asks as calmly as possible.

"That's what I would like to know Dario! What is going

on?" his dad yells angrily. At the same time, looking around the house, suddenly noticing all the furnishings.

"Well, well ... you've made yourself comfortable here, I see. Looks pretty fancy to me ... some of the guys thought someone had been coming and going from the house and were concerned, so I have had someone staking it out. When I got the call that they saw you and some girl pull in a little while ago, I had to check it out for myself. So where is she? I am assuming it's Taylor, isn't it?"

Dario seems so calm and unconcerned. I don't understand how he controls his emotions like that. His confidence reassures me, and being in this room makes me feel invincible.

"I don't know what you are talking about. Whoever told you they saw me come in here with a girl completely misinformed you. I am here by myself."

"Well, then you won't mind if I take a look around then, will you?"

"Not at all."

"So how long have you been coming out here? And why didn't you ask me or mention anything about setting up your little camp out here in your grandfather's house?" His dad continues to interrogate Dario as he vigorously walks through the house looking for me.

"I didn't think it would be a big deal if I hung out here, so that's why I didn't ask or tell you I guess. And I've been coming here since I got my driver's license last October. I've always remembered grandfather talking about hanging out here, and it just seemed like a cool place for me to do the same and fix it up."

Dario follows him through the house, while his comment echoes in my mind: Wait a minute, did he say October and a driver's license?

I interrupt Dario's thoughts. *"You turned 16 last October? I turned 16 in October. My birthday is on the thirteenth; what day is yours on?"*

The second he said he was born in October, I knew our birthdays had to be on the same day.

"I was born on the thirteenth as well Taylor. Now don't ask me anything else until I get rid of him."

The birthdays make sense, considering our souls are connected and have now become one. Now that my body has stopped shaking from the scare of Mr. Mancini's arrival, I slowly slide down the wall to sit on the floor, thankful that it's carpeted. Sitting here awaiting his departure, I recognize the intensity of the bond that Dario and I have. At first, I thought the whole Split-Apart thing was cool and interesting, but now I realize the full impact of what lies behind it.

Dario's dad has searched the whole house, unable to find any trace of me. Unfortunately, he now decides to take advantage of this time to have a heart-to-heart conversation with his son. He tells Dario that he disapproves of me, although he does think I am a nice girl ... just not the right girl for his son. That's promising, right?

It sucks to sit here and listen to Dario's dad tell him how to live his life! Dario is ignoring half of what his dad is saying to him, and Mr. Mancini doesn't even listen to how Dario responds. I find their discussion mind–numbing to the point that I drift off to sleep on the floor of the hidden room. I have no idea how much time has passed when I awake to the soft whisper of Dario's voice.

"Taylor, Taylor ... hey baby, my dad is finally gone. Let me help you up off this floor. Why don't you come and lay down on the bed if you want to sleep more?"

It's a relief that it is all over for now. "How long have I been asleep?" I ask. "I feel like I have been in here forever."

"It has only been like an hour, but you must have been pretty tired because you were out cold; it's been difficult waking you up."

Slowly getting off the floor, I make my way into Dario's bed.

"Please don't leave me alone," I say. "And wake me if anything else happens, okay?"

He lies down next to me, wrapping his warm arms around my body as I drift back to sleep. "You're safe," he whispers, "and I won't leave you I promise. I'll be right here."

Deliverance

I am awakened abruptly by Dario telling me that we need to leave the house immediately. This isn't something I want to be hearing right now. These unexpected situations seem to be becoming the norm in my life. I'm starting to think that maybe I should just accept them for what they are: a never-ending rollercoaster of twists and turns.

"What time is it?" I ask in a state of deliriousness.

"It's two in the morning. Some of my dad's guys have arrived out back in the garage and I'm not sure what they're up to, but we need to go—now."

"All right then, let's go." I start walking as quickly as I can toward the garage, confused and sleep-deprived.

"You're going to have to lie down in the backseat and hide, just in case someone is still watching the house, which I'm sure they are."

I have no problem hiding from these crazy criminals, but the sick thing about all of this is that I think I am actually starting to like the craziness, in a twisted, yet exciting kind of way. While I lie on the floor of the back seat, Dario pulls out of the garage, closing the door and drives quickly away from the house.

"Did you see anyone watching?" I don't ask this out loud, afraid someone might hear me even though that's impossible from inside the car.

"I didn't see anyone, but just in case, stay down. I'll let you know when you can get up."

The car's acceleration tells me we've pulled out onto the two-lane highway. I lie in silence, waiting. After about 10 minutes, Dario's informs me. *"You can come up front now; I don't think anyone is following us."*

I sit up and glance out the back window to assure myself. Not seeing anyone, I climb from the back seat to the front.

"You know what, Dario? This is going to sound completely off the wall, and I know that it seems really weird, but I think I'm actually starting to enjoy all this crazy, sick chaos that seems to surround you."

Dario looks at me, reaches his hand over to mine and squeezes it. He smiles and then laughs out loud. With tenderness, he says, "That's good. Because that is exactly what my life is in a nutshell! Complete and total chaos all the time! Welcome to my life!"

And then his voice shifts. Now I hear anger and almost a call for help. "Why can't I find a way out of all of this bullshit?!"

I know that Dario must be in a state of turmoil with his father. He knows that I heard him say that I'm all wrong for him. I have to say, I'm proud of the way Dario stands up to his father ... it's got to be really hard ... I mean ... Mr. Mancini is not someone you want to be on the bad side of. Dario squeezes my hand once again ... I know that he just heard me think that.

We drive in silence for a few minutes, and then I decide that I need to get his mind off his father ... we both do.

"Not to change the subject or anything, but I'm starving. Is there any possibility of grabbing a bite somewhere?"

"Sure. What are you in the mood for? We could go to the Hard Rock Hotel and eat at Mr. Lucky's—it's one of my favorite late-night eating spots."

"Sounds perfect! I've never been to a Hard Rock Hotel before. I know that there is a café in London. Are they the same?"

"The hotel is way different than the café. It can be completely off the hook and a great place to hang out ... You're going to love it. I'm sure of it. It's the perfect place for us to settle in and just talk."

The drive to the Hard Rock continues in silence, mainly because we're both still half asleep. The rain from the evening has left the desert so clean and the air so fresh.

Pulling up to the Hard Rock, I'm a little surprised when Dario drives into the parking garage. Why not use the valet like always? Then I learn from reading his mind that he just wants to keep a low profile the rest of the night, which I completely get at this point.

Walking through the hotel, I'm amazed at how everything in Vegas seems to be busy at any time of the day. I swear people just don't sleep in this town—including me, apparently. I can't believe that I'm actually going out to eat at two in the morning.

For someone who wanted to keep a low profile, Dario isn't doing a very good job of it—already three people have said hello to him in the short five minutes we've been here. I wonder how long it will take to get back to his father that we are here.

This hotel is different than any of the others. There's a mind-blowing energy here. It's younger, hipper—all of my favorite tunes are rocking across the casino floor. As we approach Mr. Lucky's, the hostess greets Dario by name and informs us that his regular table is available and to follow her.

The table is in the very back—obviously a place where he can see everything and everyone for that just-in-case situation. I only know this because his worrisome thoughts are flowing through my mind, including thoughts of the gun he has down the back of his pants. He's thinking he should check to make sure it's safe, secure and ready for action!

"What? You have a gun? Why do you have a gun?" I whisper to him, realizing I should have asked through our minds, but the shock made me forget myself.

"I always have a gun; you just haven't noticed before or paid any attention to it."

"Really? That kind of freaks me out!"

Sitting quietly, I'm trying to wrap the whole gun thing around my head—why haven't I noticed that he has a gun? Do any of the other kids know he carries one? What about my parents, did they notice? How could I be so unobservant when I've spent hours with him? Maybe it's his eyes and lips ... sometimes, it's all I see.

While all this is jumping around in my head, I find myself people-watching. Especially this time of day, everyone's out in rare form, and I think even more so here at the Hard Rock. I love the craziness of this city!

Dario interrupts my thoughts,

"I agree this place does attract the craziest, and usually the coolest, people of all. This is why I like hanging out here," he says as he reaches once again for my hand, this time lifting it up and brushing it with his lips ... those amazing lips ... as he connects with my eyes. How can I ever doubt him?

Dario's prediction was right. I do love this place. I can't believe all of the exciting and interesting outfits everyone is wearing, which makes me realize I really need to go shopping and glamorize my wardrobe some more.

"I'll go shopping with you; let me take you shopping. We can take Arianna with us—she loves to shop and has impeccable taste," Dario proposes.

"Right now?" I ask, wondering if the mall would be open.

"No, the malls are closed now. You're so cute when you ask like that. Later, when they're open, we'll go." He chuckles as he pulls me in for a hug.

Yes, I'm thinking I like Mr. Lucky's and the Hard Rock a lot.

Our food arrives and I realize that I'm famished ... really famished. I don't know what it is, but since we moved here, my appetite has taken a different turn.

While we eat, Dario uses his phone to text someone—something about a room. Within minutes of Dario sending the text, a man in a suit approaches our table and slips Dario a key while shaking his hand. Then the man disappears just as quickly as he appeared.

"Who was that, and why did he slyly give you a key card?"

"Taylor, one thing you are going to have to learn about Vegas is that everybody knows everybody, and someone is always watching, and someone is always talking about someone else's business. So the less information going across the network the better, get it?" he shares in a low whisper.

"I think I get it ... like when your father showed up at the house a few hours ago. The only thing I don't understand is, don't people have anything better to do?"

Dario doesn't even bother to answer my stupid question. He just sits there shaking his head. Is that a smile I see spreading across his face? Is he giving me grief for being naïve? Or is he just amused?

After our meal, he leads me hurriedly through the casino, down a hall and onto an elevator that takes us to the top floor. Soon, we find ourselves opening the door to a lavish suite.

"I love Las Vegas. It's like living in a movie of pure perfection!" I say with excitement as I throw off my shoes and start jumping on the bed. I catch the view of the Las Vegas Strip through our window, a view that takes my breath away, I swear, every time I see it. Dario's enjoying himself, laughing at me,

"You're crazy!"

"I know! Get up here with me ... This is so much fun!" I shout at him.

"No. I'm not jumping on the bed," he answers, laughing and shaking his head.

"Are you scared? It's okay—I'll hold your hand." I stretch my hand out, taunting and teasing him.

"You're certifiably nuts!" he answers while laughing at me. I love how he loves seeing Vegas through my eyes—how it makes him feel alive again. I love to see him laugh.

Jumping down and sitting on the edge of the bed, I pat on the mattress next to me for him to join me.

He first secures the door, takes the gun from behind his back and places it on the nightstand. Then he joins me. Before he can even think about it, I do a swift jump-attack onto him, pushing him back on the bed, pinning him down.

"How do you like those stealth moves?" I ask as I lift both his hands over his head, pressing my body onto his.

All I can think of right now is his amazing face, those eyes and those lips. I'm seduced by his mesmerizing, irresistible stare.

"You have incredible stealth moves," he thinks as he kisses me, sending a chill through my body that flows right into our kiss. What an unbelievable sensation! It's like nothing else matters in this world except for this moment. This time—Dario and Taylor time.

We kiss through the night and into the light of the coming day, when the sunrise makes us both aware of how exhausted we are and how we need to get some serious sleep.

Dario gets up and closes the curtains across the windows as I climb under the covers, into the smoothest sheets my feet have ever felt. I love the sensation, not to mention the warmth of the duvet I'm buried under. Within moments, Dario joins me under the covers, still clothed seeing as I am still wearing my sundress. He pulls me toward him as he lovingly folds me into his arms. I wouldn't trade being in his embrace for anything.

As we drift off to sleep, I start to think of the cave and how being there with him was one of the most invigorating experiences of my life. I can't get it out of my mind—the beautiful red-orange rocks, the luscious warm water of the pool, and the soft white sand. Dario hooks into my vision as we drift off to sleep, and he finds me in the cave waiting for him.

"I thought you were tired?" Dario asks.

"I am. That's why I am sleeping in your arms right now. I

can honestly say I couldn't feel more relaxed if I tried. I am still amazed that these waters healed your wound. This really is an extraordinary place ... What do you think it all means?" I ask Dario as I lower myself into the pool.

Dario joins me. "*I don't know, but it sure is magical, I still can't believe it myself.*" With this he passes his hand right through my body, giving me a small taste of his being.

"*You are such a tease.*"

"*I know. Isn't it great?*" He laughs at me.

In return, I move my hand through him, smiling and showing him what a real tease I can be.

We play around with each other, running our hands through each other's energy, tempting each other until it turns into one intense encounter as he pins me up against the wall and finally pushes his entire body into mine.

My body shivers with passion as liberating vibrations of energy send both of us into an unadulterated ecstasy and we become part of the universe as a whole. Then blackness engulfs the two of us.

36

Strange Encounter

Our intense burst of energy must have **knocked us both out, big time.** Now, waking up in the hotel room, I am completely dazed—and I have no idea how long I've been asleep. I head to the bathroom, confused and almost wondering what day it is. I splash my face with some water, and when I walk back into the room, I find Dario slowly waking up.

"What time is it?" he asks, groggily.

I look around the room for a clock but can't find one.

"I don't know. There isn't a clock in here."

"Oh yeah ... I put it under the bed last night—the light was just too bright in the dark," he says as he reaches to retrieve it. Taking a quick look, I almost have a heart attack realizing that it's one in the afternoon!

"Oh no, I'm going to be in so much trouble!" I say, remembering that my mom and dad think I'm at Skyler's with Mckylee. What have Mckylee and Skyler been doing this morning? And more importantly, what have they told my parents? I rifle through my purse looking for my cell phone. I should never have turned the ringer off last night. Finding it, I see that I have 9 missed calls, 11 texts, and 6 messages. Oh my gosh, what was I thinking?

Reading my texts and listening to my messages, I learn that the girls are worried about me and need to hear from me ASAP! One of the messages calms me, though. Due to my dad being the romantic that he is, Mckylee left a message telling me he surprised our mom with an overnight trip to Los Angeles today, so I'm off the hook! Someone is in my corner for sure.

I take a deep breath and heave a sigh of relief. Dario tells me he knew everything would be all right. Right, like he really knew it would all work in our favor.

I dial Mckylee. "Oh my-gosh, am I the luckiest girl alive, or what?!" I blurt out before she even has a chance to say hello.

"You so are! Where have you been? I couldn't believe it myself, but when I couldn't get a hold of you this morning,

I didn't know what I was going to tell Mom and Dad. Around ten o'clock, we were supposed to call to check in with them, but when Mom answered the phone, she was so excited about their trip to L.A., she didn't even ask about you. How perfect is that? You are so freaking lucky, Taylor!"

"I know, I know. I'm sorry for not being around, but we had a kind of crazy night last night and I turned off my phone and didn't think that I would sleep all day. I'm so sorry Mckylee ... I owe you. We had such an amazing time. I'll have to fill you in later. What are you two doing today?"

"Besides worrying about you? Right now we are at the Fashion Show Mall shopping."

"You're shopping? I need to go shopping." I share with her.

"Tell them that we will meet them there in 45 minutes and to wait for us," Dario shares.

"Hey, Dario says if you will wait up, we will meet you there in about 45 minutes. Is that cool with you?"

"Sure, that'll work. We just got here not too long ago anyway, so we will see you then. Just call us when you get here."

"Perfect. See you soon," I say and hang up.

Dario then calls room service and orders some coffee and pastries, before jumping in the shower. Part of me is now contemplating joining him. But what am I thinking? I haven't even seen him naked yet. This whole mind-connection thing has me all freaked out again. I know he's listening to me, but I'm glad he's letting me have my thoughts to myself.

Once he gets out, it's my turn. I step into the shower and let the hot water flow over my body, relieved that I'm not facing any serious consequences with my parents and, even more importantly, that I actually got some sleep last night. I dry off and soon realize that I left my bag out in the car last night, so that means I have absolutely nothing to wear except the same clothes I wore yesterday. Gross!

Dario interrupts my thoughts. *"I took care of that, while you were in the shower ... I ran down and got our bags."*

"Thank you so much for reading my mind!"

I wrap a towel around me and when I re-enter the room, I find a cup of steaming, hot, delicious coffee awaiting me.

"You are way too good to me, you know? Thank you," I tell him as I sip the coffee, then grab my bag and head back into the bathroom to get dressed. Afterward, I return to find Dario eating a pastry and watching sports highlights on the telly.

"I'm ready whenever you are," I say as I grab a bite of a yummy-looking blueberry muffin.

"I was thinking we could just stay here another night. I mean, now that your parents are out of town, what do you think?" Dario asks.

"That sounds good to me; I obviously don't have to be home anytime soon. I just need to talk to Mckylee and see what she is doing and if she will cover for me."

"Perfect. Then we'll just leave our things and we're out of here," he tells me as he grabs his gun, puts it down the back of his pants again and leads the way out of the room.

"Do you really have to take that thing everywhere with you?"

"*Well, where would you like me to leave it? Where the maid could possibly find it?*"

"No, I guess not. I was just wondering," I say out loud as the elevator opens, packed full of people. We enter silently but continuing our conversation.

"*The thing I find quite interesting is that I've had it on me ever since you've known me, and now it's a big deal?*"

"*I didn't realize you had it on you until yesterday, so of course it didn't bother me.*"

"*Taylor, I'm not going anywhere without it so let's go back to you not knowing I have it. Put it out of your mind, okay?*"

"Fine. What gun?" I say as I get out of the elevator and follow Dario to the car.

• • • • • • • • • • • •

The mall is super, crazy busy, to the point that it is almost bothersome. I'm happy to see Mckylee and Skyler, though. Mckylee looks amazing—her hair is so long and straight, and her makeup looks nice, yet natural. I've never seen her look so grown up and so pretty.

"Wow. Who did your hair and makeup? It looks awesome," I tell Mckylee as I touch her soft, silky hair.

"Skyler did it. I love it, and I can't believe my hair looks so long when it's straight. I never knew I could get my hair this straight. Isn't it amazing?"

"I wonder if my hair will do that. Can you do my hair like that too?" I ask Skyler.

"Yeah, of course. It's not hard. It takes a while to do,

though, but I can teach you how. And once your hair is straightened, you don't have to wash it for a few days, so it's worth it."

"Oh! Is that why the other girls never want to get their hair wet?" I say, thinking that I've finally figured out why Kayla hardly ever wants to get in the water when we go swimming.

"Exactly!" Skyler says.

Walking through the mall, all I can think about is how I have to seriously do something with my hair. I can't stand my long, curly rat's nest another minute. Maybe I'll get some beautiful blonde highlights and some sort of new style. That's it. It's time for a Taylor hair makeover. I can't fathom why Dario would ever want to be seen with me, really! I've never actually liked my hair, but now I can't stand it!

"I like your hair. It's beautiful and natural and curly," Dario tells me sweetly, injecting some conflict into my thoughts. "Well ladies, let's get some shopping done. Isn't that why you all like to come to the mall?" Dario asks.

All of us nod our heads in unison, almost as if he pulled on three puppet strings at the same time.

"Let's go then!" Skyler answers with enthusiasm.

Store after store, bag after bag, we're having a very successful day of shopping, all on Dario's tab. I can't believe he is paying for everyone's things, but he seems to be having a grand time doing so. All of us are completely taken aback by his generosity and stumbling over ourselves to thank him. Note to self—take Dario with us shopping all the time!

Mckylee and I finally get a chance to talk for a few minutes. Leaning in, she nudges me and says, "So, what is he like … did you …?"

"No, it's not what you think. I really love being with him … and he's … he's … well, he's so gentle and kind with me. We talk a lot, eat at his favorite places … and he holds me. We even slept last night—but not like what you think. I don't know Mckylee, I think he actually respects me and wouldn't do anything to hurt me."

"You mean you didn't …"

"No, we didn't …" I know instinctively that what we did is so much more than she or anyone would ever understand. "Dario is having fun showing me Vegas. You will cover for me again since Mom and Dad are in Los Angeles …?"

"Yes. but you have to tell me everything. *Everything.* Promise?"

"Sure … and thanks," I say. I give her a hug, knowing that her *everything* will not be everything as Dario and I know it.

I never knew shopping could be so exhausting and soon feel the need to rest. "Hey, does anyone want to get a coffee with me?" I ask, pointing toward a coffee shop.

"That actually sounds good," Mckylee answers. We all walk over and order our favorites, and I pick up the tab before Dario gets the chance. As we sit in the mall enjoying our coffee and people watching, Dario interrupts our girly chit-chat.

"Hey, Taylor, we need to get going pretty quickly. I have the rest of the day planned, plus some special things for us this evening."

I can't see what's in his mind, although I'm trying. He's learning how to block his thoughts from me. Sneaky—and a trick I need to get better at. I tend to be such an open book.

"Sounds good. I need to use the ladies' room first. I'll be right back. Can you watch my stuff?" I ask, pointing to the bags leaning against my seat.

"Sure, we'll wait here for you," Mckylee answers.

I walk into the closest department store, knowing they will have a ladies' room. After asking the lady at the makeup counter for directions, I head to the back corner of the store. Then, to my surprise, I notice a woman following me. I'm pretty sure I have seen her a couple times earlier today in several of the other stores. Actually, now that I think about it, I remember seeing her just over by the makeup counter. There is no way this is just a coincidence, right?

I decide to test my paranoid theory by making a quick turn, getting off the main aisle and going through the men's department. I glance over my shoulder discreetly to see if she is still behind me; to my relief she is gone.

"Is everything okay?" Dario asks in the midst of my thoughts.

I assure him everything is fine, that I thought I was being followed and it's just my mind playing tricks on me. We both share a laugh between us. I can feel myself smiling as we do.

Happy to finally find the ladies' room, I hurry so I can get back to everyone. But while washing my hands, I look up into the mirror, and to my horror, there she is standing behind me—the woman that's officially following me! I jump at the sight of her staring at me in the mirror. Instantly, I turn around and pull myself together. "Why are you following me?" I ask. "What do you want?"

"I'm sorry. I didn't mean to frighten you. I just need to talk to you, and you're never alone. I know he is listening, so I need you to quickly tell him everything is fine and follow me."

"What? Why would I follow you? You just scared me to death, and now you're telling me someone's listening to me? Who's listening? You're crazy, and I have to go. My friends are waiting for me." I push past her, wondering how she knows Dario is listening to me. In the meantime, I try to block out all that is going on so Dario doesn't panic or question the situation.

"I know about you and Dario and the powers!" she says loudly just as I'm exiting the bathroom.

Turning abruptly, I glare at her. I'm a little bit dumbfounded, but also scared and suddenly wondering ... is she connected with Mr. Mancini somehow?

"I don't know what you're talking about. And stay away from me," I tell her as the door closes behind me.

I feel beads of sweat across my forehead as I walk briskly back to everyone. I turn around to check and see if she is behind me, and thankfully, she isn't. Something tells me I'll be seeing her again, though. I can tell she isn't going to give up easily. How does she know about Dario and me? How does she know about our powers?

I so want to think about her, but I can't, not now, because Dario will hear me and want to find out what's going on. He already has enough crap on his plate. Quickly, I put the encounter behind me and integrate myself among the crowd of other shoppers. That allows me to clear my mind and put on a happy face as I approach everyone.

"What took you so long?" Mckylee asks.

"Yeah, what did take you so long? I almost came looking for you," Dario chimes in.

"Nothing. Can't a girl just go to the ladies' room without getting interrogated? It was kind of far away," I snap at them as I pick up my bags and tell everyone I'm ready to go.

"All right then, is everything okay?" Mckylee inquires, looking at me as if I had grown a third eye.

"I'm sorry ... I'm just tired and hungry and ready to get out of the mall. That's all."

"I understand. So what's the plan for tonight? I told Mom and Dad that we would be staying at Skyler's again, if that is okay with you."

"Of course it is. Do you mind if I just stay with Dario again?"

"Taylor, what's with you? ... I already said you could, but can you keep your phone on this time so I can get a hold of you? Please?"

"Yes, of course. I'm sorry I turned it off last night. I'll never do that again," I assure her as we walk toward the exit.

"So we'll see you tomorrow then." Mckylee says as she gives me a hug and thanks Dario for all the gifts. Skyler also gives me a hug and thanks Dario as they walk out of the mall.

Standing there silently, I watch the two of them giggling

happily as they head off to Skyler's car. Dario stands in front of me.

"Okay, what's going on? What happened to you when you went to the ladies' room? You were kind of freaking me out, and then you went offline for a few minutes. Why were you blocking me out of your thoughts?"

"I wasn't doing it on purpose. I don't know. Nothing was going on. Why is everyone making a big deal out of me going to the ladies' room? Can we just stop talking about it?" I try to ask this calmly, knowing that if I keep up the edgy attitude, he's just going to keep thinking something is wrong.

"Okay. For now. I still think something happened back there to you and you aren't telling me, but you're here safe with me now, so I guess it doesn't really matter. Taylor, it's you and me. We are different, and there may be people who want to keep us apart, including my father. I think we need to keep our channels open in case something odd happens. Agree?" he says. Then he grabs some of the bags from me so that he can hold my hand as we walk to the valet to get the car.

37

Deceived

We arrive back at the hotel around five o'clock. Dario pulls into the valet and tells the guys to have our shopping bags brought up to our room as he slips them some cash.

Turning to me, he asks, "Are you ready, Madam?"

"Ready for what? Where are you taking me?"

"You'll see. Just trust me."

We walk through the casino and down a long hallway,

stopping at a door marked "Spa". Dario opens the door for me, and I take in the intriguing aromas.

"What are we doing here?"

"You'll see," he says, as two ladies approach us. "Hello, Mr. Mancini. It's such a pleasure to have you back. And you must be Taylor. Welcome."

"Hello," I say hesitantly. I've never been to a spa before, and I'm really not sure what to expect.

"Relax and enjoy yourself," Dario says. "We are going to get a couple's massage, and I guarantee, you will love it!"

"Wow, this is so cool. I've never had a massage before."

Dario chuckles to himself as the ladies lead us in separate directions to get ready. "I'll see you in a minute. You're in good hands," he assures me. Then he walks down the hall and disappears around the corner.

A nice lady leads me into a dressing room area that's more like a living room, with beautiful chairs and lounges, two different beverage stations, and baskets of fresh fruit throughout the room. I follow her to a locker, where she informs me to take off all of my clothes and put on a robe and slippers provided for me and to meet her at another door. I take my clothes off shyly, throw on the robe and slippers and meet her as directed.

Soon, we come to another door that opens to a semi-dark area with two tall, strange–looking, cushioned tables and soft music playing in the background. Dario is lying face down on one of the tables. He lifts his head to greet me. "Nice of you to join me. Trust me, you're going to love this." He flashes me one his fabulous smiles, then places his head back down into what looks like a hole in the table.

The attendant leads me to the other table. As she pulls back the sheet on it, she says she'll be right back. She directs me to take my robe off and get on the table, face down, like Dario.

"Dario don't look!" I say laughing.

"I will be the perfect gentlemen, I promise."

He was right; getting a massage is the most wonderful thing ever! I can feel all the tension from every point of origin in my body disappearing. This is so awesome! I could get used to doing this all the time.

"Can you stop thinking so much?" Dario interjects. *"You're hurting my head."*

Taking Dario's advice, I force myself to relax and enjoy this heavenly experience. After our incredible massages, we are led in our robes to some special chairs in a very tranquil room, where we are both handed a glass of champagne, non-alcoholic of course. I look over at Dario, *"You are the most romantic guy ever!"* I hold my glass up to toast him. "To life, love and you."

"No, to you," he says, as our glasses softly clink against each other.

I love the way the champagne bubbles tingle in my mouth. I decide it's my favorite drink—much better than the wine Mom and Dad let us have in England. And I like it better than the margaritas Kayla ordered for us the first night we went out to the cantina.

"You seem a little preoccupied. What's going on in that pretty little mind of yours?" Dario asks with a chuckle.

"You are so funny, seeing as you always know what's going

on inside my mind. I am just having a great time and wondering what's next without looking inside your head, that's all."

"Well then, for your next surprise, after you finish your glass of champagne, you can go and get that new look you've been wanting. But don't go too crazy on me. I like you just the way you are."

"Really? I get to get my hair done after this?" I'm so excited, even though I already kind of knew what was next. As soon as he told me about the couples massage, I couldn't help but hear him think that my hair was going to be just the way I wanted it.

Sitting here completely relaxed, I close my eyes and take a few moments to relive the massage I just received. I tell Dario, *"Thanks for sharing such a wonderful experience with me."*

Finishing my champagne, I walk back to the dressing room so I can move on to the next excitement of the evening, and soon, I'm sitting in a chair at the hair salon.

I never realized that getting a new me could be such a long process. The stylist is beyond excited in helping me with my tangled mess, but after an hour, I have only just gotten through the highlighting process. Dario has left to take care of a few things, which actually makes me happy because I know that he'll be concentrating on other things and not on what I'm thinking and doing. It gives me some time to review my encounter with that strange woman at the mall.

Who is she and how does she know about Dario and me? These are the two very important questions I need answered. The whole situation is so bizarre. Somehow, though, I feel that I will find out what's going on soon enough.

"Find out what soon enough?" Dario interrupts me as he walks back into the salon.

"Nothing. I'm just thinking about my hair and what it's going to look like, that's all." As he approaches me, the look on his face is one of surprise.

"Wow! I love the hair—it looks amazing!"

I must have been pretty deep in thought because I'm now realizing, as I look in the mirror, that the stylist is almost finished blow-drying out all my curls. The color is unbelievable, it has touches of blonde and light brown with ever so faint red highlights. I love it!

"What color would you call this?" I ask the stylist.

"Why? Don't you like it?" he asks.

"No, no! I love it! I just don't know what color it is."

"I would call it a medium strawberry-blonde. You have a lot of natural red in your hair, so that really came out when I put the highlights in," he explains.

"It's awesome! I love the cut and I can't believe my hair is straight! Thank you so much!"

I never knew I could be so pretty, and my hair seems so long, even though it was cut. Who would have known that there was so much length in all my curls? A little bit of makeup and some clean clothes and I'll be ready to go. As the stylist finishes up, he gives me some tips on how to take care of my hair and a bag of hair products to help keep it straight. I thank him profusely, and after three hours in the salon and spa, I am finally leaving with Dario.

"Hey I don't want to pressure you or anything, but we have reservations for dinner in about forty-five minutes so I need you to be dressed and ready to go in about thirty, okay?" Then Dario drops a bombshell on me. "By the way, we're having dinner with my family again."

"What? What do you mean we're having dinner with your family? Your dad hates me and makes me feel really uncomfortable."

"He doesn't hate you, but I didn't have a choice. He said if we didn't show, he would send someone for us. So I'm sorry, but we have to go, Taylor."

"Fine, but I am only doing this for you. I can't believe this; he scares me to death, to be quite honest with you."

Feeling completely overwhelmed, I enter our room knowing I'm better off just letting my frustrations go. I will never win this one. His family is like peanut butter and jelly ... they will always be together, no matter what!

"I really have nothing with me to wear to a dinner event with your parents," I tell Dario. Then I notice a large box on the bed—and the smile on Dario's face.

"I knew you would be upset, so I took the liberty of taking care of your wardrobe issue. Open the box."

The box itself is lovely; I can only imagine what's inside. I slowly take the lid off and sort through the tissue paper to find a dress that's a fabulous shade of midnight blue, and there's also a pair of stunning silver heels to match.

"It's amazing."

"And you will look amazing in it."

I enter the bathroom to get ready, completely beside

myself that Mr. Mancini wants to see me at dinner. I can only imagine what he has in store for Dario and me.

After getting dressed and touching up my makeup, I glance into the full-length mirror on the wall and barely recognize myself. I can't believe I am the same girl who was running through the fields of England in jeans, T-shirts and tennis shoes just a few months ago. Now I'm a glamorous young lady with my own knight in shining armor.

I take a deep breath and open the bathroom door. I can tell that Dario is completely amazed and taken aback by how extraordinary I look.

You would think someone dressed this nice and feeling this good about herself would be excited for the evening before her. But I'm very nervous about what's to come. Walking mindlessly through the casino holding Dario's hand, I catch a few glimpses of people staring—something I've never encountered before. I love the way my hair is flowing across my back and its new softness.

Dario tries to comfort me by telling me everything will be fine, although we both seem to have knots in our stomachs. We arrive at the car, which is parked at the valet in the front of the hotel. Dario opens my door, gives me a slight kiss with his soft, luscious lips, and tells me again how beautiful I look. He has a way of mesmerizing me, and if it weren't for the situation, I would feel reassured. It's not that I don't trust him; it's his father—he's a different story.

Dario drives away, heading out toward the east side of town.

"Where are we going?"

"We are going to this wonderful little Italian restaurant in Green Valley that my family loves. It has an amazing view of the Strip."

I wonder if everyone will be there again like the last time we had dinner with his dad.

"Yes, everyone will be there," he answers me.

"Great, I can't wait," I reply. I do enjoy his mom and sister though, so I'm hoping it won't be completely disastrous.

We get to the restaurant pretty quickly. My stomach is doing back flips as we walk through the crowded tables. Dario was right; the restaurant is very nice and has an astounding view of Las Vegas. Of course, we find his family in the back at a large table where they can see everyone and anyone coming or going at all times. I'm guessing that they locate themselves this way because they have many enemies who might try to make a hit on them, especially when they're all together. They need to protect themselves as much as they can. I make another educated guess that everyone at this table has a gun or two on them.

"Welcome, Taylor and Dario," Mr. Mancini greets us, standing up. He gives me a kiss on the cheek and whispers in my ear that I clean up well and look amazing. Blushing, I thank him and join Dario at the two seats saved for us next to his dad at the table.

"I hope you don't mind, but we went ahead and ordered while we were waiting for you," Mr. Mancini informs us.

I wouldn't have expected anything different.

"No, that's fine dad; we didn't expect you to wait for us," Dario says.

Seeing as my stomach is still in knots, I'm not even hungry. Not only that, but for all I know, I could have been summoned here to be poisoned or something because they don't want me in Dario's life. Mr. Mancini made that pretty clear last night when he came out to the house.

Sitting here trying to keep my mind on more positive things, I'm drawn to the pure beauty of Dario's mother—how can anyone be that perfect looking? She seems to control everyone around her—especially Dario's father. He is so besotted with her, along with everyone else. I wonder what her magic power is.

"I know. It's almost weird, isn't it?" Dario echoes in on my thoughts. *"The weirdest thing is that I've only noticed it since I have been with you. I don't even feel like I know her anymore; I feel so estranged from her lately."*

"It's strange because I didn't feel this way around her the first time I met her; something is definitely different," I reply.

Dinner arrives, and the sight of all the food makes me feel sick. I decide that I need a little fresh air, or at least to step away from the table for a few minutes. Excusing myself, I head toward the ladies' room for a moment of sanity. I feel like everyone at the table is so phony with one another—well, except for Dario and me. We couldn't be phony with one another even if we tried. OMG, I feel so uncomfortable with all of them in that room. It's as if there are undercurrents of things that are best left unsaid. The vibes are heavy, and they're everywhere.

"Don't leave me here alone too long." Dario requests of me as I walk away.

I'm just glad to be by myself for a minute; it gives me great relief. Finding the ladies' room, I enter the back stall and stand against the wall, relieved to be away from all the eeriness. Leaning my head back, I gather myself together. I take a deep breath. Then, knowing I should return to the family gathering, I force myself to open the door and leave the stall.

After washing my hands, I reach for my lip-gloss in my purse and bring it up to my lips. Then suddenly, my hand stops in midair. I can feel the color draining from my face and my jaw dropping. In the mirror, I'm looking at the face of the woman who has been following me!

"Leave me alone! What are you doing here? Did you follow us here?!" I demand of the strange woman. I know that I must get away from her. Now.

"Wait ... wait ... don't leave. We don't have much time. I need you to eat this now!" she insists, trying to put something in my hand that looks like a flower that hasn't bloomed yet, like a bud.

"What? No, I don't even know you!" I shout, pushing her hand and the flower away and reaching for the door.

Then my curiosity gets the better of me and I turn to her. "What is ..."

Suddenly, she reaches up, grabs my face and shoves the disgusting thing into the back of my throat, forcing me to swallow it before I can try to stop her or call for help!

"It's the bud of a lygos flower. I don't have time for this; we don't have time for any of this. Swallow it ... all of it."

As I attempt to fight her off, she twists my arm and says

that if I keep giving her a hard time, she'll call in the forces. That stops me for a minute. What do "forces" mean?

In my moment of hesitation, she grabs my hand and pulls me out of the bathroom. Within seconds, I'm outside being shoved into a van. Before the door is closed, the van takes off abruptly, slamming me to the floor!

I try to get my bearings, but just then, the woman shoves a needle in my arm! I struggle to get my mind around what's happening, about what's just been injected into me, but all I know for sure is that I'm losing consciousness fast...

Dario ... help ... D a r i o ...

Catch a glimpse of

Book Two in the Vegas Dazzle Series

DARK MOON

1

Vanished

A rush of terror fills my body, leaving me **breathless.** Something is wrong. *Taylor ... Taylor ... What's going on? ... Are you all right? ... Where are you? ... Can you hear me?!* I pray for her to hear me, even though I'm getting no response, and I can't hear her at all. Panicked, I leave the table abruptly, running through the busy restaurant to find her. I faintly hear my dad shouting out my name behind me, but I continue my pursuit despite the consequences.

Bolting into the ladies' room like a madman, I shout out her name.

"Taylor! Taylor! Are you in here?" With no response, I begin to check each of the three stalls. Nothing. There is no sight of her—there's no one. What have I done, this is all my fault! Tony and Mateo come crashing through the door.

"What the hell's going on Dario? What are you doing in the ladies' room? Where's Taylor?" Tony blurts out at me with a confused look on his face. The hostess interrupts us.

"Excuse me, but what's going on here? You guys can't be in here. What are you doing? And you need to stop shouting. You're scaring the guests!"

"Did you see a girl come in here with long, brownish-blonde hair and a blue dress? Did you see her?" I frantically ask the hostess.

"Yes! I saw her. You don't need to shout at me!"

"Where is she then?" Mateo asks before I can even get the words out.

"She left with some lady. They left in a rush out the front door. If you ask me, she didn't look like she was really into going with her though."

"What did this lady look like?" I ask, worried, while trying to wrack my mind for any woman I could possibly know that would ever force Taylor to go somewhere with her.

"Excuse me, what's going on here? I need you all out of the ladies' room now! Dario, what's going on anyway?" Angelo, the manager, asks me as I notice my dad and Vincent standing off to the side behind him giving me their pull-it-together stare.

What the hell is going on? Where's Taylor, what's happened? Someone please help!

"I need to get out of here! I've had enough of this bullshit!" I say to Tony and Mateo as I push through everyone standing in the hallway looking at me like I'm out of my mind. Bypassing my dad and Vincent and ignoring their harsh stares, I abruptly barge out the front doors into the dark, lifeless parking lot. Why can't I get a read on Taylor?

I don't understand why I can't hear a single thought in her head—not one. It's like she doesn't even exist. Something is seriously wrong. Who is this woman the hostess is talking about? Why was she forced to leave with her? Why didn't I hear that she was in trouble? Maybe I'm thinking too much into this whole situation. Maybe she just ran into a family friend or something and just got out of here? She really didn't want to be here anyway. I need to get back to the hotel right away in case she shows up there.

"Shit, Dario! What just happened in there? What's going on? You're kind of tripping out," Mateo demands as him and Tony appear behind me.

"Do you think the Larson brothers are behind this?" Tony asks.

"F— if I know what the hell's going on! I know one thing for sure, I'm going to get to the bottom of this, and whoever is behind this will have hell to pay! I'm heading over to the Hard Rock. Maybe she's there?"

Walking to my car, I try to call her, but it goes straight to voice mail, usually meaning her phone has been shut off. This makes me even more furious. I get in my car and yell for the guys to get in. Once the doors slam shut, I speed out of the lot, skidding onto Eastern Avenue toward the hotel. My mind is racing. I can't drive there fast enough. Pulling up to the front of the Hard Rock, I park the car and toss my keys to the valet. I try to stay calm as I race into the hotel. Mateo and Tony immediately join me as we head straight for the elevators and up to the suite.

Sticking the key-card into the lock, I pray Taylor's on the other side of the door with a damn good explanation of what the hell just happened back at the restaurant. But the reality of it all is if she were here, I would know it. I would feel her ... hear her ... and right now I can't do either.

Without delay, I open the door, finding absolutely nothing. The room is exactly the way we left it a few hours ago. My heart sinks. I don't know what to do. What if someone is hurting her, or worse yet, killing her? Shit! The worst part of all of this is that I have no idea who could possibly be behind it. There are so many suspects. Grabbing my phone out of my pocket, I call the one person that might just possibly have some answers for me. I push the button labeled *"Dad"* and listen to the phone ring on the other side, hoping he'll be there for me ... hoping he'll help me. After a few rings he picks up.

"Hello, Dario. Have you calmed down yet?"

"Yes, I'm calming down. What's going on? I don't understand who would take Taylor? The hostess said it was some lady. Who could that possibly be?" I really want to ask if he is behind this, but I know that would be crossing the line.

"Dario, I'm as confused as you are. It's beyond me why anyone would think taking her would have any power over our family, or think that she could possibly be held as some sort of leverage. We barely know the girl. You've only been hanging out with her for what, a brief moment in time?"

"Exactly, so I need someone to explain to me what the hell is going on! What am I going to tell her parents if she doesn't show up? What am I supposed to do here?"

"Dario, you and the guys need to meet us all back at the house, and we'll try and get to the bottom of this. You don't have to tell her parents anything right now."

"Sounds good, we'll be there pronto," I tell him as I motion the guys to follow me and head back down the hall toward the elevators.

"What did your dad say?" Tony asks.

"He wants us all to meet back at the house. He doesn't have a clue what's going on either, but we're going to get to the bottom of it," I say over my shoulder as we walk across the casino floor.

Taking a quick look around, I hope to maybe, possibly catch sight of Taylor as we hurry toward the valet. The casino is starting to get crowded. The floor seems to be busier than when we went up to the suite a short while ago. Not really paying any attention in my pursuit toward the valet, I collide with some guy, practically knocking him over.

"Hey man, I'm so sorry," I announce to the stranger who seems to be somewhat familiar to me, but I'm not sure why.

"No problem, is everything okay? You seem a little hurried? Hey, don't I know you?" the stranger asks in what I think is an Italian accent.

"Yeah, everything's fine, and no, I don't think you know me. I for sure don't know you!"

"Yeah, I do know you, you're Dario Mancini. We go to school together at Vegas Valley High."

"Yeah, whatever you say," I say dismissively. "But I still don't know you, sorry."

"Not a problem. See you around," the stranger states.

Even though I could really not care less, there is something odd about this guy that I can't put my finger on. It forces me to stop and ask, "Hey, by the way, it seems a little unfair that you know my name, and I don't know yours?"

"Salventino," he answers.

"Cool. See you around," I say back to him before I continue my way through the casino. I'm still convinced our connection goes beyond school, but I just can't put my finger on it.

• • • • • • • • • • • • •

Pulling through the front gate of my house, I start to have a sick feeling in my stomach, mainly because I feel so helpless and unsure of what is really going on. The thing that sucks the most is that I can't share with anyone how I know Taylor really is in danger and things really aren't right. What the hell am I supposed to do, and why can't I get a read on her? Where could she possibly be, and the real question—with who?

"Dario, are you coming?" Mateo shouts at me from outside of the car. I didn't even realize the car had come to a stop.

"Yeah, I'm coming. Sorry about that, I'm a little out of it," I explain as I get out of the car and follow him into the house—my house. Before I can even shut the door behind me, I see Air running toward me from the family room, embracing me with a big hug.

"Dario, are you alright? I'm so sorry. I don't understand what the heck is going on. Dad has been on the phone since we got home. To see Dad baffled is a first. He always knows what's going on in this town, and most of the time before it even happens. This is all just way too crazy!"

"I'll be okay Air, we just need to find out what has happen to Taylor," I say gently, pushing her off me. "Hey, where is Dad? In his office?" I ask her as I walk down the hall, following Mateo and Tony's lead without completely blowing her off. But in reality, she can't help me right now, and I need to get to the bottom of all this quickly.

Entering my dad's office, I can tell right away he really has no idea who's behind all of this. Everyone in there has the same look on their face and seem to be as baffled as I am, which is good and bad. It's good to know I can still have a little faith in my dad, but on the other hand, I still don't know what has happened to Taylor.

Coming in on the tail end of some plan being executed that seems to be taking every possible measure to find out what the hell is going on, I can only wonder if all of this goes way beyond my family and my dad's shit. The deeper

I search inside of me, my gut tells me in some strange way that she's okay. I can't even explain it completely, but ...

"Dario, I am so glad you are here. Come in and sit down over here next to me, we need to talk," My dad directs me as he has one of the guys pull up a chair for me to sit in. "So what do you think has happened to Taylor? Did you two have a fight or something before you joined us at the restaurant? I need all the facts."

"No, nothing like that, what could we possibly have to fight about? Everything was fine ... I just don't understand ..." I tell him, searching through my mind for some sort of evidence that could possibly explain all of this madness. "Wait a minute! You know what, I totally forgot about this because it seemed so insignificant at the time, but I got this text a few days back. I don't know how much use it can be, seeing it came from an unknown number, but ..." I say, while searching through my phone to find it. "Here, here it is,"

Dario who's your cute little friend you've been spending a lot of time with? You better keep her close to you. What is her name? Taylor? We're watching you, and we're especially watching her ...

"It didn't seem like a big deal at the time ... but maybe I was wrong ..."

"Dario you really need to tell me these things as they happen. I could have had someone with you two at all times. We could have at least kept a better eye on Taylor. I don't understand why you fight me so much, and you don't let me help you. You do realize you are not alone around here—don't you? Look around this room Dario—this is your family, whether you like it or not, and the sooner you figure that out the better off we will all be."

Taking a look around the room I see all the familiar faces that I have known my whole life—the faces of men I know would do anything for me. What is wrong with me? Why do I insist on taking on the whole world on my own? Now look at what I've done. How will I ever live with myself if anything happens to Taylor?

"You know what Dario, I think Vincent and I have everything covered here. I think it's best if you go back to the Hard Rock and wait for her there just in case she shows up. Take Tony and Mateo with you in the chance that you run into any trouble." My dad's right. Someone needs to be there just in case.

"We'll head back to the hotel and wait for her there. Hopefully, this is all just a big misunderstanding and she's back at the hotel waiting for me. I'm sorry," I add, feeling defeated and most of all, like an idiot.

"Dario, why didn't you tell us about the text?" Mateo asks, genuinely concerned.

"I don't know Mateo ... because I'm an idiot!"

"You know we're here for you no matter what, right? You're our brother," Mateo says.

"I know, Mateo. Thanks. I really don't want to talk about it right now, I just want to get back to the Hard Rock, and hopefully Taylor will show up soon." I try to convince myself everything is going to work out. But I don't really know at this point.

• • • • • • • • • • • •

Back at the Hard Rock, the energy of the people is start-ing to vibrate the casino. The place is packed and there are people everywhere. It seems like everyone I know is here except the one person I am really looking for. I can't wrap my head around any of this.

"Dario, why don't you go upstairs and wait for Taylor, while Tony and I scope this place out and see if she is down here somewhere," Mateo says to me as he nudges Tony.

"Sure, I need to clear my head anyway. Maybe I will remember something else that might help us find her."

"We will stay in touch—call us if you need anything, all right? We're here for you," Tony tells me as he gives me his "I mean it" look.

"I got it! Let me know if you find her or hear anything! I'll see you later," I reply before heading off across the casino floor toward the elevators.

Back in the room ... still no Taylor. I lay down on the bed, crushed—devastated. Staring up at the ceiling, I replay everything in my head ... the entire day ... the whole week. What am I missing? What can't I see? There has to be some answer somewhere in this head of mine. Exhausted, I close my eyes. Still unable to hear Taylor, I lay in a deep sea of blackness, but then, out of nowhere, his face appears.

Clearer than ever, I remember where I saw Salventino before. He was the guy that kept talking to Taylor the night we were at Unity, the club at the Beauvallon. I remember seeing his face through Taylor's eyes and thinking it was quite strange that she happened to bump into him twice in one night. But even more twisted, she had conversations with him. Then I just happen to bump into him on the night that she goes missing? In the hotel that Taylor and I just happen to be staying in? There is no way in hell that was a coincidence.

Who is he, and what does he know? I have to find him right now. I am positive he can fill in the blanks to whatever the f— is going on around here!

About the Author

Pam Langsam was born in Dallas, but has spent most of her life living in Las Vegas. When she's not writing, she loves to travel and explore the world. Pam believes that everyone creates their own destiny by living out their dreams and believing in themselves. She lives with her husband and son with their two cats and black Labrador, living each and everyday to the fullest. Visit her at www.pamlangsam.com

Live life passionately,
Believe in your dreams,
You can make anything happen.
—Pam Langsam